Dawn Light
On the Chesapeake

Harv Nowland

Dawn Light
On the Chesapeake
by Harvey L. Nowland Jr.

Printed in the United States of America

ISBN 978-1-60477-095-7

Unless otherwise indicated, Bible quotations are taken from the King James Version of the Bible.

Edited by Adeline Griffith
Art graphics by Justin L. Nowland

www.xulonpress.com

Table of Contents

Foreword

Reader's Rights: Concerning the reader's entitlement to be able to distinguish between fact and fiction, I agree with James A. Michener who said, "[A novel should strive] for an honest blend of fiction and historical fact, and the reader is entitled to know which is which."

At times, in *Dawn Light*, fact and fiction are easily distinguishable, while at other times it is less obvious. The acquisition of property in colonial Maryland in the story is probably fictional. Or is it? Probably, but neither you nor I will ever know with certainty.

Historical Characters: A significant number of actual historical events and characters are portrayed. Fictional characters are composites and have names that I like. Any chance resemblance to actual persons is unintentional and coincidental. After all, before long there'll be more than seven billion people in the world, and original name combinations are hard to come by.

Places: Geographical sites, such as cities, towns, rivers, and islands are factual. Nevertheless, I'll admit that I have creatively rearranged some geography. I trust this will do no permanent harm to your appreciation of Maryland or Chesapeake Bay and will not detract too much from the story.

Language: I have used some slang and word contractions as devices for expressing my understanding of the way people might have spoken during that time. Included in the linguistic license that I have adopted are phonetic expressions used when slaves spoke English.

The phonetics are mine, representing how I might hear and speak the words. Slave dialect was the most difficult part of writing this story. My friend and editor, Adeline Griffith, has been good about keeping me from doing too much harm to the characters and their speech.

No special attempt has been made to conform to any particular method of phonetic pronunciation or dialectic rules. I apologize to those offended by this self-licensing authorization. If I have stumbled onto proper usage, it is just that . . . a stumble.

Acknowledgements

One purpose I had in writing this story was born out of a desire to understand more about the people whose family name I bear. The first chapter actually occurred as written. However, in the book my family name of Nowland has been substituted with the name O'Connell.

If you should you ever find yourself near North East, Maryland, I invite you to stop at the St. Mary Anne's Episcopal Church, which was built in the early 1700s. The graveyard that surrounds the church is one of the oldest in Maryland. It contains graves that date back to the 1600s of several of my kinfolk, as well as some Susquehanna Indians. The markers of my Nowland ancestors are found close to the present church building.

My good friend—and long-time editor for Larry Burkett—Adeline Griffith, has provided her expert editorial talent to this endeavor. I am grateful to her because I have benefited from her suggestions and skills, and I believe the readers will also.

As I have noted in the Foreword, the geograph-ical designations on the map found in the book may not be accurate, but this has nothing to do with the artist's intelligence. He was simply following the description found in the book.

My thanks to that artist, our grandson Justin L. Nowland, for creating the ink drawings of O'Connell Manor and the map of the uppermost reaches of the Chesapeake Bay area. He graciously applied his artistic talent to this venture. An artist since he was a young boy, he will soon graduate from Belhaven College in Jackson, Mississippi, where he has had a four-year scholarship as an art major.

None of this would have been accomplished if it were not for the patient encouragement of my best friend, my wife Bobbie. Through her love she has always expressed her belief in me and has continu-ally shown me how to keep my eyes on the Lord and His horizon.

Chapter One

Pleasant Places and Goodly Heritage

The day was hot, even for July. Scattered clouds were moving swiftly, and it would have been uncomfortably humid had it not been for the cooling breeze coming off Chesapeake Bay.

Harvey and Bobbie had come to North East, a sleepy little town at the northeast end of the bay, to spend a Saturday with their friends, Ken and Debbie.

Harvey thought ice cream was in order. "Let's walk into town and browse in the stores. But, we're only going to take enough money for ice cream—no other shopping."

Bobbie could not have cared less about shopping on a day such as this. It was supposed to be a day for relaxation and visiting.

"Sounds good to me," Ken remarked. "What about you, Deb?"

Ken and Debbie had been friends with Bobbie and Harvey for several years. Even though they had not met until later in life, they felt as though they had grown up together. Ken was an elder in the church in which Harvey served as pastor, and Debbie was the pastoral administrative assistant.

"I don't want to shop in this one-horse town anyway . . . nothing's expensive enough," joked Debbie. "And besides, we'd better not let the guys think we have money, Bobbie, or we'll end up buying the ice cream."

They decided to walk rather than drive the few blocks to the center of town. Harvey had been doing some reading about the history of Cecil County, Maryland and especially about North East.

"Cecil County," he explained, "was named for Cecilius Calvert. He was the Second Lord Baltimore."

"Boy, that's really interesting, Harv," Ken teased. "I can't wait to hear the rest of the history of this exciting place." He looked at the women to see if he was going to get a laugh, but they were talking to each other about their families.

Walking slowly along the sandy path, Harvey continued his monologue about how the mouth of the river, for which North East was named, had been called Gunter's Harbour when first visited by white men in 1608. That first white man had been none other than James Smith, from Jamestown, Virginia.

As they approached the small St. Mary Anne's Episcopal Church, Harvey said, "Let's cut through here. I saw some guy searching the grounds with a metal detector when we drove in this morning. I wonder what he was expecting to find here."

"Same as us probably—bodies," Ken responded.

Entering through the iron-grated gate, the breeze seemed unwilling to follow them into the cemetery. Even though the air became still, it was cooler here. The old oaks and yellow poplars provided a cooling effect and shaded the ground—shaded it so well that little grass was able to grow.

Sun dappled through the trees and caught Harvey's eye as it reflected off a small brass plaque on the side of the brick wall of the church. The plate revealed that the Queen of England had given a Bible to the congregation in 1714 and that, on occasion, it was still in use.

Bobbie, Debbie, and Ken strolled along together, chatting about their favorite flavors of ice cream and debating the important issue of whether this was a one- or a two-scoop day. Harvey walked slowly and deliberately behind them, studying the headstones as he went.

Suddenly, he shouted, "Look! Look over here, Bobbie! It's our family name!

There, just a few feet from the east side of the small church building were five headstones in a row, all bearing the name *O'Connell.*

The other three turned back to see what had caused his excitement.

Ken said almost sarcastically, "So what's the big deal, Harv? I didn't know how much you liked cemeteries. I suppose that now this is where you'll want to be buried. Right?"

"No. You don't understand; I've just never seen a headstone with our family name on it. At least not one that wasn't a close relative of mine—you know, someone I had known personally. You see what I'm saying? Would you look at these? Here's *Alan O'Connell*. And look: this one says *Sarah O'Connell, our daughter*. And here's *Nathan O'Connell* . . . *Thomas O'Connell* . . . *Edward O'Connell*. Oh, this is amazing! It's wonderful!"

Harvey was particularly pleased because he had long wanted to know the origins of his family. Many of the men on his father's side of the family had been commercial fishermen on Lake Superior and Lake Michigan. But, no one in his family seemed to know much beyond that fact, except that the family had come from "somewhere out east, probably Boston," they would always say. Of course, Harvey knew that when you were from Wisconsin "out east" could mean anywhere on the other side of Lake Michigan.

Harvey and Bobbie lived in Kennett Square, a small town in Southeastern Pennsylvania, where he served as senior pastor of a church. They enjoyed living in the area, with its proximity to Amish country; Philadelphia; Washington, D.C; New York City; Chesapeake Bay; Delaware Bay; and the Atlantic. It was a nice place to live. Now here they were, just a short distance from Kennett Square, and at least some part of his family had lived here at one time—and died here as well. He was excited.

"Look at these dates. Some of them are so old and worn you can hardly read them. Look at this one:

July 4, 1692. I wonder if some of these others are even older."

Turning attention to the ladies, he asked, "Does anyone have a pencil and paper?"

Because of the comments they had made about shopping, the women had not brought their purses with them.

"Sorry, Honey," Bobbie said. "Why don't you come back here after we get our ice cream cones and copy some of the information?"

Ken and Debbie didn't share his enthusiasm, and that was understandable. Ice cream was more important to them than headstones today. But, he did expect his wife to show a little more interest.

"Wow, 1692! Can you imagine?" Harvey said, gently stroking the aged stone. "I wonder how old these others are. I think I'll try to do some of those rubbings on these headstones. I think they're easier to read when you do that—at least that's what I've heard. Hey, can you wrap your mind around this date: July 4, 1692? Isn't that something? That's over three hundred years ago, isn't it? Today's July 11th, so that's about three hundred years . . . no, I mean that's exactly three hundred years and one week."

He was reminded of a passage from the Bible. "Let's see," he mused, "there's a Scripture—it's somewhere in the Psalms—that goes something like, *'The lines fell to me in a good place, and I've got a good heritage.'* No, I think maybe it's, *'pleasant places.'* Yes, I think that's it. *'The lines have fallen to me in pleasant places; yes, I have a good heritage.'*

Or, maybe it's a *'goodly heritage'*. Anyway, I'll have to look that one up."

"Come on Harv, these guys aren't going anywhere," offered Ken. "Let's catch up with the girls. You can come back later and check this stuff out. In fact, I'll come back with you and help do the tracings if you want."

Ice cream was no longer on Harvey's mind. All he could think of were the headstones and those who had been buried in this old cemetery. He wondered who these people really were and whether it could be possible that he was actually a descendant of the men and women buried here.

He wanted to spend more time looking over other parts of the cemetery to see if other potential family members might be buried here. But, he knew he couldn't talk the others out of their appointed mission—not now. Besides, it really was an ice cream sort of day.

"Yeah, you're right, I'll come back later. Who did we say was buying?"

The women had already left the churchyard and the men hurried to catch up with them. They walked into the Kool-Kone ice cream parlor and Bobbie and Debbie had to sample a few flavors before both of them settled on butter pecan. Ken wanted chocolate with cookie dough, and Harvey tried the black raspberry.

They sat around a small table chatting, each enjoying their choice of flavors.

However, Harvey couldn't stop wondering if those graves might really hold the remains of kinfolk to whom he was directly connected. He also reflected about what the Bible said and whether these folks had indeed been a "goodly heritage." Even more important to him was whether they had been a godly heritage.

The day was hot, even for July 11, 1992. Yes, it was an ice cream sort of day. Yet, he couldn't keep from imagining what the "other O'Connells" had been doing on a day much like this more than three hundred years ago.

Chapter Two

A Small Cemetery at Gunter's Harbour

The day was much too cool for July 4, 1692, and another O'Connell headstone would soon be placed in the small cemetery on the banks of Gunter's Harbour. Only two family members remained alive in Maryland now.

Threatening gray skies seemed determined to further dampen the spirits of anyone daring to show the slightest hint of happiness in the small cemetery. The dampness chilled Elayne, causing her to shiver. She pulled the black shawl more tightly about her, folded her arms across her chest, and then drew closer to her brother Edward as he placed his arm over her shoulder.

The dark dress and countenances of those who gathered were good matches for the skies. Even the small oaks, pines, and poplars seemed to grieve for the cheerless mood of the mourners. The events of the past few days had left Edward and Elayne in deep sorrow.

Almost thirty years had passed since Queen Mary II had granted land holdings to the family, along with the authority to trade slaves. The Queen, a Protestant, had been crowned after her Catholic father was deposed in 1692. Even though she was sovereign in her own right, her husband William III wielded the power. However, the Queen governed the realm when her husband was off to war, which was often; and it was during one such occasion that the O'Connell family gained her favor, although what had brought them to such favor was unclear.

Family legend was that one of the O'Connell brothers had brought some rumor of an Irish rising to the Queen's ear, but this was never confirmed with any particulars. Nevertheless, the family's close acquaintance—whether perceived or actual—with Leonard Calvert, brother of Cecilius Calvert, the second Lord Baltimore, had brought the O'Connell clan to the sympathetic attention of the royal family.

William Clayborne, a member of the Council of Virginia, established a trading post in 1627 on Kent Island, at the mouth of the Susquehanna River where it emptied into the Chesapeake Bay. Once the area was opened to settlement, more than one hundred Englishmen came with the hope of a lively fur trade.

The successful fur trading led to expanded merchant opportunities, and the need for provisions increased as more people came. Then, the increased population and the high cost of bringing large quantities of food from England created the incentive to grow crops. More and more land began to be cleared and cultivated. Tobacco soon became the money crop, and then the slave trade began to flourish.

The O'Connell family and the influence they had held was fast dissipating. First Alan was gone, then Nathan, and now Thomas. Only Edward remained alive of the O'Connell men, and Elayne was the sole surviving daughter of the family—a spinster.

In the beginning it had all seemed like such a wonderful opportunity and so adventuresome. The Queen had given large tracts of land in the Maryland Colony to the family. The slave trade was quite brisk and very profitable. Even if it was not promoted, the slave trade was protected by the Queen herself. Consequently, the family business was afforded the security of the Royal Navy on the high seas. The land had been reasonably productive, and it all seemed quite proper and prosperous—at first.

The Reverend Jonathan Topping was at his pompous best at the graveside. His expensive clothing, which was intended to clearly identify his imagined social position, only made him look out of place. Actually, under other circumstances he might have been respected and would have had no need of the rich fabrics that made up his wardrobe.

However, this was a man of great personal insecurity and a man who lacked both integrity and passion. He found his importance only when he was able to raise himself (at least in his own eyes) above others.

He found himself wondering how many more of the family it would take to fill the small cemetery here at Gunter's Harbour. He'd had the "privilege" of burying every one of the O'Connell men.

Topping's voice droned on, "And none shall be denied that wonderful haven of beautiful rest prepared for us by God Himself, just as He promised when . . . ."

Edward pulled Elayne closer to himself, wondering with disdain, *Can this man actually sleep at night? He's never cared much about anyone but himself, and he's certainly had no deference for any of our family, except when it comes time to bury one of us.*

Topping's mind also wandered as they stood around the grave with their heads bowed. He was thinking, *One of my brothers should have been the recipient of the Queen's generosity and protection, rather than these coarse Irish pretenders. Or, even better than my brothers, it would have been more advantageous if it had been my sister Cynthia's husband, Daniel Wells.*

In Topping's mind, that would have resolved any possibility of sibling rivalry with his brothers. But, alas, his brothers had all returned to England, and he was left alone in this forsaken place with his sister, who was now widowed.

Now, he pondered, *here I am intoning platitudes over the grave as I've done for the others, just as a priest of the Church of England must do, and it's all so tedious.*

Then a faint smile came to his face as he thought, *I've become rather good at this pretended behavior, as though I've been Thomas's most beloved friend, which is sheer nonsense. And this ill-mannered O'Connell peasant brood is completely unaware.*

Perhaps Topping's musings were well founded. What would become of Dawn Light, the O'Connell holdings, now? Who would tend the farm and the trading? Edward had always been more interested in the social graces than in overseeing the family business, and it certainly would not be the unmarried Elayne. Who, indeed?

Just then, another funeral procession entered the small cemetery. It was the Dixon family; they would bury one of theirs today also. Their aged patriarch, Darby, had outlived three wives and most of his children. Only one son, Ben, who had remained in Maryland, and a married daughter, now living in England, were left behind.

Noticing the approach of the Dixon family, the Reverend Topping rolled his eyes. He thought that he'd better prepare yet again for more pious pattering nonsense over another grave. *These Dixons may have been English, but they live as if they're cut from the same bolt of coarse Irish cloth as this other brood.*

It was to be a day for burying, and the day was much too cool for July.

Chapter Three

Call of the Family

The year was 1694. Almost two years had passed since the death of Thomas, and the O'Connell holdings in Maryland had fallen into great disrepair. Most of the slaves had been sold in order to provide money for living expenses. Edward had proved to be a clumsy manager of workers, property, crops, money, and of his own life.

In December, 1693 — the same year the College of William and Mary was founded in Virginia — Edward had died too, as a result of feeding the livestock, of all things. As he approached a horse's stall, the surprised animal kicked out, breaking Edward's leg. Improper care allowed an infection to set in, and in a very short time the gangrenous limb caused Edward a rather unpleasant death.

There was more intoning by the Reverend Topping, and another O'Connell headstone scarred the ground of the small cemetery at Gunter's Harbour.

Elayne became despondent over the death of her last surviving brother. She seldom ate properly, found it impossible to manage the manor, was left helpless with her grief and depression, and had determined that she would leave Maryland and return to England.

However, before leaving, Elayne wrote to her nephew in Dublin and offered the manor in the new world to him. Sean O'Connell was his name. He was the son of her deceased brother, Nathan, the closest male blood relative that might be able to maintain the holdings and remain under the blessing and protection of the Crown.

Elayne knew that he duly met the qualifications of blood and law, but she had not seen him since he was a small child. She was unaware that this legal heir was otherwise ill-suited to the task in Maryland. He had no experience in the farming life, was young and unmarried, not particularly drawn to labor of any kind, reckless, and very headstrong.

Across the expanse of ocean, in Dublin, the day was overcast but warm. A breeze brought the pervasive smell of fish up the Liffey River from the Harbour. Women hurried about with their daily purchases from every sort of merchant that plied their goods on the streets, but no one was in such a hurry that they could not stop for a bit of gossip.

News had reached Dublin that Mary the Second, Queen of England, Ireland, and Scotland had died. Everyone in the streets now speculated what would happen now that the queen was dead, leaving her husband and cousin, William the Third, as sole ruler.

In Ireland, only the degree of oppression varied when a new ruler took the English throne. Nevertheless, until William actually would begin his solo monarchy and the effect of his ruling was felt by the Irish, they could spend much time gossiping and complaining about the variant bad possibilities of William's rule.

Sean had slept late; perhaps more accurately, as he himself would have described it, he slept until his usual hour for rising—just before noon. He dressed in what he thought to be a fairly clean shirt before he pulled on coarse Kersey wool breeches and forced his feet into heavy wet brogans that hadn't dried since last night's outing.

He then laced up his leather singlet; he preferred this sleeveless vest to his only other outerwear, a sleeved jerkin. Then he removed his money pouch from under the sleeping tick, where he always placed it at night. He left his cramped third-floor quarters, which nestled under the roof of a decaying building.

The narrow stairs spiraled downward. As he pushed the door to the street open, leaving the darkness and stepping into the light of the street made him squint. Walking slowly from the Wood Quay[1], he tried to ignore the pervasive smell of fish as he turned up the Viking path toward the region once known as Fish Shambles, near Trinity College.

Recognizing some of the younger women who bought and sold in the streets, he attempted small conversations with those lasses who seemed willing.

But his mind was set on more important matters—a habitual objective.

Soon, he stopped in front of a familiar red door, looked about, stretched in the sunlight, and was about to step into the inviting dank of his favorite inn, The Strongbow. Just then a voice called out.

"You there! Ahoy, young sir! You there! Be ye the O'Connell gentleman?"

Sean turned about and saw a raw-looking seaman coming toward him. He countered with the challenge, "Who is it that would know?"

Even though he wasn't outwardly the belligerent type, his obstinate Irish temperament scarcely allowed Sean to avoid a challenger when the opportunity was presented.

"Tommy Beal, I am, Sir. Seaman recent come on the *Prince's Pride*, up from Southampton I have. Docked we did yesterday and I've been looking about for you, Sir. That man yonder told me it was you, he did."

"Is that so? And for what purpose might you have need of me?" Sean asked. He cast a look across the way, shaded his eyes from the sun, and saw a man whose name he didn't know but with whom he was somewhat familiar, for they had both spent a fair amount of time in The Strongbow.

Looking back at the seaman, he quickly searched his memory and could think of no sailor to whom he might owe money for gambling debts.

"Aye, it's a letter I have for you. Captain Lawless, he says to me, 'Tommy, you should needs to find this Sean O'Connell gentleman and collect a bit for your trouble.' So he says, did the captain. A man with a keen mind, the captain."

"Did he now? Do tell. Well let me see what you have then."

Sean reached out and the seaman drew a letter from his waistcoat and handed it to him. A wave of anticipation gripped Sean when he saw that his name had been penned with the careful and deliberate hand of a woman.

Sean rummaged in his pocket and then pulled out a coin and placed it in the man's outstretched hand. He thanked the seaman, who immediately began to walk into the pub, relieved of his responsibilities and well prepared for his next, more anticipated, liquid assignment.

However, with his hand on the door latch he turned and said, "Blimey, if me work's yet to be done." With that, he reached inside his tunic and pulled out a small package wrapped in oilskin.

"Here it is, Sir. This one here's for you too, so it is," and he handed Sean the parcel. "I'm supposing you'd be as likely grateful for this here bundle as ye are for the letter, Sir."

Sean felt obligated to pull another coin from his pocket, and as he handed it to him the man responded with a thankful, toothless smile.

"Aye, mate—oh, excuse me it is, Sir—thanking you I am, Sir, and God bless you, Sir. Indeed, God bless you and your family, your kin, and your kind, and may fair winds fill your sails."

Again, Sean grunted a response of thanks and then leaned against the building. He felt a strange sense of pleasure as he carefully opened the waxed seal. He unfolded the paper and glanced down to the bottom of the letter. He was surprised to see that it was from his Aunt Elayne, and he began to read.

April the 3rd in the 1694th yr of our Lord

Loving and dear nephew Sean,

My most humble duty of remembrance to you, hoping that in God your health is good. As for me myself the augue has striken me so often I scarce know when it comes and goes. I must tell you dear nephew that I am most heavy by reason of the nature of my situation and the nature of this country which is such that it seems to cause much sickness. I falter to mention some of the terrible sicknesses as the scurvy and bloody flux and diverse other kinds of such disease which make one's body very weak and poore. It is not in joy that I write such as this yet since your father and uncles have died away your poore aunt is left alone and there is none to give me hope. With no men to hunt and fish I scarce can keep the field hands working. A mouthful of bread for a penny would be good if bread could be found. Alone as I am except for the black savages that are my indenture I live in some fear. On the Sunday before Shrovetide I surprised five thieves who came to steal the last of our corne grains. When such a thing happened I could no longer bear the terrible burden of the obligation which my brothers had left upon me. It is with this appeal of regret that I ask if you will come and by reason of your authority as my near kin O'Connell male receive the responsibility of Dawn Light. I can no longer abide in this place and seek berth on the next passage that leaves for Southhampton. I should say that the land holdings have been in better repair but by reason of the death of my brothers your uncles sickness and my inability to give proper superintendance to the black savages the plantation is very weak and in need of strong keeping. I shall not await your answer as I declare to leave shortly. Perhaps we will meet in Southampton. If we should not or if by reason of God's will our lives should soon end I would not hold you responsible for to not accept this charge and withhold. Yet it is my wish that you do accept and somehow restore Dawn Light to something of its days when your uncles gave good stewardship to this land that I have come to rather contemn. Along with this letter will arrive documents that I have put my hand to and that have been witnessed so that your ownership is legal and proper. My body is tired and my spirit is weak and your Aunt Elayne asks your forgiveness if this charge I have placed upon you be oppressive and obscure. I remember with great love your dearest mother now departed to better

*worlds and have the fondest memories of you
as a child here at Dawn Light now who has
grown to a man.*

*With sincerest thoughts of valuation I am
your loving Aunt Elayne*

Sean read the letter again and then read it a third
time. Yes, that's what she had said all right. Dawn
Light could be his. He stood there dumbfounded,
as he glanced again and again at the letter. Phrases
seemed to leap off the paper. *"In need of strong
keeping . . . would not hold you responsible for to not
accept . . . yet, it is my wish that you do accept . . . I
shall not await your answer."*

His aunt's letter and the small packet of papers
wrapped in oilskin had caught up with him there in
Dublin almost a year after she had sent them.

It seemed that his aunt had a better appreciation
of him than anyone else who knew him. In fact, he
thought himself disqualified in every way to be the
sort of man his aunt assumed he was: a hardworking
man who would be eager to oversee the lands and
business of his family in the new world. Sean had
never spent any length of time in honest endeavor
and had been known to enjoy gambling and ale, and
he never refused to respond to any belligerent appeal
over even the slightest offense.

Since his mother's death so many years ago, he
had given little thought to his family or the manor
in Maryland. Nevertheless, at the consideration of

being a landowner, he could hardly deny that this was surely an opportunity not to be passed over.

With little deliberation and with less hesitation, he eagerly determined that he would accept his aunt's offer.

After making this hasty decision, he resolved that, rather than responding to her by letter, he would simply leave for Southampton to see her personally and tell her of his decision: that he would gladly accept this charge. Besides, the sooner he could get to her, the better his chance of obtaining some money, for which he was in great need.

He stepped into the inn, pausing as his eyes adjusted to the darkness, to inquire of the seaman who had given him the letter and package.

Sean saw the man who was about to finish his first jar. Approaching him, Sean said, "Good man, I thank you for providing me with this news from my family."

"Aye, Sir, glad it is I could find you as the captain told me I should. Yes Sir, glad I am."

"Well then—Tommy, is it?—let me provide you with another pint, and tell me about your ship and the captain's plans to sail from here."

"Aye, Sir. They be unloading at the dock now they are, Sir. As, for the captain, Sir, it's not likely his custom to tell me his plans." Again he shared a toothless grin. "But, I'll tell you this: the captain he won't be staying long."

"How long?" Sean asked impatiently. "A day? A week? How long?"

"Aye, Sir, 'ere's what the captain'll do. He'll get the ship unloaded he will. Then he'll bring some stores aboard and what cargo he'll find. Then Captain Lawless, what he'll do is he'll have us put canvas up, and *Prince's Pride* she'll be off again to Southampton. The captain, he likes the sea better than the docks. A few days is what I says, and no more, Sir, is what I says. A few days and no more. And what about the provision you said you was going to make for me, Sir? I could take it now I could, Sir."

Chapter Four

To England and the Colonies

S ean was able to secure passage on the *Prince's Pride*, and three days later the ship was ready to return to Southampton.

The lines were cast off at high tide, because low tides exposed large areas of mud and sand within the main channel of the river. From Pigeonhouse to Islandbridge, the width of the Liffey was virtually the same at both extremes of the tide, but sailing was always treacherous at low tide.

Sean stood motionless on the deck and watched the dark waters of the Liffey move the ship slowly past quay walls and the great walls of the bay. They became enveloped in the shroud of early morning fog that made him feel eerily invisible.

For some reason, the cold moisture of the fog pleased Sean. But as they neared the sea, the air became fresher as the fog began to lift, and Sean was glad because he wondered if he would ever again see the bay at Dublin.

Suddenly, the sails took on life. They seemed to inhale as they filled with air, and the small vessel lurched forward in response to the brisk wind that carried them southeastward out to the Irish Sea and on toward England.

The small ship heaved starboard as its sails fully caught the north wind and the sun broke through the clouds that raced before them. Sean looked over the stern and could still see the low-lying Ben of Howth. Turning forward, as they were passing Dalkey, his mind reluctantly left Ireland and began to drift toward the possibilities of the future.

Three days later they arrived in Southampton, where his excitement over the potential of a new life in Maryland, the colonial place of his birth, was quickly quieted.

Seeking directions to find his Aunt Elayne, he came across Jonathan Shore, who claimed to be a distant cousin of sorts.

"I do know her. Indeed I do, or I should say that I *knew* who she was. You see, even though I've never met your Aunt Elayne, she was the cousin of my own dear mother. Now, I know that makes you and me kin."

"You said that you *did* know who she was?" Sean asked. "What do you mean?"

"Oh, I regret to have spoken so. I thought you knew. You see, I fear I have unfortunate and disheartening news for you. Your aunt, having been in ill health when she boarded the ship in the colonies, died less than two weeks into the voyage. The captain of the vessel said she was buried at sea, possibly near Bermuda, but he couldn't be certain. I knew of no other kin, so I gave your aunt's small trunk and other belongings to my sister. There were only a few personal items of feminine interest. I could take you to my sister's home and you could see for yourself."

"No, no. That's not needed. If there was anything of value that I should know of, I'm certain that you would tell me."

"Of course, and I thank you for your trust. I regret to also tell you that not even a headstone has been placed in honor of her name — not here in Southampton or on the Isle of Wight. That's what I'm told."

Although Sean had no money to set such a stone, nevertheless he said, "I had no idea of her death and wonder what change this will present to my plans now."

Realizing that the man would not know what he meant, he added quickly, "I've no experience with these things, but do you not think it must be important to memorialize my aunt in some way?"

"You're right," the cousin agreed, "and we should see that a memorial stone is placed for your aunt."

"Yes, of course. That we must do, but I have to secure passage to the colonies and have no money for the passage or for placing a stone at this time."

"Then that's what I'll do for my newly found cousin. I'll see that the stone is placed and then . . . . ."

Sean interrupted, "Would you do as much, Sir? I've no way to pay you now, but I pledge to send money as soon as I am able."

"I'll take you as a man of your word; after all, you are my cousin. And I'll resolve to set the stone myself. You can count on that."

They agreed to the plan, and both were happy to have had this chance meeting. But Sean was already thinking that, even though cousin Jonathan Shore would bear the expense, he himself would not give much thought to repaying him.

Sean knew he'd have to raise money for passage and other expenses for the trip. For years he had found it a rather easy task to win at gaming of almost any sort—whether cards, dice, gambling tables, horseracing, or cockfights.

So Sean looked for events where he might obtain the quickest profit. Although, just a few days earlier, because of the promising outlook of his new role as a landowner he had resolved to turn over something of a new leaf, now he found it necessary—just this one last time—to resort to a method of making money that he knew all too well.

Watergate Quay stood at the foot of High Street and was bordered by the old town walls of Southampton. There was a time when French wines had been imported here for the Norman kings, and wool was exported to the continent from these piers. For centuries Southampton had been the heart of maritime activity and was England's major port.

Small wharves extended on either side of Watergate Quay, and to the east they reached an area known as "The Platform," built in the 13th century for defense of the town. Further on lay the oyster beds.

However, because of competition from London, continental trade in the port of Southampton had been rapidly declining,. Even though Southampton remained a popular port of choice for the colonies, nevertheless, the area around Watergate Quay had fast become derelict.

The district was filled with men and women who lived to take advantage of others—the sort of place that Sean knew would provide him with quick income. Early in life, he had discovered that anyone who was determined to take advantage of others could as easily become victim to their own greed.

Five weeks later, Sean found himself with his pockets full of the king's coin. He was able to obtain passage on the next available ship bound for Maryland by way of Bermuda and Jamestown. The ship was a sloop, built of strong Bermuda cedar. It was the *Southern Swallow*, out of Southampton, and Laird Murphy was her captain.

Sean stood on the forward deck. As southeasterly breezes filled the sails and tousled his long brown hair, the wind felt good against his face. Taller than most men, he struck a rather handsome appearance, and his ruddy complexion belied the fact that he spent most of his time indoors.

Sean was 25 years old, the only child of Nathan. In 1675, as a boy five years of age, he had sailed from the family manor in Maryland to England with his mother Helen. While visiting family and friends in Southampton, Helen was stricken with fever and, within three days, she died.

Sean's father Nathan died in Maryland two years later. Sean had been sent to Ireland to live with his mother's sister, Ellen, who had never married and tried her best to raise him properly. However, he grew up as a spoiled, undisciplined child, and he became a self-centered, undisciplined young man.

At the age of fourteen, he apprenticed himself to a printer in Dublin named Cathal O'Byrne. O'Byrne was a master printer but a rather strange man who claimed to be kin to Humphrey Powell, the man who printed *The Boke of Common Praier* in 1551. O'Byrne also imagined that Powell must have been the man who, in 1571, had printed the first catechism, using the Irish characters called, *Aibidil Gaoidheilge agus Caiticiosma*.

Sean learned the trade quickly and did very well as a "printer's devil," but his interest was not in O'Byrne's family history, the printed word, or much of anything else.

Besides, O'Byrne was involved in some sort of clandestine business. Day and night, visitors often came to O'Byrne's print shop, but it was not to utilize his printer's craft.

O'Byrne and the men carried on quiet talks at the back of the shop. The printer belonged to a group of men who met secretly, usually at O'Byrne's. Their goal was to find Ireland's most sacred relic: the very staff of St. Patrick himself.

Even though the monstrous King Henry VIII had ordered all of Ireland's relics destroyed, there were rumors that the staff, which had been held in

St. Patrick's own hands a thousand years earlier, had been hidden away.

One day Sean overheard part of a hushed conversation.

"You can think what you want Cathal, I'm telling you it's true. My very own mother's sister, a sainted woman, knows someone who told her that the very staff of St. Patrick had been secreted from Christ Church Cathedral and replaced with a counterfeit staff. Then, when the protesting devils came for the staff, the counterfeit was the one that was burned at the king's command."

O'Byrne replied, "I've heard as much myself, but it was told in a somewhat different way."

"I'll not care about different ways of telling it," the man was quick to answer. "What I'm telling you is that there are even rumors that claim some have seen the authentic staff as recently as two years ago in County Meath."

Just then, Sean dropped several pieces of type— as precious as gold to a printer. O'Byrne turned about and saw Sean. "Are you sticking your nose in where it belongs not, lad? You'll be paying for that type if it's rounded you will. Now get back to work."

After that, Sean never gave much thought to this business about a staff that belonged to St. Patrick. He thought he'd leave it with these old men who could bother themselves with such nonsense.

However, two years later, when he was 16, Sean lost his job with the printer. Cathal O'Byrne had been arrested, along with several other men of the covert St. Patrick's guild, with whom he had met in secret.

It seems their meetings were not as secretive as they had imagined.

One day, as Sean was setting type, the door of the small print shop burst open and several armed men came rushing inside. They were hated mercenaries of Dublin's Lord Deputy. Most of these men were English, but then there were the worst sort of Irishmen, who sold their military service to the Judiciar too.

One of the men grabbed Sean by the arm, threw him against the wall, and shouted, "Where is he? Where's the papist O'Byrne?"

Without thinking, Sean struck out with the stone that he'd been using to level type, and he caught the man in the forehead.

"Buggering papist hit me," the man shouted. Cursing wildly he turned Sean's arm loose but only long enough to get more leverage, and he came down hard on Sean's nose with his fist.

Sean had tried to strike out when the man turned him loose and shouted, "I'm no papist, I'm not even . . .," but then the blow turned everything silent and dark for Sean.

When he regained his senses, the men were wildly searching the room, overturning tables and boxes of type, as well as the printer's press.

The man who struck him now stood over him with his foot on Sean's chest. "You'd better hear me now, you filthy little papist."

Sean tried to struggle, but the man bore his weight down on him.

"You'll leave this shop and don't ever be returning. We're watching you, and all like you and your O'Byrne. If we see you near here again, it'll be the end of you. Do you hear me?"

Sean couldn't get enough breath to speak, but nodded his throbbing head enough to convince the man that he understood, and the man allowed him to get to his feet. With blood still trickling from his broken nose, he staggered into the narrow alley.

Later, under the cover of night he returned to find men lurking about. He presumed they were there to capture O'Byrne. Sean never revisited the print shop; and, if he occasionally passed that way, he always looked down the alleyway first and then walked to the far side of the alley.

Later, he learned that O'Byrne's companions were taken to London for sentencing and they were all hanged—or so went the rumor. However, no one quite knew what had become of his employer. It seems that the printer O'Byrne was arrested too, but he had escaped and disappeared.

Sean certainly did not understand the situation with O'Byrne and his friends; he only knew that he no longer had employment. He was 16, and for the next several years he did whatever he fancied, living off the money that had been left to him by his father and what he gained through his proficiency at gambling. By the age of 20, he was spending most of his considerable leisure time in public houses.

The vessel upon which Sean had been able to secure passage from Southampton was a sloop—a small ship not much longer than 60 feet. It was the first vessel that Sean could secure for passage. He knew little about vessels of any kind. Of course, he was familiar with the sight of fishermen near Dublin going to sea, but these were small boats. So, even though the sloop may have been small by sailing standards, to Sean it seemed that it would be adequate enough for crossing the ocean.

The captain was a congenial sort. An older man, he often engaged Sean in conversation, questioning him at some length about his reasons for going to Maryland and inquiring of the trade skills he brought with him. This was always an important consideration, because the English had filled the colonies with laborers of one sort or another, but they were usually indentured or convicts and, of course, slaves.

So, it seemed quite natural for Sean to take the liberty of doing some embellishing about both his background and his abilities as a skilled "master" printer that he brought to the colonies.

"Yes, I've heard that the colonies had need of printers who were highly skilled in their craft."

"Is that so?" the captain asked, "And what would be your plan?"

"Well, of course I haven't been in Maryland since my childhood, so I'll first seek another master printer and perhaps engage myself with him for a time before setting off on my own. My printing skills are quite unique and I should think they'll be in great demand in the colony."

"My, isn't that a wonderful thing, to have such a craft. Keeps a man settled, it does, and not as some of us, having to be off at sea all the time."

Sean smiled, convinced that he had greatly impressed the captain. And even though he was very uncertain of his future, nevertheless, he assured the captain, "Yes, my future will certainly be successful."

Then the captain told Sean of the printer who had brought the first printing press to the colonies. He proudly told of how his ship, the *Southern Swallow* transported both the first printing press and the printer himself, along with his wife, to Jamestown in 1682.

"Unfortunately," he went on to explain, "They went and banned both the press and the printer, and the printer and his wife had to flee for their lives to Maryland. It seems he'd been printing reports considered to be both annoying and injurious to the well-being of the Virginia colonists."

Somewhat shocked by this revelation, Sean had nothing to reply, so the captain went on.

"Seems those men with money in England never come to the colonies, but they expect quick and easy riches from their investments in Jamestown. But that printer, well, he was telling colonists to look for real gold and silver. And, I'd say that the low price of that 'brown gold' tobacco was good enough reason to turn their efforts to seek real gold. Unfortunate it was for him that the colonial governor didn't agree."

Sean said no more, because it seemed that the captain already knew more about printing—at least, printing in the colonies—than Sean did.

Sean knew nothing about ships either, but the long sea journey provided ample time to learn much.

Captain Murphy was glad to tell him about the *Southern Swallow*—sometimes for hours on end.

"Now, this vessel is rigged with what we call fore-and-aft rigging, and it's seldom found on small ships like these. But, this ship's from Bermuda, and the shipbuilders there have shown it to work to great advantage. Although I've never had the opportunity to do so, I'm confident that this little bird of mine could fly away from any pirate or privateer; they'd never board the *Southern Swallow* at sea." He laughed and then added, "Unless, of course, they've a Bermuda sloop themselves."

"We're not looking to be approached by privateers, are we captain?"

"Oh, no. You see, young sir, I'm just telling you how nimble this ship is. You see, the winds can be gusty in the Bermuda Islands, and this rigging they've given us makes for some lively movement when the winds are upward. I'll tell you this bird will fly with the wind."

"But are you saying the privateers and pirates have these same ships—the same as the *Southern Swallow?*"

"Well, truth is that I can't say they do, and I won't say they don't. Here's what I'll tell you though: the *Southern Swallow* was born for the open ocean, and her deep hull makes her a seaworthy bird. That's why I looked until I found me a two-master. Oh, a single-masted Bermuda sloop may catch me with her speed, but in rough weather they'll easily be swamped— something we don't need on the open sea. And a one-masted ship's too small for a privateer's liking."

"That's not to say a pirate or privateer cannot have a two-masted sloop though. Is that what you say, Captain?"

"True enough, that's what I say. Who's to know what they'll be up to next? Aye, who's to know? Now, have you noticed the cut of the masts on this little bird? Raked they are. And the hull is deep and what we call stiff, for it's made of that fine Bermuda cedar. And it's good for the rot too. If ever you'd see a ship that's made of Bermuda cedar that's had rotting, you can lay it on the captain of that vessel, for he cares not for his ship. You see, when you care for the cedar she'll care for you. Aye, Bermuda cedar is what makes this little bird fly; she's light and fast and strong. Much the same as us is what I say, my young sir." And he threw his head back with another hearty laugh.

When the *Southern Swallow* made port in St. George, Bermuda, Sean was ready to disembark. He was confident that the life of a sailor was not for him. Even though the seas had been fair during the crossing from England, he had spent a good deal of his time in great discomfort from seasickness.

As he strolled along the piers of St. George, he was surprised at what he saw. In addition to a fleet of 10 sloops and ketches, there were four British brigantines with menacing gun ports and dozens of small boats. He guessed that these probably were used along the coastal waters.

The friendly Bermudians were well known as excellent builders of very seaworthy craft, using that native Bermuda cedar, the same wood used in the

Southern Swallow. They built large boats for foreign clients as well as for the English, and Sean learned that they were in the midst of some of the best years ever for Bermuda shipbuilding.

The small amount of cargo on the *Southern Swallow* that had been destined for Bermuda was unloaded quickly. However, Captain Murphy had private business that kept him in St. George for several days. He usually slept aboard the ship but was gone most of the time during the day and often far into the night.

Although Sean was anxious to get to Maryland, he found that he liked the effect of having land under his legs again. His stomach certainly took advantage of the firmness of the land.

Every day he wandered along the docks of St. George, fascinated by the craftsmen who labored at their boat building. For some reason he took great interest in the way these men worked. Little instruction was given, because every man—even the youngest of them—seemed to know what needed to be done.

He was particularly drawn to three brothers who worked together as boat builders. Each brother had two sons, and despite the fact that three of the sons were no older than 10, the nine worked together in a way that Sean admired.

During his brief stay in St. George, daily he spent hours watching how quickly this family enterprise advanced in building a boat. He came to realize that they were able to make such progress because of their skilled and cooperative teamwork. Cooperation was a concept with which Sean had little experience.

The time passed quickly in Bermuda, One morning, before Sean was fully awake, he heard the first mate's harsh voice shouting for the lines to be cast off. By the time Sean had dressed and climbed to the deck, the *Southern Swallow* was catching a lively breeze and the pilot, a Bermudian, was snaking the ship among the coral reefs and out of the security of the St. George's Harbour. Safely outside the reefs, the pilot bid farewell to the captain and crew, boarded his small ketch, raised its sail, and turned back to port. Once again, the *Southern Swallow* was underway to Maryland.

Once outside the barrier reefs, the captain saw Sean standing on the forward deck, gazing back toward Bermuda and called to him.

"Say, young sir, I've some things to tell you. Come back here to the helmsman's whipstaff² with me, if you please."

Sean was almost always ready to talk with the captain and actually was hoping to learn more about what had kept them at St. George for almost a week.

"I didn't want to alarm you back in port," the captain began, "but my contacts there told me there's been a good deal of pirate and privateer activity during the past month. Actually, three of our English brigantines have been prowling about lately, hoping to run into these thieving rascals."

"How is that?" Sean asked. "I'd heard that the throne actually commissioned the privateers. If that's true, why would we dread them?"

"Aye, young sir, it's true, and that's just the catch. As often as not, these commissioned privateers don't come up with enough bounty from French or Spanish ships. So, I've heard it said that's when they turn to our own English vessels. But, no one can claim that for certain, because they'll take what they want, sink the English vessel, and kill off any of the crew who won't join them. Aye, it's a bad sort are these—a bad sort."

"Well, then," asked Sean, "What are we to expect from the Royal Naval ships? I mean, will they join us and protect us until we gain port in Jamestown?"

"No, that's not to be. But we've nothing to dread from privateers, unless you've more in your sea chests than I'd reason." The captain hesitated for a moment before he broke into a good-natured grin, and Sean laughed with him.

Puzzled at first, Sean then said, "So, you're saying that our cargo isn't the sort that attracts pirates or privateers?"

"That's so. These deceitful rogues are wise enough to know what ships are at sea and the kinds of cargo each type of ship carries. They'll see a ketch or a sloop like the *Southern Swallow* and know that we're not the sort of vessel that's been trusted with any kind of precious cargoes. Any seaman knows we'll do well to carry enough provision for the crew, let alone any spoils that might attract those blackguards."

Despite the captain's assurances of their safety, Sean resolved that he would spend a good deal of time on deck from that time forward, searching the horizon surrounding the *Southern Swallow*.

His intentions to be a lookout lasted less than an hour, because his stomach determined to interrupt his plans. He fell to the deck seasick, and stayed there for almost seven days, during which time he seriously considered asking to be tossed overboard so he could die.

One morning, Captain Murphy called for Sean to have an early breakfast in the captain's quarters, but Sean declined. Even though he was hungry, he cared nothing about eating. The small ship had continued to toss in what had become heavy seas during the past several days and nights since leaving Bermuda. Sean could scarcely discern whether it was day or night. His stomach was not eager to go through the turmoil of more seasickness for the sake of a little hardtack.

"A few more hours, Sir," the captain assured him. "We've bypassed Jamestown and I don't know that you've taken notice of it but I had no cargo for them and have plenty of water and such."

Sean had noticed little in the past days, except that he had given a good deal of thought to his wasted life. He had even been wondering if God might not be executing judgment on him at sea.

"We're sailing high and the tides are running right," the captain offered. "And I calculate that we'll be snug in berth within eight or ten hours. You'll do well again, when you're ashore. You'll do well again. You needn't be ashamed; I've seen old hands at sailing who were far sicker than you, I have."

Somehow, that did not make Sean feel much better, but he did consider it a kindness that the captain had taken such an interest in him.

"As you say, Captain. And I do appreciate your concern for me. Now, if you'll excuse me, I'll go below and secure my belongings."

He was not eager to go below decks again. Even though the ship was in the somewhat shallower waters of Chesapeake Bay and was rocking only mildly now, Sean still had queasy feelings in the depths of his stomach, simply from watching the horizon changing as it moved up and down.

But, he had to go below. He wanted another look at the drawing and map before they arrived in Harbour.

As soon as he shut the small door behind him, the confined space that he had paid his passage for seemed to grow smaller as it closed in on him. He found himself fighting the strong urge to run back on deck to vomit.

Trying to keep his mind off the lingering queasiness, he sat down on the edge of the narrow bunk and, in doing so, he hit his head on the overhanging lamp. It had happened almost every time he sat down on his bunk during the crossing.

"You'd think I'd learn," he heard himself saying aloud, as he rubbed the same spot on his head that had been carelessly abused throughout the sea journey.

The small oilskin package that he had received in Dublin from his aunt was lying on the bunk. He opened it carefully, unfolded the papers, and his eyes wandered over the drawing of the house called Dawn

Light. One of his uncles—he did not know which one—had made the drawings of the front of the main house.

It looked very much like the house in England that he remembered from his childhood—the one he had first visited. The main difference was that the house in this drawing did not appear to have a thatched roof.

The drawing showed a dwelling with two floors and a porch that ran the full length across the front and appeared to continue on the right side as one faced the house. Four windows were placed in such a manner that Sean decided that there must be at least three rooms across the front of the second floor. The first floor had two doors, one on either end of the house, and only three windows. It looked very much like the house in Southampton.

Sean then unfolded another sheet of paper and laid it out on the bunk before him. This was to certify proof of his ownership. It read:

Possession of the manor house of O'Connell Manor, known as 'Dawn Light,' delivered by Elayne O'Connell, unmarried sister of the last remaining male heirs, Edward O'Connell, now dcsd., Elayne O'Connell being the tenant in possession, to Sean O'Connell, son of the dscd. Nathan, nephew of the aforementioned, and the lawful and undoubted heir of his uncle, Edward, lately deceased, before us

*this third day of June, in the year of our Lord,
1693.*

> *William Dare*
> *Edward Jones*
> *James Thompson*

Immediately after this entry, on the same paper,
it read:

> *Quiet possession of the Manor house of
> O'Connell Manor accepted and received,
> this day of, 169 .*

> *In presence of*

> > *Clerk to the Commissioners of
> > Cecil County*

The second entry required Sean's signature and
was to be signed by the same men who had witnessed
his Aunt Elayne's delivery of the manor to him.

Sean then unfolded the next document, which was
the legal patent for the land holdings. This was not
the original grant but was devised later and signed by
the second Lord Baltimore. After greeting all persons
to whom it should come, "in the name of the Lord
God Everlasting," it declared:

> *The Honorable Lord Baltimore grants unto
> Alan O'Connell, Nathan O'Connell, Thomas
> O'Connell, Edward O'Connell, and Elayne
> O'Connell, their unmarried sister, all that*

tract of land to be called O'Connell Manor, lying on the north side of the Chesapeake Bay, and on the west side of a river in the said bay, called Gunter's Harbour, on the western-most side of a creek in the said river, called Beacon Creek, and running northwesterly up the said creek of the length of two thousand perches[3] to the southernmost bound marked by an oak tree of the land of Philip Calvert, Esq., and from said oak running southwest for the length of three hundred and twenty perches until it intersects the easternmost side of a creek called Principio Creek, and running southerly down the said creek until said line reaches the bay. Containing and now laid out for four thousand acres. These lands and manor to be held by them and their heirs, in free and common socage[4], by fealty[5] only for all manner of services, by even and equal portions, the rent of four pounds ster-ling, in silver or gold, or the full value thereof, in such commodities as we or our heirs shall accept in perpetuitous discharge thereof.

Cecilius, Lord Baron of Baltimore.

He then turned his attention to the map, tracing with his finger that portion shown as O'Connell Manor. He tried to say some of the strange-sounding names on the map aloud. He struggled to remember what it had looked like when he left as a child but could not bring up anything from his stored memories.

"Sus - que - han - nah River," Sean slowly sounded aloud as though he expected it to come out correctly, and then he repeated it. *What an odd sounding name,* he thought. *It must be that one of their natives named it.*

He continued examining the map, trying to imagine the lay of the land and wondering what the Principio Creek might look like. He laid his head back on the small bunk and slept.

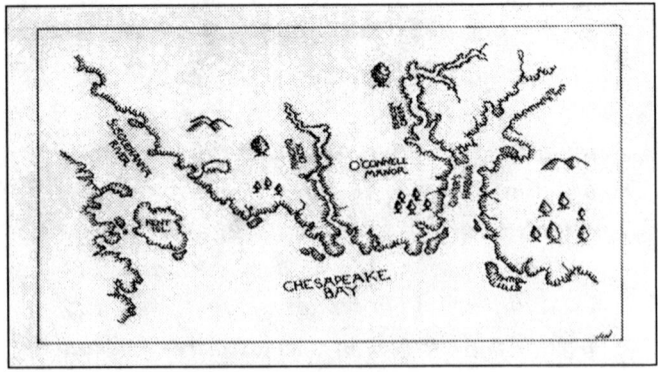

Upper Reaches of the Chesapeake Bay

He became aware of the sounds of voices that had been increasing in volume. He didn't know how long it had been since he had studied the map and then dozed off until he heard a bumping against the side of the ship. Then he heard some unintelligible orders being shouted.

Sean carefully refolded the documents, placed them in his sea chest, and closed the latch. Earlier that day he had placed his other belongings in the larger chest and was ready to leave the ship.

As he rose quickly from his bunk, he again struck his head on the overhead lamp, but this time in his excitement he scarcely noticed he had done so. Besides, it would be the last time the lamp would do him injury. Running through the narrow passageway and up to the outer deck, he stumbled over a coiled rope and fell face down. Lifting himself to his feet he glanced about, hoping no one had seen him. From the deck, he looked over the side and saw two small boats tied up to the ship.

The boats were pinnacles, or yawls—small rowboats about 15 feet in length with four men at the oars. In Southampton and Bermuda, Sean had seen boats being used for the same purpose, but for berthing much larger sailing vessels. Accordingly, those berthing boats had been larger too, often exceeding 25 feet in length, with six or eight men at the oars.

Sean looked all around him. Then he walked forward on the small ship's deck and saw a third yawl being tied up at the bow of the *Southern Swallow*. Inquisitive faces were all about, looking up at him. The first thing he became aware of was that the clothing the men wore was much less restrictive and cruder than that worn in England, or even in Ireland.

He thought, *So this is North East.* As he did, he wondered if he had made a wise bargain in coming.

Chapter Five

Greeted by a Trojan Horse

The *Southern Swallow* was being pulled snugly into her place by the oarsmen in the berthing yawls, and the men of the third boat were already secured at dockside. Sean noticed that these oarsmen were quite skilled at the task, and one of the men in each boat would speak directions to the other three in his boat. Then, at appropriate times, one man or the other would shout to those in the other yawl. Their experience was apparent, and the small sailing vessel was soon expertly berthed in the small, shallow docking area.

Southampton had been a crowded port that bustled with activity, sometimes both night and day. Even St. George's had more activity than Gunter's Harbour seemed to have. As he looked about, Sean thought it scarcely qualified as a Harbour at all, and it certainly seemed ineligible to be designated as a port. Rather than a Harbour, it was more like a small stream that emptied into the Bay and got narrower the closer they came to the docking area.

This Harbour, or river (or whatever it might be), had no need for a proper quay, as there had been in Dublin and Southampton, because there was no room for a real wharf on the banks of this shallow waterway. However, actually a rather feeble attempt had been made to build a quay of sorts. But, it could hardly be considered a proper quay, and the small ship listed landward, because it was actually touching bottom. What served as a dock was no more than rough planks that barely reached up out of the muddy banks and stretched out to the deck of the ship.

There was certainly much less activity on this waterfront than Sean had anticipated. Even though the *Southern Swallow* was a small vessel, nevertheless, several freight carts were lined along the wooden docking area, waiting for goods to be unloaded.

In one of their daily conversations, Captain Murphy had mentioned to Sean that he would notice a smaller number of horses in Maryland than he had been used to in Ireland. These animals were very expensive and difficult to ship aboard a vessel, especially one as small as his.

The day was sweltering and unusually hot, even for July. A few local merchants were there to pick up goods from the ship. Slaves were sent aboard to begin unloading the small main cargo hold. A few men exchanged local Maryland news for hearsay from England and Bermuda with the captain and his mate. As they shouted back and forth, the local gentry got the better of the bargain for the news exchange. This was because the sort of activity that would generate news in Gunter's Harbour was generally not the sort that newcomers would find interesting.

Sean was surprised at how quickly they unloaded the ship. They began with smaller items like spices and cloth and metal utensils, such as pots, nails, and tool heads. The goods in barrels would be unloaded last.

He had been the only passenger aboard the ship since they left Bermuda, and his eyes swept back and forth across the small dock and shore for anyone who might be looking for him. He had fully expected that someone from his family holdings would meet him when he arrived at North East. Everyone he saw seemed to have a reason for being there, but apparently no one had come for him.

His eyes continued searching through the small crowd of people along the muddy bank, and he noticed a well-dressed man step down from a carriage that had just pulled up to the edge of the docking area.

Sean's first thought was that the carriage seemed much too ornate for this part of the world. The carriage boasted a matched set of beautiful horses; and, based on what the captain had said about the price of horseflesh, that pair must have cost a pretty penny.

He quickly guessed that the man had to be wealthy and must hold some sort of authority because, as he walked up the gangplank, trying his best to avoid soiling his boots in the mud, all of the workers made way for him.

The man approached the captain and it was obvious to Sean that he was making an inquiry of some sort. The captain turned and pointed toward where Sean stood on the forecastle deck.

The stranger was extremely thin and, because of this, he appeared to be tall. His face had the pinched look of someone who smiled too little. His narrow dark eyes seemed to neither look directly at a person nor linger at any one spot, moving about constantly.

Although Sean was an inexperienced new arrival, he thought that the thin man seemed overdressed for this part of the world—much like his carriage, which was much too gaudy.

As the man approached, Sean hoped it was not someone from his family holdings, and he was relieved to discover that indeed the man was not. Instead, he was a certain Reverend Jonathan Topping. As he introduced himself, he tried to smile his way into Sean's confidence.

"Master O'Connell, welcome to Gunter's Harbour, this forsaken outpost of the Crown's protectorate. I am the Reverend Jonathan Topping, minister of England's Church and a long-time friend of your family. I want to be able to assist you in every way possible as you begin this sad responsibility of closing out your family holdings here in Maryland."

Sean found himself thinking, *What kind of fop is this? I've never seen any priest dressed like this, not even in Dublin or London.* Not that Sean ever purposefully went looking for priests.

"Well, yes, I uh . . . thank you, Sir," Sean cautiously replied.

"I see you are somewhat puzzled by my reference to Gunter's Harbour. It is the name that those of us whose families have long been settled here still use. Although, I must say that in these recent days it is sometimes commonly referred to as North East (named for the river), but it seems a name far too common for those of us who have long lived here. But, I must not go on so."

Something about this man caused Sean to tighten inside. It was not a feeling that could be explained rationally, but he recognized it as the same reaction he had experienced on other occasions. In times past, when he acknowledged the caution, he had been saved from rascals more than once and in more than one kind of incident.

Sean imagined that Topping could be the sort of man who might build a Trojan horse and then bring it to the O'Connell holdings to get some sort of advantage over him. Still, common manners dictated that he must respond properly to the man. But what had he meant by "closing out your family holdings"?

"Yes, well, thank you, Reverend Topping. I am pleased, of course," he lied, "that a man of your stature would trouble himself by meeting me here at the docks. I am, indeed, interested in how places are named. You must excuse me though, Sir. It is not that I am disappointed in meeting you, but I rather expected to be greeted by someone from the O'Connell Manor."

"Ah, alas, my young sir, you do not know. You must understand that there is no one left there at what was once called the O'Connell Manor. The slaves that have not been sold have either run away or have been taken by opportunistic rogues awaiting such a chance as your holdings provided."

Sean sensed more here than the words he was hearing. "Do you mean, Reverend Topping, that no one now lives on the O'Connell holdings?"

"Well, Sir, of course I have not been there to see for myself, you understand; but, alas, others do inform me that indeed no one lives there any longer. The manor has been abandoned and is in great disrepair."

For some reason, Sean suspected that this man had, in fact, been on the O'Connell property — perhaps recently. *But, why would he deny such a thing? What difference does it make one way or another if he has or has not been on the property?*

"Perhaps, then, Reverend Topping, you would be so kind as to inform me how I might obtain both transport to my holdings and some help with my trunks?"

"Yes, yes, of course. I have anticipated just such a need. Allow me to accompany you myself." Topping touched Sean's arm to indicate that he should start down the gangplank to the dock. Sean looked down at Topping's hand, which the Reverend quickly removed from Sean's arm.

As they stepped onto the dock, Topping continued, "I have taken the liberty of arranging for your trunks to be placed upon one of my carts. Of course, you and I will ride in my carriage. My gardener and house slave will bring your chests later and assist you as you settle in for your brief stay. I can assure you, the house is in a terrible state . . . uh . . . that is, I have been informed of its poor condition."

So, I was right. He has been there, Sean thought. *Then why the pretense?*

"Ah, here is my cart now. My men will see to your trunks and bring them to the manor. Shall we go then?"

"Please, I must give my thanks to the captain first," Sean said, and he turned and stepped onto the grimy quay.

"Captain . . . . Captain Murphy!" Sean called.

The captain was instructing some of his crew but turned about when he heard Sean call his name. "Aye, young sir, what is it you'll have of me?"

"Nothing more than to say thank you for your kindness and help during the journey—a journey a bit too lacking in comfort for my tastes."

The captain laughed and called back to him, "No need to thank me. I understand fully well. I take it then that I'll not be expecting you to sign on as a crew member for our return to Southampton any time soon?"

"I think not," Sean replied. "But if ever I were to take the notion to become a seaman, I would look to sign on with Captain Laird Murphy and the *Southern Swallow*. And, you, Captain, please call on me the next passage that you make to Maryland."

"Aye, young sir. That I will. May you do well here in the colony, and may you prosper in your printing trade and stay in good health."

Sean hoped no one understood what the captain had said about his trade. As he waved a farewell to the captain, he saw two black men carrying his trunks to the dock. He then turned and stepped into the carriage without wiping the mud from his boots. Topping gave him a disgusted look but joined him.

The carriage was a fine example of excellent craftsmanship, with brass polished to a high shine and leather that was well blackened and waxed.

The driver turned to look at Topping for directions, and as he did his eyes rested on Sean. His look said something, although Sean did not know what it could possibly be. In a strange sort of way it seemed to be a familiar look. Was it a warning that passed between them? What a strange thought that was.

With the crack of the whip, the pair of matched white geldings made their way through the bustling activity on the crowded banks and then moved out with a flashing cadence.

The ride through the countryside was interesting. The Reverend Topping pointed out a house where his widowed sister Cynthia Wells and her daughter live. Of course, he knew all of the more important places of business and the homes of those who held any high positions in Maryland. He was ready to point out how significant it was that he had close friendships with anyone and everyone who might be seen as having any level of prominence.

The land looked so much different than Sean remembered. *I was only 6 or 7,* he thought, *when mother and I left for that fateful trip to England. Or was I younger?*

Everything looked so much greener than he remembered. The trees seemed smaller, and things certainly appeared to be much more civilized than his memory had made him believe. Of course, almost all of his days as a child had been spent at the manor, and he had seldom been taken away from the house. Besides, that had been many years and a lifetime ago.

The team moved along at a comfortable pace, and his mind wandered as he tried to bring back memories that had long lain dormant. He recalled the drawing of the house which his Aunt Elayne had sent him. He could not be certain if he actually remembered the manor house or if the drawing had only prompted his memories of the house in Southampton. He thought he might now be confusing the one for the other.

As the white geldings trotted through the narrow, sun-dappled road, Sean was given some rather elaborate histories of the various manors they passed as they traveled along. However, he noticed that his family was seldom mentioned, and Topping seemed to ignore them, as though they had played no part in the history of this area. In point of fact, he thought it very strange that it was never pointed out that his family had very close ties with the Lord of Baltimore.

Sean only heard the drone of Topping's voice, not his words, and he was startled when Topping said, "Ah yes, my young sir, just after this next bend in the road we will be coming to the manor entrance. We have been on the manor holdings for the past several minutes now. I fear I must have dozed off or I would have called your attention to that fact."

Chapter Six

Dawn Light

After almost an hour in the carriage, Sean finally saw the entrance to the O'Connell holdings. Half of the wooden gate was open and the other half was lying on its side. Obviously, someone had broken it down to gain entrance. The sign next to the gate was weathered, but even in the gathering evening gloom Sean could read the faded letters: "Dawn Light, The House of O'Connell."

"Could you stop here, please, for just a moment?" Sean asked.

As the carriage began its turn into the entrance of the lane, Topping grunted an order and the driver pulled the team in. Sean stepped down from the carriage and walked past the horses.

Looking at the sign, he choked back a hot lump in his throat. Now he remembered well the last time he had seen this sign. He and his mother were being taken to the ship in Gunter's Harbour for the trip to England, and he recalled how he cried as he waved his goodbyes to the slaves who stood at the gate to bid their farewells to Sean and his mother.

How many times, he wondered, had those same slaves and his kin ridden or walked through this gate? He felt tears forming in his eyes and was glad that no one could see them in the descending darkness.

He gazed down the lane toward the house, barely visible now as the sun had dipped below the horizon. *Was that a light in the house? Did the Reverend Topping not say that no one lived here any longer?* Sean strained to see the light, but it seemed to have disappeared. Perhaps the tears in his eyes had given the appearance of light. As he thought about it, he decided, *"It was probably simply my active imagination.* Sean climbed back into the carriage, and they continued down the lane toward the house.

"It was once a marvelous place," noted Reverend Topping. "For many years it was a gathering place for important people, even though it was so far away from Gunter's Harbour."

Sean was wishing that Topping would be quiet, but that was not to be.

"Oh, yes, many important people," Topping continued. "When Alan, Nathan, Elayne, Thomas, and Edward were alive, I can tell you that Dawn Light was a haven for many a weary soul, and that included myself. I might add that many a gala gathering occurred here as well, and I must say that it was then as it should be."

"As what should be?" Sean asked.

"What should be? Well, of course I meant what it had been like in England. I speak of, uh . . . well,

I speak of the social graces, refinement, and such. Naturally, even though your family was Irish, still they were somewhat suited to carry on English tradition. After all, this is a rather wild domain, full of ill-bred people—much like Ireland. Nonetheless, the manor was beautifully decorated and furnished. I have an eye for that sort of thing, you know. I would dare to say that the Dawn Light manor was something of an island of English tradition; even though, as I've said, your family is Irish. An island, yes, and at its best it was a tranquil island in a sea of wilderness. Quite exquisite. Oh yes, it was very civilized, you see."

Sean did not see, and the man was beginning to get on his nerves. He had to be civil, and yet he wanted this man to leave—now. He was eager to spend this time alone so he could savor these moments that he would never be able to recapture. Sean felt as though the Reverend Topping was somehow tainting these first impressions of his return to his family's home. *How can I get rid of him?*

As the carriage pulled up before the house, Sean saw that it was not as large as he had imagined it would be. In the growing gloom he could see, however, that the house would be more than ample for him.

Sean swung down from the carriage with effortless ease. "It is rather dark now. Would you honor me with your presence as my first overnight guest? You will certainly not want to return to Gunter's Harbour in the dark." Sean hoped that his offer would be refused.

"Well, yes, quite right. How very kind of you, indeed. However, as I've already suggested, it may be that the house is in no condition for guests at this time. Besides that, I have already arranged to stay at the Crown Ordinary. The inn is a brief ride past your gate. In fact, the truth is that the inn sits on your manor property. So, in a sense at least, I will be accepting your very kind invitation by staying on your property."

Sean breathed a silent sigh of relief. *The bloated toad cannot leave fast enough for me. What makes me feel such animosity toward this man? I scarcely know him and, after all, he has been my benefactor of sorts since I first stepped on Maryland's soil.* Still, something troubled Sean about the Reverend Topping.

Sean had not planned to arrive in the dark. In fact, he had not planned at all; that is, he had given no thought to when he might arrive at the manor. *What a fool I've been*, he thought, *I should have made provision for lights. In the rush of leaving the docks, I even forgot to get candles.*

"You will be in need of some light," said Topping, as though he had read Sean's mind and knew of the requirement. Just then, the carriage driver scratched a flint to light the wick of the candle in one of the carriage lamps. As he did, he also offered candles to Sean and lighted one. As the candle flickered to life, he saw the driver looking at him again in that peculiar way.

"Where are the manners of this savage, Reverend Topping? He stares at me in a most discomforting way."

"Does he now? I am sure we can correct that; and I will . . . ."

Before Topping could finish, something caught Sean's eye. "Never mind then, Reverend, it's probably simply my mood tonight."

As he said that, Sean looked up and saw, or thought he saw, a light in the upper window at the far end of the house. The light vanished as quickly as it had appeared. There had been no tear in his eye this time. It definitely was a light.

He turned his attention back to Topping, and there was no indication that he had seen the light in the windows.

"I should be able to find my way about now. I thank you for the assistance and the candles. Might I expect that my belongings will arrive some time tomorrow?"

"Perhaps," replied Topping, "But do not be alarmed if you should hear the cart late tonight. These blacks can get about in the darkness about as well as we do in the light of day — the barbaric savages."

He motioned with his hand toward the driver, indicating that they would now be leaving. "I will be off now. When you return to Gunter's Harbour, I would consider it an honor were you to choose to be my house guest. We have many rooms. You can stay for several days, if needed, to carry out your business as you sell off your property."

"Sell the property?" Sean snapped, "What could possibly make you think I would be selling the property? I thought I had misunderstood you earlier today when you made a similar suggestion, but I obviously did not. Why would you have such thoughts?"

"Oh . . . well . . . yes," Topping stammered, "You see, I simply assumed you would do so. With the terrible condition of the property, and the fact that all of the furniture was taken by the slaves who ran off, and . . . and the fact that you have no help because of that, well I, uh, I simply assumed that it would be easier to . . ."

Sean didn't let him finish his sentence. "Let me caution you, Reverend Topping, to never assume that Sean O'Connell will take the easy way out of any situation," he said boldly, almost believing it himself. "In fact, never make any assumptions about me in any way. I sincerely appreciate the help you have given me this day, Sir. However, I will thank you if, in the future, you will wait for me to ask for your help. I do not wish to express ingratitude or be in a position of insulting you further, so may I ask that you take your leave of me at this time, Sir?"

"Well! I should think that a civilized person would know how to treat one's betters, especially when one has gone to so much . . ."

"Betters?" Sean bellowed. "I'll tell you about 'betters.' You had 'better' get your carriage, your savage, and yourself off my property right now. You may stay at the inn on my property tonight. However, if what you have told me of that inn being on my property is true, you may never be able to stay there again."

Without so much as waiting for an order, the carriage driver cracked the whip over the heads of the geldings. They responded smartly as the driver turned them into a tight arc, and they were striding for the gate with the Reverend Topping crying out his complaint.

"We'll see about this. You'll learn better than to speak to me in that manner. I have never been so . . ." The creaking of the carriage and the drumming of the horses' hooves covered any further sound of his voice.

Sean wasn't sure what had brought about his outburst. He thought that perhaps it was hunger or the fact that his long sea trip was giving him a moody sort of sentiment. But then he thought, *No, I just do not like the man, and that's why I said what I said.*

The dim flickering of the candles in the carriage lamps bobbed and weaved down the lane. Sean did not wait to see if the carriage would make it through the gate. He turned to step onto the porch and enter the house.

Holding the candle high in front of him, he looked about the room he had entered. It was sparsely furnished, and the furnishings that were there were rough—not at all what he had expected. It certainly did not have the appearance that Topping had described. He quickly found a reflector lamp and placed the candle in it. He could see now that there were a few more lamps but little else.

As he lit two more candles, he suddenly had the strange sense that someone had been there very recently. He bent over to examine what he thought might be food crumbs, and the hairs on his neck stiffened when he heard a soft thump. It seemed that the sound had come from the second floor on the other end of the house, where he had imagined seeing the light. Taking a candle lamp with a reflector from off the wall, he lit it and cautiously entered the next room. The small room was completely empty. He heard the thump again.

Entering the hallway at the back of the room, he turned sharply to the right to go up a narrow stairway. He tried to walk quietly, but each stair creaked with every movement of his weight. There was that sound again.

"Who is up there?" he called. "I am Sean O'Connell, the master of this house, and I say, 'Who is up there?'"

Although Sean was unarmed, he boldly proclaimed, "If you don't want to take a blade in your belly, you'll be wise to show yourself now."

A quiet scuffling noise assured him that he was not alone in the house. He cautiously continued up the stairway. At the head of the stairs he saw a thick handled broom. He picked it up and carried it as one would a weapon. *I wonder if I should have been so bold in speaking about my nonexistent blade. And how impressed will the intruders be with my broom?* He found himself smiling at the thought. The smile quickly faded when he heard another thump.

He paused to listen as he came to each door, pushing the door open cautiously with the broom and then entering with the candle held high before him. He entered two rooms this way and found each of them empty—completely barren of any furnishings.

As he pushed on the third door, he felt a pressure holding it shut. He stepped back and raising his foot with the full force of his weight kicked the door open. A voice cried out and he could hear a body fall to the floor with a muffled scream and unintelligible words.

Holding the broom like a sword, Sean quickly entered the room to take advantage of whatever gain of surprise he might have made. With the candle held high, he looked behind the door, but he was not prepared for what he saw.

Chapter Seven

Startling Sight at Dawn Light

At first, in the darkened room with grotesque shadows being cast by the candle, the body appeared to be that of a grossly deformed man, hunched over and writhing.

Sean held the stout broom defensively between himself and the twisted mass on the floor. Raising the candle higher, he saw two heads. It was a man and a woman, or by the appearance of their faces, a boy and a girl, and they were Negroes.

"Get up, you two," Sean snapped. "What do you think you are doing on my property? Who are you? I said to get up!" With that, he kicked out at what he hoped was the boy's anatomy and not the girl's.

The boy almost grabbed for Sean's foot but thought better of it. Instead, he arose, helping the girl to her feet as well. Now Sean saw that there were not two heads but three. The girl/woman clutched an infant to her breast, still sleeping after all the disturbance.

Sean could see now that this was an unusually large boy. He stood every bit as tall as Sean himself, with broader shoulders and a look on his face that expressed more wariness than fright.

"I asked who you are and what are you doing here?"

"Us is stayin' here. Nobodies be here. Us is here," the young man responded.

"Well, who is 'us'? And what right do you have to be here? What is your name?"

"Us be here all de time since when. I be Samson. She be Kezie, and that be baby Mbfwana," the young slave said as he glanced down at the short broom that Sean held.

"Do not use those savage words in my house! Do you hear?" Sean looked down at the broom in his hands and suddenly felt very foolish and more than a little self-conscious. "What sort of name is Ma . . . fababa?" (He knew he hadn't pronounced it right but it was as well as he could do.) "You must give the child a proper Christian name."

Sean could scarcely believe the words coming from his own mouth. To be encouraging any other person, least of all a black savage, to do anything that might be considered "Christian," was hardly a normal practice for him.

"Why are you in my house? I want some answers. Where did you come from, and why are you here? Do you know I have a right to kill you for being here?"

When Sean said that, he felt even more foolish. Even if he were to have really desired to follow through on his loud threats, he had no idea how he could overpower this man.

Samson looked confused but appeared to be determined to answer properly. "Us be here all de time since when. Missylain she say Samson no go way. She go way. Samson no go way. Kezie no go way. Missylain she go way. She say Samson no go way."

"What are you trying to tell me, you ignorant savage? What has been "mislain?" Is that some of your mumbo-jumbo black Africa talk? Don't think I am unaware of such things, so don't try to do anything strange. Who is this woman and this child?"

"Missylain she house. Samson, Kezie, Mbfwana us house."

"For the last time, stop that. I forbid you to use that mumbo-jumbo language."

Then, quite suddenly, "mislain" became clear to Sean. This black savage was talking about his Aunt Elayne. When she left, she must have told these two savages that they could stay on until someone else came to live here.

"Look here, do you mean 'Miss Elayne?' Did Miss Elayne tell you that you could stay here—you and Kezie and the child?"

"No baby. Baby is no. Missylain she no Mbfwana say. Missylain she house. Samson house."

"Yes, yes, I understand. But, now I am the master of this house. I am Sean O'Connell. You can no longer stay here. You must leave now. Do you understand that, you black savage? You must leave now, and I mean right now!"

Samson looked at Sean with pleading eyes. Yes, Sean could see that he understood very well. But what he didn't know was that Samson was not concerned for himself. His concern was for the woman and the baby.

Sean wondered who they really were. Was this a family? Was she his wife? How silly, as though savages had either wives or families. He understood little about these slaves, never having been around them. But, he did know that his family here in the colony had made a fortune in trading them. He had been told they were not human in the same sense as Englishmen were—or even the Irish. But then, who was? Still, Sean thought, *They do need shelter of some sort—at least during the night.*

The room they were in should have been a bedroom or perhaps a sewing room. It could have been where Sean had slept as a boy; he just could not remember. Like the other rooms, there were no furnishings, and Sean wondered what could possibly have happened to the furniture?

The first room he had entered in the house had only the crude table and chairs. What had become of the furniture brought over from England? He knew his family well enough to know how they would have lived.

Sean suddenly realized that the two slaves were staring at him, waiting for his next words. "Yes. Well then, you must leave tomorrow. You may stay on the porch tonight. I shall remain in the house, but you must stay on the porch. Is that clear?" He was not about to allow this savage the opportunity to slash his throat while he slept.

Just then they heard sounds from the front of the house. It was voices, and then he heard a horse whinny. "Get downstairs, now." He prodded Samson and Kezie before him with the broom.

As they made their way down the narrow staircase, he heard loud knocking on the door and a voice calling loudly, "You is trunk, Mas'. You is trunk."

Sean went to the door, making sure that Samson could not attack him from the side. He carefully opened the door, putting his shoulder to it in the event that he would have to close it again quickly. If it had not been for the sparse light of the candles spilling out through the partially opened door onto the porch, he could not have seen the two men. Their blackness almost melted them into the dark of the night.

"Revren Toppin say trunks be here."

"All right, then. Just leave them on the porch for now." Sean would not allow four of these savages into the small room with him.

The spokesman looked through the partially opened door into the dimly lit room, startled to see the other two. "Samson. Kezie. You is house. Nobody is house. Revren Toppin say no is house."

"Never mind. Just do as I say. Leave the trunks outside. I do not want them in the house." Sean was sensing fear. Those outside knew the ones in the room with him, and that did not portend good.

"Revren Toppin say trunk be here. Us is do."

"Well, your Reverend Topping is not here. I am master of this house, and I say the trunks remain outdoors." Sean could not believe that he was actually arguing with these savages. He was now sensing a strong apprehension. As he turned to tell Samson to leave too, he caught the glint of steel from the corner of his eye.

The blade came slashing down toward him as Samson cried out and threw himself at Sean. Sean's first thoughts were that his worst fears were correct: Samson was attacking him! But now he saw that it was the other man who had come with his sea chests who was wielding the knife. He had slipped in through another door for the attack.

The swish of the steel whistled past his ear. Samson knocked the man down and Sean turned in time to see the man who had been talking to him as he lurched through the door and came at him with a sword.

Sean slapped down hard upon the man's forearm with the stout broom handle. The sound it made told him the blow did damage as the man cried out in pain. The knife rattled to the floor. Stooping to pick it up, Sean felt the warmth of blood running down his neck even before he felt the cut of the blade, and he dropped to the floor.

Samson was lying on the floor, stunned from a blow the other man had delivered. The attacker raised the sword to strike another blow. Sean looked up into the man's frenzied eyes as he prepared to take the life from Sean.

Then, slowly, the man lowered the sword as a puzzled look came across his face. His mouth fell open and blood began to slowly trickle and then gush from his mouth. Trying to clutch at his back, his breath made horrible rasping sounds. He turned awkwardly and dropped to his knees. With his mouth open, he fell on his face with the large knife protruding from between his shoulder blades.

Kezie stood there, staring in horror at what she had just done. Meanwhile, Samson had regained his senses and was on his knees, strangling the man who had attacked Sean with the knife.

"Stop! Stop! Enough! It is enough!" But Samson seemed determined to kill the man. "Samson. I command you as master of this house to stop what you are doing!"

The angry look began to melt from Samson's face as he looked up at Sean. "Mas' Shawn. Us is house. Missylain us is house. Mas' Shawn is house." He rolled off of the man he had been strangling, who was now gasping for life's breath.

Sean took up the sword. Placing his foot on the chest of the man on the floor, he laid the point of the weapon in the fold of his throat.

"Now, tell me, who put you up to this cowardly deed. Was it Reverend Topping?"

With some difficulty because of the sword on his neck, he answered, "Revren Toppin say kill bad man no good. Say us is kill bad man. Mas' kill us?"

"So, I am a bad man, am I? We'll have to see your Reverend Topping about all this." Sean took the point of the blade from the man's neck. "Stay where you are. Samson, take the other man out to the cart. This one can deliver the body to Topping with our compliments."

"Samson is Mas' Shawn house. Samson do."

Kezie picked the baby up from the corner where she had protectively laid him. Strangely the baby still slept peacefully, despite all of the commotion. She followed Samson out the door as he dragged the man's body to the cart. Sean reached down as Samson dragged him and removed the knife from his back, wiping the blood off on the man's ragged shirt.

"Now, you! Get up! And do not be so unwise as to try something foolish, or you will ride back a dead man too." But, Sean had no need to warn the frightened man. As he stood, his right arm was hanging at a strange angle. The blow from the stout broom handle had broken the bone just below the elbow, and it now protruded through the skin.

"Outside with you, now!" Sean commanded.

As they stepped into the dark night, Samson was struggling to remove one of the chests from the cart by himself. Brushing the attacker aside, Sean reached for the other handle of the trunk and still holding the sword ready to strike, they swung it down easily and placed it on the porch. The light from the fully opened door revealed a look on Samson's face that might have been appreciation.

Sean then instructed the attacker. "You will drive this cart to the inn and you will awaken the Reverend Topping and give him my regards along with this slave's body. If I ever set my eyes on your face again, I will kill you on the spot. That is, unless Samson here has done so first." A knowing look passed between Sean and Samson.

The man struggled to get up to the cart seat with one arm. Samson stepped up to the lead horse and gave its rump a sharp slap. The horses jumped out smartly, with the driver struggling to maintain his balance with one arm and at the same time control the heads of the horses.

Samson stood watching the cart race down the lane and voiced some strange oath, which Sean could not understand. "Here, now. I told you I would have none of that foul heathen talk in my presence." This time as he said it, his tone was much less emphatic.

Samson turned to face Sean. "Missylain she talk you come Mas' Shawn. Us is wait. You come. Good Mas' Shawn. Us is house now. Samson is house. Kezie is house."

"Yes, yes, I know, and the child 'is house.' But if you use that child's heathen name in front of me again, I'll whip you for it." Sean had never whipped any man, and he felt foolish and ashamed for having said it. But, he had heard from others that this was a common punishment for the savages.

"How is it that you seem to be talking so much more plainly now?" As he asked the question, Sean hoped that the answer was not that he was getting used to the strange dialect of the Negro.

Sean turned to enter the house and Samson, Kezie, and the baby followed closely.

"Missylain she talk Samson big trouble if Revren Toppin say Samson talk good talk. Missylain she say Samson no talk good talk to Revren Toppin. Misylain she say Samson talk good talk Mas' Shawn. Kezie no talk Mas' talk. Samson talk good Mas' talk. No talk good talk to Revren Toppin."

"Yes, yes. Of course, I see. Miss Elayne warned you to always pretend you did not talk or understand very well. That was very wise of her. Look here now, Samson, it will not do for you to sleep on the porch tonight. We may be in for another surprise visit from Topping. You, the woman and the baby can sleep here in the downstairs rooms. We will bolt the doors and bar the windows. I will sleep upstairs. But you will stay here."

The words were scarcely out of Sean's mouth and Samson was on his way to secure the house for the night.

Kezie stared at Sean, clutching the baby close to her.

"What are you staring at?" No answer. "Stop looking at me that way." She kept looking. Suddenly she dropped to her knees and began a sing-song chanting. Sean began to admonish her but slowly realized she was expressing gratitude toward him. She stopped as Samson returned to the room and gave her a hard look.

"Kezie say, she is house. She glad she is house. She glad Mas' Shawn is house. She say she glad."

"Good. I rather had that impression, especially after your explanation. Now, I am going upstairs. I do not want anyone to leave this house until daybreak and then not until I say you can leave. Do you understand? If you should hear voices, the slightest noise, or any strange sound, you are to awaken me immediately. Do you understand?"

"Samson talk good talk. Samson he say yes, Mas' Shawn. Kezie do cut, Mas' Shawn?"

"Kezie do cut?" Sean repeated. He had forgotten the wound he had received from the cutlass. Fortunately the blow had been a glancing one. Although the wound had produced a great deal of immediate bleeding, it had almost stopped now altogether.

Sean surprised himself by removing his shirt and allowing Kezie to look at the wound. She dared not say a word, but Samson assured Sean that the wound was not deep. Sean wished he had some rum to pour on it for cleansing, and he also could have done with some to drink. Kezie took water from a small crude bowl on the floor under the table and gently bathed the blood from his neck and shoulder. Then she stepped back and smiled at Samson.

Sean thanked them, took two of the candles, and started up the stairs. When he came to the first empty room, he realized that he had nothing to either sleep upon or to use as a cover. He decided that he was tired enough to do without such niceties and laid down on his side on the hard floor. Even though he now somewhat trusted this savage Samson, nevertheless he cradled his head on his arm and positioned his body so that his feet were against the closed door. He laid the sword and knife at his side. If anyone tried to get to him, at least he would have a brief warning.

Sean's mind was racing with thoughts of the events of the day. He even wondered what had made him come here in the first place. *Just what is this spurious Reverend Topping up to? Less than half a day and I have made an enemy of a notable church figure, have nearly lost my life, have more or less established myself at the manor, and have fallen heir to two young slaves and their child.*

So, this was the Maryland of the year of our Lord 1695. He had been there for less than twelve hours, yet it seemed he had encountered enough trouble to last him a lifetime. What would tomorrow bring?

All he could hope for was that the name of the O'Connell holding, Dawn Light, would bring better fortune to him at next dawn's light. Even on the hard wooden floor, sleep came quickly.

Dawn Light

Chapter Eight

First Day at Dawn Light

Sean woke up with a dusty shaft of sunlight on his face. After the long sea journey, filled with many sleepless nights through storms and rolling waves, he had slept very soundly here on land. It was *his* land. At least, in a way it was. He was happily surprised at how well he had slept on the hard floor.

He tried to move his head to look about the room, and as he did his temples began to throb. The small room had nothing to indicate that people had used it recently, and the small window was grimy from lack of care. Webs, both old and new, proclaimed that spiders had made it their domain.

As he tried to sit upright, a sharp pain reminded him where the blade had found its mark in his neck the night before, and his back and shoulders felt the effect of the hard floor upon which he had slept. A brief moment of fear surged through him as he suddenly realized that he had rolled away from the door during the night, and the knife and sword had been kicked aside. However, he was still alive and thought that was a good sign, because it must mean that the savages either were trustworthy, frightened, or had run away.

He managed to get to his feet without too much difficulty but was slow in doing so because his muscles were stiff, and he felt slightly nauseated and dizzy. He attributed the light-headedness to a lack of food. He bent over slightly in order to look out the small window when he heard, "Hello in the house there! Hello in the house!"

The call was coming from someone who could speak the King's English, and Sean thought that was a good sign. At least he knew it did not sound like Topping, and he was very glad for that. Sean hurried out of the room. Then, remembering the weapons, he returned for them and went quickly down the stairs.

As he entered what he now saw was the eating room, he saw Samson and Kezie standing by the cooking fireplace, which was only used during the winter. They were smiling and waiting obediently for permission to go outside. The baby was awake and cooing. Without speaking to them, Sean hurried to open the door to the outside. There was a great need for fresh air within the room and someone definitely needed to tend to the baby.

He opened the door and was immediately greeted by the source of the voice.

"I say, hello! You must be Sean O'Connell. I'm Ben Dixon. I've done business with your family for many years and have known them well as good friends and neighbors." As he spoke, he glanced at the bloody knife and sword Sean held in his left hand.

Sean remembered that, when they had first met yesterday, Topping had said something very much like what Dixon was now saying. Nevertheless, he replied with what he hoped was a reasonably cordial voice.

"Welcome then, O'Connell friend and neighbor. Welcome to Dawn Light. Yes, I am Sean O'Connell, just arrived yesterday from England by way of Bermuda and Jamestown."

Sean strode toward the man. Even though he hadn't noticed Dixon glance at the weapons, he suddenly was embarrassed and turned to place them on the porch. Dixon dismounted effortlessly from his horse and took Sean's extended hand with a firm handshake.

"Well, Sir," Dixon began, "your handshake tells me that you have lived a gentleman's life. Of course, that does not necessarily mean that you *are* a gentleman, and that is not to suggest that my callused hands mean I am *not* a gentleman, you understand."

He stood expressionless for a moment, and then his face broke into a great grin. His warm laugh made Sean think that this Dixon might very well have been a family friend and could easily become his friend as well.

He was not a large man, not nearly as tall as Sean, nor was he particularly stocky or muscular. But, he had a certain way of moving and a particular look that made Sean think that this Dixon fellow could probably handle himself well in almost any situation that demanded quick, strong action.

"What brings you here, Sir? I was unaware that many knew I had arrived."

"Mind you," Dixon began, "I am not the meddling kind, Sean. But when I had word that Reverend Topping had set himself to 'help you,' shall we say, well, I immediately thought you might truly be in need of some real help. I honestly was a good friend of your fine family, and I'm not about to allow mischief to come upon any member of your family if I'm able to prevent it."

So, he did know something about Topping. There was more here to be discovered, and Sean believed that he might have found a true fountain of helpful knowledge in Master Dixon.

"I have nothing to offer you, Sir. Not even a cup of cold water, I fear, for, although this is my land, I know not so much as if there might be a well or spring located nearby."

"Aye, there is a spring," replied Dixon, "and Samson here knows where it is. Am I right, Samson?" Samson had recognized Dixon, grinned, and without responding started off to the side of the house.

"Then you know Samson, do you, Dixon?"

"Know him? That I do. Oh yes, that I do. But, enough of this talk for now. It's my privilege to serve you, Sir. My wife prepared some cornbreads and sent over a portion of ham, and here are some of her elderberry conserves—fit for a king. Well, they might not be fit for a king; and, being from Ireland, I suppose it depends on what you might think of the king anyway." There was that great grin on Dixon's face again, "But it's good fare for new neighbors and friends."

Sean liked what he heard from this man. Yet, his instincts would now allow him to let his guard down, open up too much, or place too much trust in this man . . . not just yet.

They turned to enter the house and Kezie was scurrying about trying to prepare the crude table for the master of the house as best she could. Dixon swung the basket upon the table and Kezie began to remove the food. Samson appeared in the doorway with the baby on one arm and a leather pail of water in his other hand.

"Us is de house here, Mas' Dixon. Mas' Shawn gon eat food good."

"I have no slaves, Sean. Some indentured servants help me farm. But, this Samson's a fine slave," Dixon offered with an understanding smile. "He and his mother served your family well. His mother died in childbirth before your Aunt Elayne returned to England. He's one you can trust, even with your life. I don't know about this girl, though. But, if she is with him—and it seems this is their child—chances are she too can be trusted."

"Why do you suppose these two slaves are still here? What do you think happened to the others? It appears as though someone has pretty well taken what they wanted from the house, including the slaves. No one was here yesterday, except for these two and their child. When Topping's slaves appeared last night, they seemed very surprised that Samson and the girl were here."

"But, might I ask, why do you suppose they came at night? Did Topping send them to do you some kind of mischief?"

"You might say that," Sean responded. "I'd forgotten that you hadn't heard . . . or, I should say that I hadn't told you. Last night his two men came here under the guise of delivering my sea chests, but they really came to kill me, and they came close to doing so."

He turned his head to show Dixon the gash on his neck. "My life was spared by good fortune because of these two," he said pointing to Samson and Kezie. "I can tell you, it is quite awkward to owe one's life to such as these."

"Yes. Well, I do not at all wonder at the surprise of Topping's assassins, and I speak the truth when I say I'm not at all surprised of the attempted harm that occurred either. I'd say you were spared more by God's grace than simple good fortune. If you want my opinion in the matter, I would say that you might be able to find all of your family's house furnishings somewhere in one of Reverend Topping's houses. I'm not at all astonished that his slaves were surprised when they saw Samson and the woman either, because that simply gives evidence to their knowledge that all of the slaves that had lived here either have been kept by Topping or sold off."

"Sold off," Sean said incredulously, "by Topping?"

"Well, I'll say this much: you don't have to wonder where the proceeds may have gone. The likelihood is that those who tried to kill you last night may even have belonged to your family's holdings right here at Dawn Light."

"I rather doubt that," Sean replied. "For wouldn't Samson have told me so? Besides, did my family not leave an overseer behind to care for these holdings?"

"Of course, of course, but you will have to understand that these savages are unlikely to offer any information that is not squeezed out of them," Dixon said matter-of-factly.

"But, let's get to these cornbreads and ham before we have to fight the slaves for them. They appear to be in need of a good meal themselves. And I can tell you this, young Sean: I have no desire to enter a challenge over the food with Samson."

Samson's eyes lit up. He thought that Dixon meant that he and Kezie were about to get some real food too. Samson had been worrying over Kezie and her need to produce milk for the infant, because she had become very thin. At the same time, in her concern over the baby, Kezie hadn't noticed that Samson was getting thin too. He had tried to provide her with as much food as he was able to scavenge and always gave her extra portions in order to give her strength for the needs of the baby.

Even though the hour was early, Ben Dixon and Sean ate as though they had been working a long, hard day. Sean hadn't realized just how hungry he had been, and as he ate the throbbing in his head settled so he barely noticed. They paid no attention to Samson and Kezie, who looked longingly at the food as the men were eating. At last, when they had had their fill, Ben told Samson to take the remaining food outside to eat. There was no need to repeat the instructions. Sean laughed as Samson and Kezie rushed out to the porch to enjoy what was left of the breakfast banquet.

Dixon dipped two more ladles of water into their cups and leaned back in the chair. "An overseer? . . . Of course, you wondered about an overseer. He was one of the best this land has ever seen; I vouch for that. He served your family for years. Gilbert Singer was his name. A good and honest man he was."

"He was? Why do you say that? Where is he now? Where has he gone?" Sean asked.

"Found him myself, I did. I hadn't seen him for several weeks. We often helped one another, picking up supplies and one thing or another. But, because I hadn't seen him for quite awhile, I decided to take a ride out here to Dawn Light. I arrived just after first light, thinking to have myself a hearty breakfast here with him and his wife—an excellent cook, I'll add. When I arrived, I called out to him. But, there was no answer, and there wasn't a soul here—not the Singers and not one slave."

"Well, would that be so unusual? Would they not be in the fields or some such thing?" questioned Sean.

"No. Not the fields. Not in February. But, it was in the field that I found him and her as well. Both dead and had been dead for some time. Animals had been feeding on them. It was not a pleasant sight."

"But, how did you know it was the Singers? I mean, if the animals had been eating on the bodies, wouldn't they . . ."

"I see your point. Fact is, the bodies had been eaten upon quite savagely, but the faces were recognizable enough. No, it was the Singers all right; I have no doubt. At first I thought the slaves had revolted and killed them, and it was made to appear so. Some slave clothing and a few of their crude tools had been left near the bodies. Both their heads had been broken with rocks. It took me almost three days to bury them in the hard ground."

Walking to the window, Dixon pointed and said, "Come here and see. Out there, under the largest beech tree, lie the both of them. Since they killed the both of them, I buried them there together. I for one know who it was that did it. Or, at least I know who ordered it."

Sean walked to the window to see where Ben was pointing. "It was the slaves, wasn't it? Who but the slaves would do such a thing? But what would an overseer have that anyone would kill them for?"

"What they had was the very thing that the Singers were overseeing: land, Sean, land. At least, someone wanted Singer's authority over the land as overseer, and that wouldn't be a slave now, would it? When I came back to the house, after burying them, I went inside. There was nothing left of the splendid furnishings your family had brought with them when they first came. And not one stick of the other furnishings, which they had acquired from families here. Not one piece was left, I tell you. It was gone. All gone, except for some crude furnishings made by the slaves. We have just eaten at some of it."

"But, Ben, how can you be sure it was not the slaves?"

"You tell me why I am sure. What would slaves do with fine furniture? Where could they use it without being discovered? If they had stolen it, where could they possibly hide it without being found out? I tell you, Sean, many a family had to turn their heads on this matter. But, not me, Sean—not Ben Dixon."

Dixon then told him how he had spoken boldly to Topping about the matter. Dixon had even recognized a small table in Topping's entry hall at his principal residence that had belonged to the O'Connell family. But, when he confronted Topping with his theft, Topping easily dismissed it by saying that they had given it to him as a gift.

"A gift he said, mind you, of appreciation for his thoughtfulness toward them. And then he says to me, 'You, Sir have the audacity to accuse me of being a common thief? We'll see about this!'" Dixon spat and said, "Thoughtfulness, my horse's ears."

"Sean could feel his emotions getting out of hand. He wondered if he might not be placing too much trust in a man he had only just met. He was beginning to question who he might really be sharing bread with. This Dixon seemed to know too much about what allegedly had occurred. Was it possible that he could be placing himself at the mercy of another like the Reverend Topping? Might all of this talk from Dixon simply be another pretense to lower Sean's defenses?

He looked across the table into Dixon's eyes and immediately had the answer to his questions. Somehow, deep inside he knew that here was a man he could trust.

Who killed the Singers?" Sean demanded. "Why was something not done of it? Is there no order here in this blasted place? Is it Topping? It is, is it not?"

Chapter Nine

Covering the Tracks of a Trojan Horse

The Reverend Topping awoke with a start. *Was that someone calling my name? I believe I heard something—my name being called. Or was I just dreaming?*

He slept fitfully through what had remained of the night and he had suffered with terrible nightmares. In his dreams he realized that it was a mistake to allow Mose to run loose. Since he had attacked Sean O'Connell and injured him but had failed to kill him, Mose had now become a serious liability to the Reverend Topping. And how he did dislike liabilities, especially one such as this, because it might mean he would have to get rid of his own property.

He dressed quickly and went down to the small common room of the inn. The innkeeper, Oswell Hodge, and his daughter Maudie were cleaning up the table. The other guests who had spent the night were already gone. They had loudly protested to the innkeeper about the boisterous voices and other commotion of the past night.

In fact, each guest had declared they would never again stay at the Crown Ordinary. Of course, the innkeeper promised them that such an outrage as had occurred during the previous night could be laid at the feet of the boisterous Topping and his slaves and that it would never happen again. He further assured them that, if they would just return, he would not charge them for breakfast.

Still they threatened that they did not know if they would ever return. But then they relented, when he offered not to charge for the livery, and they assured him that they would at least consider returning on other occasions.

"Why did you not call me earlier, Hodge? I should have had my breakfast earlier."

"Very sorry, we are, Reverend Topping, your honorable sir. But, you see, we was very busy calming me other guests down—the ones what's rest was disturbed by you and your slaves last night—not that it was your Reverend's fault, oh no. Here now, Reverend, why don't you have some breakfast? Be quick, Maudie, and get the kind Reverend some tea and breads for him, and be sure they're warm."

"No, no. I'll not have time. Have you seen my savage, Mose, this morning?"

"Aye, Reverend Sir, your honorableness. If it's the one what's got his arm busted, I've both seen him and heard him. Such groanings and carrying on. Why, you'd think the black buggar's broke arm hurt him like an Englishman's. He's out there in the livery. But, I'll have to be telling you, Reverend Sir, that I'll have to charge you extra for letting him sleep out there. Scares the very devil—beggin' your pardon—the very devil out from the other animals, don't you know?"

The enterprising innkeeper was trying to recoup some of the losses that were the result of his recent burst of generosity with the other guests. Besides, he felt it was Topping's fault that the other guests had been upset over the previous night.

"Maudie, is it?" asked Topping of Hodge's daughter. "Have Mose get my carriage. My other slave has it down by the creek, where he spent the night. Have them bring it here at once."

"And Maudie," her father added, "You wouldn't be takin' long now, would you, girl? We've got us a whole day's work to do before noon. Don't make me take the stick to you now, darlin'."

"Yes, Father," she assured him as she ran out the door.

Reverend Toppings head was spinning. *How am I going to cover my tracks this time? There were so many witnesses, especially after the tragic bungling of my orders last night. Then, of course, there is the problem of knowing how to explain to young O'Connell why my slaves tried to murder him. But that shouldn't be too difficult. The others in the community hold a high regard for me. Who will doubt the word of a priest of the Church of England?*

Even though he was not sure who the guests were, he was certain that some of them must have heard the conversation with Mose the night before. *Mose, that's it! I'll just have to get rid of that bungling savage — just like in my dream. But, how did it happen in my dream?* He tried to recall just how it had gone.

Often, especially in the recent past, Topping had received ideas through dreams. It seemed this might be one of those occasions. Yet, to get rid of Mose would be a grievous thing to Topping. It was not that he would lose any love over Mose, but he did care about the value that he represented as a slave. Still, he would have to remember what the dream was all about before he could do anything at all.

Just then he heard a carriage coming up the road as Maudie came running back into the room to give her report. "Sir, your reverendness, the black buggar was coming right up the road as I was running through the forest to get him — frightened me he did. I didn't want to arouse the other buggar with the broke arm just yet."

The carriage came to a rattling halt, and the driver was quick to come to the door and let Topping know that his carriage was ready.

"Yes, I'll be there directly," Topping snapped. "Go to the barn and get that lazy Mose. He'll have to follow behind us. We'll be taking the long way back, because I have some business to attend to at the ford of Little Beacon Creek."

The driver look puzzled. Topping took the opportunity to repeat his orders. But it wasn't so the driver would understand; it was so he could be certain that everyone heard the reason he was going to return the long way. He wanted the innkeeper in particular to hear the instructions he gave to the carriage driver.

His dream was coming back to him now. *Mose will drown in the creek, just like in my nightmare. Such a shame it'll be, but with his broken arm and all, poor Mose would be unable to maintain his balance once he has fallen on a slippery rock and hit his head. They will never find the body. Pity to have to lose such a possession, especially since Croaker will be killed during the attack too. But, that's the best way.*

Yes, the dream was all coming back to him now. *It will be a good way to cover my tracks. Even if someone finds the body later, what will it matter? He's just another savage. His decomposed body will be taken as a runaway. Yes, that's it—a runaway. That no-good-for-anything Mose will be a runaway—and after he was treated so well. I will report him as such: just another ungrateful runaway.* The dream was becoming clearer as his only way out.

"Why, I'll even offer a reward for his return," Topping said aloud. "Alive, of course."

"Reward?" Oswell Hodge heard that quite clearly. "A reward you say, Reverend Topping, your grace? A reward for returnin' someone alive? Returnin' who?"

"I was just thinking aloud. These lazy rapscallions are always running off. Sometimes I think I spend more for rewards for their return than I do on feeding them." That was not really too much a stretch of the truth, for he spent little on either food for his slaves or rewards for runaways.

"There's ways I know to keep 'em from runnin' I do, your worshipness, and if you'd like I could . . . "

"Yes, yes. I know there are ways. But my Christian conscience does not allow me to mistreat even a slave that way," he said piously.

The innkeeper looked at Topping with a questioning glance, as if to say with his eyes that they both knew he was lying. "Now about paying me for your slave in the livery, will you be paying me now Reverend? Or, must I wait for the payment as I did the last time?"

"No. Of course, certainly I'll pay you now." Topping did not want this man to be troubling his mind about any of the happenings of the past night. The best way he could think to prevent that was by paying him now for everything he asked—and maybe a bit more.

"Here you are, my good man. And even though the surroundings are not to my liking—a bit too crude for my tastes—nevertheless, I see you are an honest man who keeps an honest inn."

Topping hated having to flatter this oaf, but he knew it was best to do so, because in that way he could be certain that he would not remember too many details about the previous night's activities.

"I'm sure this will take care of your troubles from last night" he said as he dropped some coins in Hodge's hand. "As you see, I have an almost uncontrollably generous spirit, and I have added a bit more for the inconvenience of having my slave in your barn. I am happy to pay you for your honest labors and for a good night's rest. I always appreciate good service when I receive it," he said, lying again.

The innkeeper took the money greedily, not once thinking that this was anything more or less than what Topping had said. He would soon forget about the disturbances of the previous night, and he would probably tell others how Topping had commended him for keeping such a fine inn.

Although the way things were developing had not been a part of the dream, as Topping remembered, nevertheless it did seem that events were working out very well for his benefit.

"I'll also thank you to have my cart repaired. I have not the time to examine it myself, but I'll expect you to use your own good judgment as far as the extent of the repairs needed. The wheel and axle will certainly need attention. I'll ask that you have the work done and then I'll send someone out within a fortnight to return it to me. You will be paid then. Does that suit you?"

"Yes, Reverend Topping. Yes. I'll see to it. Dependable I am, your worshipness. You'll see how well it is I'll see that your cart is repaired." The calculating Hodge was already estimating in his greedy mind just how much the repairs would cost and then how much more he could add for his profit. "Yes, Reverend Topping. Yes, indeed, your graceness. I'll see as how it gets done, and done real good I will."

"Well then," Topping began, as he lowered his voice in a confidential tone, "I suppose I can depend on you to tell no untoward stories about the past evening also. Am I right? These savages are such an untrustworthy lot. They are more bother than I some-times think a person of my standing should have to endure, patient man that I am. Yet, even though they take every advantage of my kindness, I still treat them reasonably. I believe you will remember how kind I am with my slaves simply because of the manner in which I have dealt with you also, eh, Innkeeper?" Topping's inquiry was accompanied with a knowing wink.

"Oh, I'll remember, Reverend Topping. Yes, honorable sir, I'll remember," Hodge responded. However he really had not the slightest notion as to what Topping was rattling on about, what "untoward" meant, or why he winked. Maudie looked even more confused than her father by the Reverend Topping's comments, but she stood there listening with a look of contentment and admiration for the good words being said about her father.

"I'll remember," the innkeeper repeated, as if to convince himself. And remember he would, but what he was going to remember was not what Topping had in mind.

Chapter Ten

Obadiah and Ezekiel

The weeks passed quickly. Sean soon learned that Samson was even more reliable a slave than he had expected. Samson seemed to know the manor holdings as well as if he had been part of the family. Certainly, he knew more than a slave normally would, and it appeared to Sean that he must have been favored and well trusted as he was growing up on the manor.

Sean had not tried to determine the exact cause of the frightening experience of that first night in his new home back in July. He had not attempted to confront Topping either, and it was obvious that Topping was adept at avoiding him.

He had made the trip to Annapolis to secure signatures for the proper transfer of the land to his name. It seemed to Sean that everyone with whom he spoke was somewhat suspicious of him, but he saw no reason that they should be and decided that perhaps it was simply his imagination.

When the papers were appropriately certified, he was pleased to discover that his Aunt Elayne also had left a generous trust for him. This astonished him, particularly because he had been under the impression that she had been left with nothing but the land.

However, the Crown's Solicitor in Annapolis assured him that the money his aunt had left for him was a sum she had specified as belonging to Sean. The solicitor noted with some cynicism that the poor woman did not have the money to spare, no matter how small the amount. "In fact," he said rather sarcastically, "she did without so others could have what she herself couldn't enjoy."

If the solicitor's comments were intended to reprimand or offend Sean, he took no notice, because this windfall would allow him to send money to repay his cousin in Southampton for setting the stone in memory of his Aunt Elayne, and it would buy the supplies he needed.

When Sean returned to Dawn Light, he was very pleased to notice how Kezie worked alongside Samson from early morning until dark. The baby was always close by, and Kezie made certain that he was comfortable, well-fed, and either in or out of the sun—depending on the weather. Sometimes she had him wrapped in a large cloth and arranged in a sort of hammock across her back.

Each day Sean was able to see some small, but often dramatic, improvements in the house and land. He had Samson tie a log to the harness of the largest horse and drag it down the lane toward the gate in order to level the roadway.

Tall weeds had taken over the garden at the front and sides of the house and these had been cleared away. Sean cared little about flowers, but he did insist that the weeds be trimmed regularly. However, because it had become so overgrown, the weeds had seeded and it was a continuing bother to keep the weeds out.

One day Samson suggested, "Mas' Shawn, seems be horses likes to graze on them weeds."

At first, Sean allowed Samson to put his plan into action, which pleased Samson immensely. But, soon Sean became unhappy with the byproducts left behind by the horses as a result of that experiment. Samson had no idea why that should present such a problem to the master.

The free flowing spring from which they drew their water had not been tended in awhile, so one day Sean and Samson repaired the wobbly structure that covered the spring. It was a sort of lean-to, and the roof was intended to keep leaves and bird droppings from fouling the water source.

They also dug a new course as an outlet for the small stream from the spring to run into the creek behind the house, which Sean felt was to the advantage of keeping the water clean. Previously, when it had become filled with twigs, a hard rain would back up into the spring itself.

Sean's idea worked perfectly, and he found that his plan brought him not only a better water source but a sense of great satisfaction. Either he had never been given the opportunity to make such decisions or he had ignored the opportunities. He simply couldn't remember, but he reveled in the pleasure of these small accomplishments.

The small "necessary house" behind the living quarters did not require much attention. His aunt had always seen to it that the slaves had kept it clean. Of course the slaves had never used it, preferring a more natural setting, so it was only a matter of sweeping out the spiders that had taken residence there.

"Samson, I'll not tell you to do differently, but you must do this: you must clean the areas you and Kezie use and be more careful about where you dump your night water. And, make certain that future deposits are made at an appropriate distance from the house—I'd say, back behind those trees." He pointed to a clump of pines almost 100 yards away then added, "or perhaps even beyond that." Samson was only too happy to abide by his master's instructions.

Of course, there would be no major crop production this year. Still, Sean was pleased with what he thought could be described as a small miracle: the transformation of an abandoned and run-down manor to something of what it might have been in earlier days when his father and uncles tended the land. Despite the fact that the harvest was minimal and required little attention, there was much to do as the October air spoke of cold days to come and Sean and the others were wisely preparing for the winter.

Wood had been cut and laid up. A few animals had been purchased with the financial boon from his aunt: a good mare for riding; two draft horses; a colt that was barely saddle trained; some chickens, pigs, and the animal for which Kezie seemed especially grateful—a milk cow. He was also able to buy corn for feeding the animals and enough to provide for the household through the winter months as well.

Sean had made friends quickly in the area. He was a much different man than the one who had arrived at Gunter's Harbour. He recalled some of the thoughts he'd had about becoming a landowner. He had imagined it as a way for him to become some sort of landed gentry, sitting around drinking tea while the slaves jumped with glee just to have the opportunity of performing his every command.

However, the reality of his life was very different from what he had imagined, and it was so much better. Although he would have been unable to explain the feelings he had, he felt certain that the responsibilities of the manor made him feel more alive than he had ever been.

Every new day found him taking a greater interest in the land, and he never shirked work, joining Samson often in uprooting a stump or levering a large rock from an area that was to be planted in the spring.

The work was hard and the horses could only be used to move large stones or pull stumps. Everything else that was done in the field was accomplished by hand through hard physical labor.

Sean had many questions of his neighbors, who were few and far between. He felt the information he had been gathering about crops and animals made him fairly well prepared for the coming spring. Already determined to raise all of his own food in order to be as self-sufficient as possible, he also decided to plant tobacco as the major crop on his land. After all, tobacco was the coin of this colony; however, he knew that growing tobacco would require good information, good seed, and probably more slaves.

Ben Dixon had proved to be all Sean had expected and more. Ben had quickly become his best friend and advisor. He decided that he would follow Dixon's advice to begin a small farming operation in order to have a minimal need for extra help with the tobacco crops. That way, as he was able to expand his land and the crop increased each year, he might be able to afford to buy more slaves from the profits of the year before. At least, that was the plan.

They had decided on a cooperative effort. Even though Ben's father, Darby Dixon, had left his holdings to Ben, only twelve acres were cleared and these would be used for producing corn, their main source of food. In the past, many colonists had been so eager to become wealthy that they became focused on growing tobacco and failed to plant corn for food.

In fact, the problem had become so serious that the Maryland Assembly passed a law requiring that two acres of corn be planted for every worker. This unusual law was of great benefit, because it assured that colonists wouldn't starve even if there was a bad harvest.

Together, Sean and Ben had agreed that most of Sean's land would be used for growing tobacco. He was excited about the way things were turning out, and for the first time in his life he was looking forward to the future, rather than simply living day by day.

The Dixon's had arranged for Sean to have some of their furniture: a bed with a rag and cornhusk tick, a table, and some chairs. That allowed Samson to move the slave furniture from the eating room back out to a small one-room cabin. It was the same cabin in which he had been born and where he had lived with his mother right up until she had died giving birth to the last of her nine children. The child had been stillborn.

Of course, since Elayne's departure, Samson did not know where any of his siblings were, but one of Topping's slaves once told him that they had been sold to a plantation buyer from Virginia. That meant he would never see any of his family again.

Kezie took great pride in the fact that this was the cabin of Samson's mother. She kept the dirt floor so well watered and swept that it was hard as stone. One day, when Sean had his first look inside the cabin, he was surprised to see that the floor was dirt. Later that day he told Samson that they would need to build a wooden floor in the cabin. The idea neither surprised nor excited Samson. He would simply do as the master said, even though he considered it strange. After all, the floor had always been dirt.

Four days later they tore down a portion of an unused shed and nailed boards in place to cover most of the floor of the cabin. Kezie became prouder than ever, because her home now had a wooden floor. And when Kezie was pleased so was Samson.

Even the baby, Mbfwana, had dramatically progressed. He had grown quickly and was beginning to look like a miniature Samson. He had also been given a proper name. Samson thought that the name Obadiah would suit the master.

"He be have crishan name, Mas' Shawn. He Obadiah," Samson proudly exclaimed one day. And so Obadiah it was.

Sean suspected that Samson and Kezie still called him Mbfwana when they were alone with the child. But, what did that matter? And, what mattered that Obadiah was an Old Testament name? And perhaps one could argue that it was not a proper Christian name; even Sean knew that. Yes, and he knew they were good slaves—at least Dixon told Sean they were—but what did that matter? After all, Sean had never known anyone who owned slaves before and he had never owned anyone; nor had he any close connection with anyone since his mother died years ago, so he had no one to hold up in comparison. Yes, what did any of it matter? Things were going well.

"Samson, you will have to go to Master Dixon's house tomorrow. He and some of his men will take you to Elk River to pick up food and other supplies I have ordered. You will need the large cart, because there will be furniture to bring back as well."

Samson knew he would have to go alone. Kezie would not be allowed to go, because there was so much for Kezie to do around the house in preparation for the arrival of the new furniture that Sean had ordered from a craftsman recommended by Dixon. Besides, this was man's work.

Kezie was learning to say some words in English and appeared able to understand Sean quite well. This pleased her, and Sean was grateful because he did not always have to wait until Samson came back from the fields to give her directions for doing his bidding.

However, Dixon had not learned to understand a thing she said and joked that it seemed Sean was learning to talk and hear like the savages, and not the other way around. Although Sean wouldn't declare it, he was rather pleased to admit to himself that he did seem quite adept at communicating with them.

The next day Samson arose early. Kezie prepared a large bowl of hot corn mush and he ate quickly and gulped his hot bark tea. It felt good, warming his belly on this chilly October morning.

Just before new light, Samson hitched the horses to the largest of the carts. He led them to the front of the house to see if the master had last minute instructions for him before leaving. He did.

"Samson, if you find it getting dark before leaving Dixon's place on the way back, you stay there with them. I don't want you on the road in the dark of night—not with Topping's men about."

"Yes, Mas' Shawn. I do like you tells. I be here by dark."

He headed the team down the lane toward the gate that he had repaired himself. He admired how smoothly the cart rode since he had leveled the lane with the log, just as he had been instructed to do. He turned to wave at Kezie and Obadiah, and as he looked back toward the gate he saw movement in the shadows. A chill swept over him. It was not fear that caused the hackles to rise on his neck; it was a primal anticipation and preparation for danger, and every muscle tensed as he approached the gate.

He slowed the team. "I be seed you. You bes' come out the lane," Samson said with a firm authority in his deep voice.

The man stepped out into what little light the open lane afforded. Samson strained to see if the man was armed. He stopped the cart. "Come here where I sees you bes'," he demanded.

As the man approached the cart, Samson could see that he was large and had a familiar walk — a very familiar walk. "Zekiel. Be you Zekiel?" Samson shouted.

"Be me, Samson. I don' be no bad. I come house to stays."

Samson could see now that it was Ezekiel, the one slave at Dawn Light that he had admired above all others. He knew that easy, loping walk and as a young boy had tried to imitate it. It was a walk of pride, a walk not often seen in a slave. It was a walk that said, "I am someone and nothing can change that. There is nothing you can do to me, no circumstance in which I can be placed, that can take my pride from me. I am a man."

It was Ezekiel, the closest to a hero that a young slave might have.

"Where you comin', Zekiel? Where you stays?"

Ezekiel drew very close to the cart and, in a soft voice, so as to be heard by only Samson, he began to speak in their African dialect, which translated would be:

"I am coming from the devil Topping's. He is an evil man, Samson. He beats me. He beats all the slaves, but he beats me badly. Imagine, me, the son of a chief being beaten by this devil white man. He took me with the rest of the people when he stole everything from this O'Connell clan. The devil has killed old Mose. He killed Croaker too. I escaped, because I said that I cannot be with such a devil as he is. We did not know you were alive. Where do you stay Samson?"

"I am staying here, at the place of the O'Connell clan. Kezie is with me and our man-child Mbfwana is also. But, we do not call him by his people name when the man Sean from the O'Connell clan is with us. We call him by a slave name then. We call him Obadiah."

They talked on excitedly, each happy to see the other and to know that the other was alive. Ezekiel explained what happened when overseer Singer and his wife had been killed. Ezekiel had been taken to Topping's and made his carriage driver.

Samson then explained how he, Kezie, and the baby had lived in hiding after that terrible day when Singer had been killed. He told how they had secreted themselves, sometimes in the house, sometimes in the forest. One time he had even buried himself in a ditch to avoid men who were searching. Samson told how they had existed off the land, eating berries and plants and sometimes stealing food when they could. Samson had seen Topping and his men come to carry off all the furniture and take the animals that were still alive.

All this sharing of events that had passed since they were separated took only a few minutes, but the men found comfort in being able to communicate in their own language.

Sean watched from the porch, expecting the cart to start up again and wondering why it had not. He thought something might be wrong and started walking toward the cart. As the sun rose higher he could now see that Samson was talking with someone in the lane.

"Here, now, Samson. What's going on down there?" Sean called out. "Who is that? What does he want?"

As Sean came closer, he recognized the man. It was Topping's carriage driver, the one who looked at him so strangely the night he was almost killed. It was the one whose glances suggested that they might somehow know one another.

"Who are you? What do you want here?" Sean repeated. He knew the answer to the first question, but was waiting for an explanation for the presence of this slave who did the bidding of Topping.

The two slaves quickly explained to Sean what had happened to them when Topping and his men had raided the O'Connell holdings, looted everything of any value, and taken all of the slaves, except for Samson and his woman and child. Samson then told Sean how he had seen Singer killed by Topping's men.

Ezekiel told Sean, "Croaker and Mose be mens come kill you. They be dead. Topping he all time beats me. I wants be here. I belong." He went on to tell him more of the details of recent months.

Sean was overwhelmed with the information that came flooding into his life. It all seemed to confirm what Dixon had told him—things that he had suspected all along. But, why had Samson not told him all these things before? Why now, when this man Ezekiel showed up, would he suddenly be willing to tell the whole story?

It seemed strange indeed. Stranger still, Ezekiel continued to look at Sean as though he had known him for a long time. Samson could barely hide the admiration in his eyes every time he looked at Ezekiel.

Things were happening much too quickly. Sean thought that events always happened unexpectedly and quickly in this strange new world he had inherited.

Was this some kind of elaborate plot? Sean had learned to look with suspicion upon almost every new circumstance and every new acquaintance. Each new relationship he developed seemed to have an unusual twist or contain complications that were somewhat mysterious, often inexplicable.

Nevertheless, Sean decided it was time to take a bold step. He told Ezekiel, "All right then, you can return to my manor, but do not expect me to trust you for now. I'll be watching you."

"Yes, Mas' Shawn. I be stays and work hard."

Maybe this would be the way he could get Topping into the open. Sean had often thought of how he might confront Topping and repay him for the evil reception he had given Sean. Sean had a plan.

"Samson, I want you to take Ezekiel with you today to the Elk River. You will see to it that he helps you with the furniture. You will need help with the heavy pieces and he will be there to help and . . ."

Samson interrupted with a pleading voice, "Oh, Mas' Shawn. Samson no be doin'. Zekiel, he be Mas' slave. I be doin' how Zekiel be sayin'."

"Enough of this! You will do as I say and you will do it now!" Sean emphasized his point by looking at Ezekiel. "Do you understand Ezekiel that it is Samson who is to tell you what to do?"

Ezekiel quickly responded, "Yes, Mas' Shawn. I be doin' how Samson he say. I be stays. Zekiel be good." He seemed overjoyed just for the possibility of once again being on this land.

"Then, Samson, here is what I want you to do. I want you to make a show of yourself. Talk loud and laugh. Be sure every slave and every master along the road sees you and Ezekiel together. If you should see any of Reverend Topping's slaves, be boastful about how well you are cared for at Dawn Light. Do you understand me?"

"Samson, he unerstans. He be doin' like Mas' Shawn say."

"Now, I want you to turn the cart around and come back to the house. I will write a letter that you must deliver to Master Dixon. When you arrive at his house, be sure you give him the letter before you do anything else. Have I made myself clear? Do you understand me?"

"Samson, he unerstans Mas' Shawn. Be doin' jes like you says."

Sean hurried back to the house while the men turned the cart around. He quickly wrote a letter to Ben Dixon. This could be just the opportunity Sean had been waiting for. Reverend Topping may have made his last unholy move. At least Sean hoped that it would be the last outrageous act that Topping would ever arrange among these friends that Sean had come to admire.

As he held the candle over the paper he let the wax drip and sealed the letter. He hoped that he had explained everything clearly in the hastily written dispatch and that Ben Dixon would not think poorly of him. *I hope he understands more than just the words of my letter.*

Samson and Ezekiel started out once again down the lane, billowing dust behind them. Kezie held the baby close and smiled as she saw her Samson looking happier than he had for a long time. Obadiah smiled a contented baby smile too and then nestled his face in his mother's breast, looking for something to eat.

Chapter Eleven

There's a New Day Dawning

The Reverend Topping had decided that he would go to the Crown Ordinary personally to pick up the cart that had been damaged on that night of terror and error—when Sean had failed to die.

He was arguing with innkeeper Oswell Hodge over the cost of the repairs. "I did not give you permission to spend such an exorbitant sum as you have spent on these repairs. What made you think you could get away with such treachery as this? You have proven yourself to be a liar and a cheat."

Topping was back to his obnoxious, bullying self. Because no one had questioned him about what happened at Dawn Light and no one really seemed concerned over the whereabouts of his slaves—except, of course, Topping himself—he had regained his arrogant attitude.

Hodge normally would have backed down before the blustering cleric. But somehow even this rather dull fellow knew that he had something on Topping, although he was not certain just what that something might have been.

"Here, now, Reverend, your worshipness," the innkeeper sputtered, "I'll have you know I be as honest a man as what you'll find in these parts. It was you what told me to use me own good judgment. That's what you told me, your lordship. And use it I did indeed. It's not as though you was living in London now, is it, Sir? I had me a devil of a time— beggin' your pardon—tryin' to find someone to put your cart together. We've no cart makers what I know of. And you'll see as how I got the work done for you and I'll thank you to pay me now, or you'll just not see your cart soon."

Hodge was sensing that things might be shifting his way and that he had the upper hand in the matter, at least for the moment. He had anticipated a problem from Topping, so he had the cart well hidden, and he was not about to be outdone by this Reverend Topping.

"I'll pay you, I'll pay you!" Topping was almost shouting now. His face became red with anger and he was trying desperately to remain in control. "I'll pay, all right. But believe me, you too will be paying and much more than you are bargaining for right now. I am not one to be trifled with or dealt with unjustly."

The innkeeper was beginning to wonder if he had gone too far and considered that perhaps he was not handling this transaction the right way. "Well now, your reverendness, don't be misunderstanding my meaning here, I was only . . . ."

"You can forget your meaning," Topping snapped. He knew that now he had regained the upper hand. "Just bring my cart about, and do it now. I will pay you your thieving price."

Then, narrowing his eyes, he glared at Hodge as he hissed, "You need not think the church will look kindly upon you or your family after this outrage."

Topping always enjoyed the look on the face of a man or woman when he made this sort of threat. Somehow, he could always detect when a person was really more superstitious than religious; and with that perception he was then able to artfully use the knowledge for his own benefit. After all, Topping had never received the blessing of advancement up the church ladder that he had prayed for and expected, and any faith he might have had was more obligatory than real. Besides, he also had his share of religious superstitions concerning belief.

As Topping knew, the innkeeper could hardly be considered a religious man. However, he did have an illogical belief. Like many others, he thought that in the event that Christianity might possibly be true, perhaps he should maintain some sort of connection with the church. And Topping had just cut him off from his version of having hope of eternal life.

"Now, Reverend Sir, I'll not have you consider me a thief, your grace. I'll be willing to take the loss and pay for half the price myself, and you can have the better of me."

"The better of you?" Topping was certain now that he had the man, and he reveled in the knowledge. "The better of you? My simple-minded man, I have always had the better of you and always will have. For, you see, you and I are from two different worlds, and you shall never attain the level of mine. It's done then. Here is your portion: half of the thieving money less something for the aggravation. Now, bring my cart about."

"And the church, Reverend Topping? Am I in good favor with the church, Your Holiness, Sir?" Hodge whined.

"You are to be pitied," Topping said with a sneer, "and not favored. However, I will take it under consideration. Do not think this sort of behavior can go without just recompense and some form of penance. Yes, I shall consider it." Topping had the man squirming now and knew he would be able to extort more from him in the future.

Topping gave orders to his slaves to unhitch the team of horses from behind the carriage and go with the innkeeper to fetch the cart.

As Topping climbed into his carriage to wait for them to bring the cart about, he heard the creaking of another cart on the road. Looking up, he saw a team of two outsized horses pulling a large freight cart and, behind the reins, two familiar faces.

Samson saw the Reverend Topping at almost the same instant that Topping saw him and Ezekiel. A chill of panic swept over him, because he knew this man for who he was and for what he was capable of doing. Yet, what Sean had said to him gave him a confidence unlike any he had ever had before. He remembered Sean's words: "Make a show of yourself. Talk loud and laugh."

As nervous as Samson was, the loud talk and laughter came easily. He quickly assessed the situation and said to Ezekiel, "You be laugh what I says. Don' care it ain't for laughin'. You hears?"

"I hears," Ezekiel responded, nodding his head, and he immediately burst into uproarious laughter.

Samson quickly came back with a broad smile and more of his loud talking. He knew that Topping could not hear what they were saying as the cart rattled on past the Crown Ordinary. He and Ezekiel played their parts well. They each gave Topping a look as they passed by, and if they had any fear of the man it did not show in their faces.

Topping was infuriated. His stolen-and-then-escaped slave, Ezekiel, was mocking him before the other slaves. He called to the men who had accompanied him, "Quickly! After them! It's the runaway slave. Take them both. Dead or alive, I'll pay you for them."

His men had been lying about in the shade near the roadside. Their horses were tethered to bushes, but the saddles were loose. They jumped to their feet and struggled to get the cinches drawn up and tightened. Mounting, they looked to Topping for instructions.

But, just then, Topping was watching a lone rider approaching and did not realize that his men awaited his word. Topping recognized the rider. It was Sean O'Connell. Being too late for an escape, he called to his men to come help him. But they, having seen Topping look in the opposite direction, had taken off after the cart driven by Samson and Ezekiel.

Now Sean saw Topping standing in the carriage and he felt hot anger surging up within him. His heart immediately began to pump faster. As he approached Topping, he almost jumped his mount over the carriage but managed to pull his horse in right before the carriage step.

"So, Topping, here we are. We meet again, this time under somewhat different circumstances."

Topping had reached under the carriage seat and pulled out a silver handled cane, holding it defensively across his chest. "Well, yes. How good to see you, young sir. I've meant to come by to see you, because I have heard of the terrible and unfortunate incident when you were attacked the night I left you at the manor."

"I'd say you know more about that night than you'd care to admit to me, Topping," Sean replied.

Ignoring that comment, Topping quickly said, "Well, I understand you have made some important changes on your property. I trust you are holding no grudges as a result of our first meeting. I only wonder if I . . ."

He was interrupted by shouts and curses as the freight cart driven by Samson came careening back toward them.

When they had first driven past, laughing and talking loudly, Ezekiel was watching over his shoulder and he saw Topping's men mount their horses and begin the pursuit. He also saw Sean riding up to Topping's carriage. When he told Samson what was happening, Samson almost turned the cart over as he pulled the horses' heads in and laid them in a tight circle.

He drove the horses at a furious pace back toward the Crown Ordinary inn and headlong into the pursuing riders. The three men scattered. One fell from his horse and was almost trampled by the cart horses. Another man's horse ran wildly into a thicket and he was knocked from his saddle by a tree limb. The third turned his horse, fell off, remounted, and tried to continue the chase, but his saddle had not been secured and he fell off again.

Samson was not nearly as adept at stopping the cart as Sean had been with reining in his horse. The horses decided that Samson wanted some real speed from them, and they obliged him. When Samson tried to pull them up, the lead, a headstrong mare, determined that she liked the run and turned in the opposite direction.

The cart leaned precariously on one wheel and there was nothing Samson could do. The horses ran headlong into the frightened carriage team. One of the carriage horses reared and the carriage tipped over. As Topping tried frantically to jump free, the freight cart was sliding sideways.

Topping wasn't fast enough. He tried to roll aside as he hit the ground, but the wheels of the skidding cart first shoved him along like a rag doll and then thumped over him. The spinning wheel bounced him once and then the other wheel rolled over him.

Sean rode quickly behind and away from the carriage when he saw that the freight cart was out of control. As the dust settled, Sean swung his horse around and dismounted. He ran immediately to the Reverend Topping. His head had been crushed by one of the wheels. He was dead.

Sean looked down at the pitiful sight in disbelief. Many a day he secretly had dreamed of ridding his life of the influence of Topping but not as it had occurred this moment. Now, looking at the lifeless upturned face, in the reality of death he found no satisfaction. Sean had planned on doing Topping in for what he had done to him, his family, and the Singers. But, looking at the man, he felt only a cold emptiness and sorrow in the death of another human.

It had all happened so suddenly. Oswell Hodge and Maudie watched the activity in horror from the safety of the inn's doorway. They came running toward Topping. The girl was in tears. "Oh, it's the Reverend what's dead. Oh, Father, what ever shall we do?"

"Do?" the innkeeper asked, obviously puzzled by the question. "Well, I'm thinking God would want us to have all our money back, so I know what to do."

He bent over to look under the overturned cart for Topping's money pouch. When he did, one of Topping's men ran up behind him and knocked him to the ground.

Hodge cried out, "Here, now. What's this? I need to get me money back, er, uh . . . I mean get that as what the good Reverend Topping owes me."

When Sean saw the man hit Hodge from behind and knock him to the ground, it was all he needed. His emotions had been jumping from one extreme to the other, and he saw his opportunity to do something about those very active passions.

He rose from where he had been squatting next to Topping's body. Grabbing the man by the shoulder, he pulled him to his feet, spun him about and with a swing of his arm that started somewhere from behind him, Sean's fist struck Topping's man full in the face. The blow sent the man reeling backward where he tripped over the fallen innkeeper and struck his head on the step of the carriage. He was unconscious.

Sean was pleased with the way the blow had released those stored-up emotions, but he was shocked that he had dealt the man such a hard blow and now felt the pain across the face of his knuckles.

Samson and Ezekiel came running up to Sean. "Din't mean do so for Revren Toppin, Mas' Shawn," Samson said with a pleading tone.

"I know, I know. It was all an accident. It was an accident as far as we are concerned. However, as for God . . . well, maybe it was a matter of true restitution." said Sean.

Samson and Ezekiel looked at one another, and the looks on their faces made it plain that neither of them had any idea what Sean meant. Noticing the look, Sean thought it was just as well that they did not understand.

Hodge was making another try for the money pouch. Taking notice that Sean was watching him, he said, "What do you think, Sir? Shouldn't I have me money back from the Reverend? After all, he cheated me by giving me less than half what was the cost of repairin' the cart." It was only a partial lie.

"I'll tell you what, Innkeep: you show me the bill for your cost of the repairs, hand that money over to me that you have in your waistcoat, and I'll see what we might do."

Sean was certain that Hodge was not telling the truth. He knew the man was doing his best to make the situation work out to his benefit. Even so, Sean did want to be sure the man received what was due him.

"Seems the receipt for the repairs was lost in the accident, Sir," he said making a show of searching his own pockets. But, could you let me have a bit more just so's to cover me costs?"

"Enough," said Sean. "Samson, Ezekiel, come here. I want you two to stay here and help clean up this mess. You two, after all, were in the midst of causing it all."

"You there," he called to Topping's man, who was beginning to regain his senses, "you will take the Reverend's body back to his family and tell them of the accident; and, what you tell them had better be the truth."

The man stood and, in obvious pain, he wiped the blood from his mouth. He shook his head, acknowledging the orders and started for his horse.

"Samson," Sean continued, "Give me the Reverend's money pouch. Oh, and, Samson, give me the letter as well."

Samson reluctantly took the pouch from Topping's body and handed it to Sean who quickly assessed the contents. He pulled the letter from inside his shirt and handed it to Sean, who seemed relieved to have it back in his possession.

"I know every farthing that's in this purse," he said to Topping's man. "When I talk to the family later on, there had better be none of it missing. Have I made myself clear? Do you all understand me?"

All seemed eager to quickly agree with this insistent young man's orders. Sean walked to his untethered horse that had been enjoying the freedom of nibbling some long grass.

Gathering up the horse's reins he said, "I'll be back, Innkeep. There are some unanswered questions that I will have the truth about. You do know what the truth means, do you not?"

"Oh, yes. Yes. Yes, indeed, truth. Yes, Sir. That's what it's about. That I do, Sir, bless me, yes. My, yes, the truth you'll be having from me, Sir," he replied, much too sincerely.

"Mind you," Sean continued, "I'll be looking in on Topping's family, and I'll be looking in on you as well. Remember, it's the truth I want. You and I will have some talking to do about running an inn on my manor, as well. Again, so there is no mistaking my meaning, am I making myself perfectly clear to all of you?"

Sean knew from the way Hodge and Topping's men glanced at one another and the way they assured him that they did understand, that he would have no further trouble from any of these. He was certain that he would now be able to get to the bottom of these incidents that had been caused by Topping.

"Innkeeper, don't forget the matter of operating an inn on my property. I advise you to have all of your papers ready for me to see the next time I come. You may well be looking for a new business—or perhaps the stocks."

Sean mounted his horse and began the ride back to Dawn Light. When he turned the first bend in the road, he looked back over his shoulder to make certain no one was following.

He stopped the horse, dismounted, picked up some dry tinder and struck a spark from his flint to it. Fanning the flame, he held the unopened letter to the fire and it was consumed in seconds. Thoroughly stamping out the smoldering ashes, he remounted and headed home.

As he rode along he talked to God—a very curious diversion with which he was not familiar. He would not have said he was praying, but in his own way he apologized to God for the bitter plans he had laid out in the letter—plans in which he had wanted to involve Ben Dixon. They were designed to result in the humiliation of Topping. But, Sean was beginning to realize that it was not up to him to make such plans for the life of another.

Besides, it seemed to him that God's plan that had resulted in the death of Topping was much harsher than any plan he might have invented.

He was very relieved that the letter had never reached Dixon.

Chapter Twelve

Reverend Topping Has a Niece

Somehow, the whole world seemed different now. In the weeks since Topping's death, Sean felt more relaxed and sensed that prospects for his future had greatly improved.

Sean allowed his horse to set his own pace along the road to Gunter's Harbour. The pleasant day set his mind to recounting the events of the past weeks. Despite some of the harrowing, life- threatening incidents, he felt a real sense of peace in being here in what might become his permanent home.

Topping was dead and he could not say that he was grief-stricken over that matter. It was not that he was glad that Topping had died, but he did have a strange sense of relief in the matter. Then there was the issue of the letter. Topping's death had prevented Sean from making a terrible mistake.

Recalling that fateful day when the Reverend was killed, he thought of how he had sent Samson and Ezekiel off to Dixon's with the letter he had written. He heard himself breathe a loud sigh of relief.

He had written the letter to Dixon in anger, hoping to involve Dixon and some others in a conspiracy that he had hoped would lead to Topping's humiliation and eventually reveal him for the callous person he was.

However, Sean had never considered that some sort of revenge might lead to the Reverend Topping's death. He had been a fool to write the letter and he knew it. In fact, that is why he started out after Samson and Ezekiel, hoping to intercept them before they could deliver the letter. Despite the tragedy of Topping's death, he felt fortunate that events kept that letter from being delivered and his appalling thoughts revealed.

Able to think more clearly now than he had on that fateful morning, Sean knew—or at least hoped—that Dixon would not have gone along with his idea. If he knew Dixon at all, Ben would have refused to do so.

The letter which had been written in angry haste, spoke of a plan to set a trap that would force Topping to show himself for the thief he was. Since that day, he had gone over the plan in his mind again and again. He knew that even if Dixon had agreed to help him with the plan, there were too many things that could have gone wrong. Yes, he was very glad the letter had been destroyed. He would not want Dixon to know the sort of criminal thoughts he'd had on that day.

There was another thing. Ever since Topping's death, the words Sean had said to Samson kept repeating themselves in his mind. He had no idea where the thoughts came from, and he certainly had felt no obligation to say such things to Samson. Yet, he remembered the words as though he had just expressed them: "As far as God is concerned, maybe it was a matter of true restitution."

Such an odd thought for him to have: "As far as God is concerned." After all, it wasn't as if he had ever given much thought to whether there even was a God. Besides, if by some chance there truly were a God who delivered providential restitution, Sean wondered how his own life might fare.

But why bother? Sean brought his horse to a halt in front of a beautiful house.

He vaguely remembered that Topping had mentioned who lived there on that fateful day when the Reverend transported him from the ship to Dawn Light. He was not at all disappointed in what he saw. The house had been easy to find and it was just as Ben Dixon described it. There was no mistaking who had lived here, because he saw Topping's ornate carriage under an open shed at the back of the house.

He was not certain what he would say or how he might say it. In addition, he found it somewhat strange that Mrs. Dixon was so insistent that he should come and pay his respects to the family of the deceased Reverend Topping. Nevertheless, having little experience with this sort of thing himself, he had deferred to Mrs. Dixon as a woman who was conversant with proper behavior.

Standing on the porch was a woman that Sean judged to be too young to be the Reverend's widow. She was quite easy to look at and just as his thoughts began to wander, the door opened and another woman stepped out onto the porch. *Now that is most certainly Topping's widow*, Sean thought. *She looks as though she might be the elder sister of the younger woman.*

He became aware that he had been standing there next to the horse staring at the women, and suddenly he sensed his face reddening. He felt very self-conscious, because he did not even know the relationship of the women to Topping. He tied the reins off on the hitch and walked to the gate.

He placed his hand on the gate latch but waited as he said, "I am Sean O'Connell. I have come to pay my respects and offer condolences to the widow Topping and to the Reverend's family. May I step inside the garden?"

The women looked at each other with what he took to be mild shock or perhaps displeasure; he was not certain which. The younger woman began to say something but was immediately prevented from doing so by the other.

The older woman then said, "Yes, Mr. O'Connell, you may step into the garden. Please come to the porch and sit with us." The younger woman said something, but it was spoken too softly for Sean to hear.

He had not really noticed the garden, because he was staring so intently at the women. But, when he came inside the gate he was surprised to see beautifully trimmed bushes and shrubs and even a few flowers that the frost had not yet touched.

As he stepped onto the porch, the older of the two women extended her hand toward Sean and said, "I am the Reverend Jonathan Topping's sister, Cynthia Wells, and this is my daughter, Julia. Please, sit here."

Sean took the seat that was offered, first allowing the women to be seated opposite him. He realized that he had not uttered a word since stepping onto the porch and had ignored Mrs. Wells' offered hand. He was also painfully aware that his jaw was slack and he was staring at Julia.

"I am, thank you," he stammered.

"Isn't that nice? You are what, Mr. O'Connell?" Mrs. Wells asked.

"I am seated," he said self-consciously.

"Yes, that is nice. I can see that you are," she smiled and glanced at Julia who was smothering a giggle behind her handkerchief. "We can see that he is seated, can we not, Julia?"

"I . . . oh, well, I meant to say, I am pleased to meet you both. I am very sorry about your brother, Mrs. Wells . . . your uncle, Miss Julia. I must admit that the Reverend Topping and I were not on the best of terms, but I do regret what happened to him. I was there when it happened, you know."

"Yes, Mr. O'Connell. We are quite aware of your part in his death. That is to say, we do not lay blame at your feet, but we are aware that you were there and that you were not the best of friends. I understand, and I admire you for coming to see us upon my brother's death. We do admire him for that kindness, do we not, Julia dear?"

"Oh, yes, indeed, Mother. We do admire Mr. O'Connell . . . uh, for his kindness," she said as she averted her eyes from Sean's.

"Well, Madam, and Miss Julia, I confess that I thought I was coming to see the Reverend's widow and was not aware that you would be here. Actually, I mean I did not know that he had a sister and a niece here."

"Mr. O'Connell," began Mrs. Wells, "you are not entirely wrong. For you see, I am widowed. But, did you not know that Jonathan was unmarried? There is no widow Topping. You see, he never married, because when he entered the priesthood he was determined to rise quickly in the church. I must tell you that he thought the assignment he was given here many years ago was going to become a stair step to higher things in England. I fear he had his heart set upon being an Archbishop. Alas, it never happened. Unfortunately, as you may have observed, it made him a singularly bitter man."

"I'm sorry to know that. I mean, I don't regret that he wasn't married. Well, that is, I'm sorry to hear that too. But, it is sad to know that a man's unrealized dreams could turn him so bitter. Would you ladies please forgive my boldness in coming here without announcing myself first and for the clumsy way I have been handling myself?" He was addressing Mrs. Wells, but he was looking at Julia.

"Of course, young man, it is perfectly understandable. We do not stand on propriety in this matter. You must know that we also feel somewhat awkward. Let's simply put that behind us, shall we?"

He managed to get his eyes off Julia long enough to nod affirmatively.

"Well then," said Mrs. Wells, drawing her shawl about her, "I notice a chill in the air since the sun is no longer striking the porch. Perhaps you would join us in the parlor for tea? The hour is close enough for afternoon tea, isn't it, Julia dear?"

"Why, yes, Mother, I suppose it is," Julia replied. "Shall I have Missy prepare it?"

"No, you stay here with Mr. O'Connell, and I'll call Missy. Give us a few minutes, then come to the parlor, and we'll have the biscuits ready," Mrs. Wells said as she got up to go inside.

Sean jumped to his feet as she arose, but in doing so his boot top caught on the edge of his chair. He lost his balance and fell clumsily across Julia, almost knocking her to the floor. He ended up sitting at her feet and felt his face flush red. He knew it was more than embarrassment that reddened his face.

Mrs. Wells spoke first. "Are you all right, young man? I trust you've done yourself no injury. Are you hurt?"

Julia could not contain her glee this time. While giggling, she said, "Mr. O'Connell, was the chair not comfortable enough for you? Do you fancy the floor instead?"

Sean's response was not typical of him. "Yes, the chair was comfortable enough but not nearly so pleasant as sitting at the feet of such a lovely young lady."

It was Julia's turn to blush and her mother came quickly to her rescue. "Well, Julia, perhaps you had better come in with me to prepare tea after all. And you, Mr. O'Connell, can enjoy the solitude of our garden until the biscuits are ready."

Sean could see that his remark had caused some suspicion in the mind of Mrs. Wells. "I am sorry, Mrs. Wells . . . and I apologize to you also, Miss Julia. Please forgive me, ladies. I do not know what has come over me. I am not usually the rude person you have seen today. Perhaps I should leave. Might you excuse me for now and be so kind as to allow me to come back another time when I might announce myself properly?"

"Nonsense," replied Julia's mother. "You will wait right here until we call you, and it shall not be but a moment or two and we'll make a proper announcement. Come along, Julia." With that said, the two women disappeared into the house.

Sean thought he could hear two voices giggling this time as the door closed. He took his seat again, grateful that he had not been excused but not certain as to why he was acting the part of such a bumbling idiot.

As the door closed behind them, Mrs. Wells, still smiling, said to her daughter, "Julia, what ever has come over you? You are behaving like a girl who has neither manners nor sense, rather than behaving as a proper young lady should."

"Oh, Mother, I know. But, isn't he simply lovely? I'm so glad you did not send him away. Did you see his eyes when he looks at me? I thought . . ."

"Julia, that's enough now. Never mind what you may have thought. I'll not have you doing any such thinking. Call Missy in here and have her help you prepare the tea biscuits. She made too many this morning and I know there are more than a dozen on the sideboard. Warm those up; they'll not take long to heat. I'm sure water is already boiling for the tea." Regardless of her tone, secretly Mrs. Wells agreed wholeheartedly with Julia's assessment of Sean.

"Yes, Mother," Julia replied as she went off to get Missy.

Julia heard Missy humming on the back porch. She was busily scrubbing *hopniss* (the wild potatoes local Indians had taught them to eat) for the supper meal. Julia called to her, "Missy! Missy! Come help me heat some tea biscuits and boil some tea. We have company, and I hope your biscuits are as tasty as usual."

"You know they be tasty liken to always, Miss Julia." Missy came into the cooking room wiping her hands on her apron.

The two young women were about the same age and were quite close emotionally, despite their cultural differences. If they had been from similar backgrounds there is no doubt that people would have considered them close friends. But, because one was a slave and the other was the mistress, such could never be—at least not in public.

Julia's life was a series of pampered days and boring leisure. Missy's life was a monotonous ordeal of continuing labor and little rest. Even so, Julia did not look down upon Missy nor did Missy resent Julia.

Meanwhile, left to himself on the porch, Sean did not know what to do. So, he decided to do what Mrs. Wells had suggested. He walked about the garden, trying to enjoy it. He thought that he must have Samson and Ezekiel do something besides simply cutting weeds down. However, he decided that he wouldn't know how to begin such a task. Actually, he did not see that much of the garden, although he continued to walk aimlessly about. His mind was wandering back to try and recapture the incidents of the past minutes with Julia.

What a fool I've made of myself, he thought. *Yet, Mrs. Wells has invited me to stay. What a beautiful young woman! I wonder if she has any suitors. Come, now, Sean, what difference would it make if she did? Would she consider me in the running? That is, if I should want to become a suitor. I suppose that I could always . . ..*

The voice of Missy calling from the front door startled Sean, "Miss Wells say be comin' in the parlor." With that, she ducked back inside the door and Sean wasted no time in responding to the invitation.

As he entered the parlor, he quickly saw that it was furnished very much the same as any family of means might furnish their comfortable principal house in Dublin or Southampton. The chairs were placed intentionally and not in the haphazard way his were at Dawn Light. Intricate cloths and doilies were placed on tables and candle lamps were next to every chair. Next to a fireplace was an ornate bookcase with more volumes of books than Sean had seen in his entire life. From the comments Dixon had made to him, Sean wondered if any of these furnishings might really belong to him, perhaps having been stolen by Topping from the O'Connell Manor.

His question was about to be answered—at least in part. The two ladies were seated before a small serving table where Missy had placed the tea pot, cups, and a heaping platter of biscuits.

"Please, Mr. O'Connell, sit there," Mrs. Wells indicated, pointing to a large chair across from the ladies.

He took his seat and she continued, "You should know, Mr. O'Connell, that these chairs in which we are sitting and this serving table were purchased by my brother from your estate. It seems your family fell upon hard times, especially after your uncle Thomas was killed when he had been kicked by that horse— such a tragedy and a very painful death. Your Aunt Elayne had no income from crops or animal sales. So my brother, God rest his generous soul, helped your aunt by purchasing some of their furnishings. I am simply delighted that we could offer you that chair for your comfort. This is a lovely serving table, do you not think so? It also was your aunt's."

"Oh, yes, Mrs. Wells. Lovely. . . lovely I should say so." But, Sean was not looking at the table when he answered, he was looking at Julia.

Taking his seat, he was graciously served delicious hot tea, wonderfully warm biscuits with jam, and delightful conversation.

Mrs. Wells said, "Would you care to read some verse for us, Julia? Perhaps Mr. O'Connell would like to hear some Baxter, or he may prefer Donne. Which of the two do you prefer, Mr. O'Connell?"

Before Julia could respond, Sean said, "I'm afraid I have not been one to read much poetry, so I must confess that the names are not familiar. Still, Miss Julia, perhaps your mother would like to hear you read, and it would certainly be a pleasurable opportunity for me. May I ask you to favor us with some readings?"

"I don't know, Mr. O'Connell. You see, mother loves to hear me read, but I fear that it may be something of a disappointment to you because . . ."

"No, please do. I don't see how you could do anything that would disappoint me, unless of course you should decide to not honor us with some verse."

"There, you see, my dear? Mr. O'Connell would like to hear you read too. Please, Julia, perhaps some Baxter, of whom the young sir has never heard." As she said this, she assumed a curious mock surprised look as she glanced at Julia.

"All right then," said Julia as she stood to glide across the room and directed her attention to the top shelf of the bookcase that contained a number of small, leather bound books. Running her finger across their spines she selected one and returned to take her place.

Sean stood to help her be seated and he moved her chair slightly closer to his side of the table. The effort did not go unnoticed by either of the ladies.

"Mr. O'Connell, the verse I have chosen to read was written by a woman, and I . . ."

"A woman? A woman poet?" Sean interrupted. As he did, he realized that he might be showing more ignorance than he should. "I mean, I didn't know women could do such things and I know so little of the . . ."

"Yes, well then, as I was saying," Julia continued, "I want to read the verse of this woman, Anne Bradstreet, because this particular poem is quite significant to both me and to mother. Shall I read it then?"

"Oh, dear, Julia, I wish you hadn't chosen her. It's true Mr. O'Connell, it is one of my favorite poems. However, I think I shall be unable to hear it read aloud without shedding a tear. You see, the poet Anne Bradstreet is writing about her own husband," and her voice filled with emotion.

"I'm sorry. I'll choose another, Mother."

"Not at all, dear. You've chosen well. You see, Mr. O'Connell, the death of my husband, Julia's dear father, was an unexpected tragedy. He had become so very weak, and his joints ached so and, oh, the bruises. The physician didn't seem to understand and he thought it was scurvy. But in two months he was dead. This verse meant much to me while my husband was alive. It still means a great deal to me. But, go on then, dear; read it please."

Julia smiled at her mother. Then, sitting back and drawing in a deep breath, she said, "The name of this poem is 'To my Dear and Loving Husband'," and she began to read.

If ever two were one, then surely we.
If ever man were lov'd by wife, then thee;
If ever wife were happy in a man,
Compare with me ye women if you can.
I prize thy love more than whole mines of
*   gold,*
Or all the riches that the East doth hold.
My love is such that rivers cannot quench,
Nor aught but love from thee, give
*   recompense.*
Thy love is such I can no way repay,
The heavens reward thee manifold, I pray.
Then while we live, in love so persevere
That, when we live no more, we may live
*   ever.*

Sean had never heard such words. The verses seemed to flow like liquid sounds of delight from Julia's lips. He was unsure of whether it was the impact of the words themselves or the combination of the words and Julia's lilting voice. He was stunned and his face reflected how deeply the reading affected him.

"How beautiful, Julia," Sean blurted out. "I mean . . . I mean you read beautifully; that was beautiful. Never have I been so captivated by words. Surely Mrs. Wells, you and your daughter have honored me by allowing me the privilege to hear this poem that has meant so much to you."

"Yes, Mr. O'Connell, the poem is very significant to us, especially to me. I do miss my husband so very much. He was a good and kind man. You would have liked him. And I dare say that he would have liked you as well. Don't you agree, Julia dear?"

"Mother," Julia responded in a mildly scolding tone, "Mr. O'Connell should not be made to feel so uncomfortable." Looking directly at Sean, and then lowering her eyes she said, "But I am pleased that you enjoyed my reading."

He was about to answer her when the mantle clock tolled five times and he was surprised when Mrs. Wells asked, "Well, Mr. O'Connell, the time is moving toward the dinner hour, would you care to join us for that meal?"

Sean knew that the invitation was simply a kind way of announcing that he had probably overstayed this first visit.

"I do thank you, Mrs. Wells, but I must be getting back to the manor. I apologize for taking so much of your time."

"Not at all. You must come back and visit us another time. Perhaps then you might join us for a meal. Would you like to invite Mr. O'Connell back, dear?" Mrs. Wells asked Julia. She blushed at the thought of inviting Sean, and he quickly responded to Mrs. Wells in order to spare Julia further embarrassment.

"That is much too kind of you, ladies. What I must do is have you as my guests for tea at Dawn Light. Would you consider doing so? You must forgive me for being so awkward. It has been many years since I have had the pleasure of the company of ladies. I fear that I have forgotten how to behave properly. Am I being too bold, Mrs. Wells?"

"No, not at all. You have behaved in a perfectly proper way, hasn't he, dear?" She looked at Julia with the hint of a smile on her face.

"If you would come and honor me with a visit, perhaps you could bring your books and read again. Maybe I would learn to appreciate verse more if I could hear it read with such emotion. I would come to fetch you both and bring you back home. You'll not have to answer me now but please, ladies, will you at least grant me the honor of giving my invitation your consideration?"

"Yes, of course we shall. Julia?" she asked looking at her daughter for a response. Julia was avoiding the question by gathering the tea cups.

"Thank you, Mr. O'Connell. I am certain that mother will communicate with you."

When Sean left, Julia and her mother lingered in the parlor. "Isn't it so, Mother? Isn't he simply lovely?"

"Julia. What sort of talk is that? He is a rather handsome young man, but don't be expecting too much. I think we may have done a bit too much talking. I fear he has not had much of a genteel upbringing. Why, from his ignorance of Baxter and Donne I wonder if young Mr. O'Connell can read, or if he is a Christian man at all."

"Oh, Mother. How can you say such things? Not every man is a reader, as the men in our family are . . . or were. Mother, would we consider going to visit his house as he invited us? I have a wonderful idea. I could take some of the best Christian verse, perhaps even the Bible and read to him. Could we, Mother?"

"Hush, now, dear. I'll think about it. But for now, let's simply wait a few days before we make too many plans. Knowing men as I do, he may never call again."

As Cynthia Wells arose from her chair to leave the room she was thinking that, knowing men as she did, she would probably be seeing more of the young Mr. Sean O'Connell than Julia would be prepared for.

Riding back to Dawn Light, Sean recounted every moment there in the parlor. He was relishing those thoughts and turning them over and over again in his mind. He decided that he had never before had such fine tea and the biscuits were very much out of the ordinary. Yes, one might judge this to have been an extraordinary day in Sean's life.

The conversation with Mrs. Wells and Julia had been the most stimulating in his recollection. Never in his life had anyone read words with such emotion and meaning as Julia had. He was certain that she was a young lady that would make her mark in this world, and that mark would be one of excellence.

He remembered many things about that afternoon, but what he could not stop thinking of were Julia's beautiful green eyes and her quick smile.

Yes, I'll have them come out to Dawn Light for tea. I wonder what sort of tea they had. Delicious it was. Very unlike the bark tea to which Kezie has introduced me. Very fine tea, steaming hot tea, unusually fine tea, I'm sure.

In fact, Sean believed he could still feel the tea warming him as his horse headed home.

Chapter Thirteen

Ezekiel Has a Secret

When Sean made the decision to allow Ezekiel to stay at Dawn Light, even before Topping had been killed, he knew the choice had been a wise one. Winter came early that year, and the cold weather, freezing rains, and snow prevented them from working in the fields.

Nevertheless, there were many things to be done around the manor. Tools were repaired. Wooden handles were made to replace those on shovels, hoes, and the other hand tools that were broken or worn out. They were carefully cut to fit the worker and then smoothed by rubbing them with stone. New harnesses were braided for the horses.

Sean was being frugal with his money, but he bought those necessities that would be needed as soon as spring came. Dixon had already made arrangements to obtain seed for both him and Sean.

Just as the cold weather of winter had begun before December, spring also came early. There had been unusual amounts of snow and ice that winter, leaving the fields very wet. However, as soon as it was possible to do so, the men began to work in those parts of the fields that began to dry.

The spring air seemed to breathe new life into everyone at Dawn Light. Obadiah was not much more than a year old, but it was obvious that his mother Kezie would give birth to another child by the year's end. That would be another benefit for Sean, especially if it were to be another strong boy to work in the fields.

Ezekiel had proved to be an even greater asset than Samson. The two slaves worked together as though they were one man. The uncanny way Ezekiel had of anticipating what needed to be done on the manor was something that Sean had not expected during the first days that Ezekiel was with them. However, as time passed, Ezekiel's knowledge of the land he had worked for so many years with Sean's father, uncles, and aunt proved invaluable.

Samson always watched Ezekiel as they worked. If Ezekiel laid a hoe down in order to begin another task or look for a tool, Samson would know what to do.

"I know what you need, Ezekiel. I know where the heavy metal bar is. I will get it for you," Samson would say (always spoken in their African dialect unless, of course, Sean was nearby). Off he would hurry to bring the needed tool to Ezekiel. Ezekiel would watch him go, and a faint smile would cross his face.

Although Samson was not aware of it, Ezekiel was watching him too. Before long, Ezekiel would try to get Samson's opinion on some work problem he was trying to solve. At first it was simple things about which he would question Samson, but he'd never ask him directly.

"Hmmm," Ezekiel would say aloud to himself, "Mas' Shawn says we brings hay from Mas' Dixon. Don' see how he 'spects we be doin'."

Then, Samson eagerly made a suggestion. Despite the fact that they had fieldwork to complete, he said they could get their work done before midday, and then he would hitch the horses to the cart while Ezekiel ate his lunch. Samson offered to eat while they drove to the Dixon's.

Another pleased smile crossed Ezekiel's face. "That be good, Samson. Wish I thinks that my own self."

Sean spent almost as much time in the fields working alongside Ezekiel as Samson did. He enjoyed the quiet banter between the two men, sometimes in their version of English but mostly in their savage tongue.

Although Sean would occasionally rebuke them for speaking their dialect, it did not really bother him that he could not understand them, because his trust for them both was growing. Sean could see how deeply Samson admired Ezekiel, and the older man did not hide his favor toward Samson.

Sean knew little about farming of any kind. As the weeks passed into months, even Sean knew he would need more help than Samson and Ezekiel could provide. He asked Dixon for advice in the matter. He thought that he might be able now to afford another slave or maybe two. Even though Dixon had no slaves, he had an eye for such things and was perfectly willing to help him procure them.

Sean putting his trust in Samson and Ezekiel could have been a grave mistake had they been two other men. But these were men of honor. Sean could not help wondering what sort of life Ezekiel had had before being captured and becoming a slave. Samson, of course, had been born and was raised right there at Dawn Light. Sean could imagine that Ezekiel might have been a leader among his people in Africa. He was certainly a leader on the manor.

Before acquiring the new slaves he was considering, he did a strange (if not dangerous) thing. He decided to seek Ezekiel's counsel in a matter that had concerned him.

One day, Sean sent Samson to Dixon's to pick up some supplies that Ben had purchased for Dawn Light on a recent trip to Gunter's Harbour. Samson did not question the master, but he thought it was somewhat strange that he would send him alone, without Ezekiel. Samson sensed that it seemed to be Sean's desire to see the men together all the time, and Sean would occasionally remark, "The two of you work better as two men than I've seen any four or five men work." When Sean said that, Samson would look at the ground to keep from grinning with pride.

As soon as Samson started down the lane, Sean called Ezekiel back from his fieldwork and asked him to sit on the porch. Somewhat reluctantly, Ezekiel came to the house and took the chair on the porch that Sean offered.

"Ezekiel," he began, "I want to ask you some questions, and I want you to answer me without lying. Do you understand what I am saying?"

"Yes, Mas' Shawn, I unerstan. I don lie, Mas' Shawn. I make truth talk."

"Yes. I believe you. I know you tell the truth. I simply mean that I don't want you to hold anything back from me. Here is what I must know, Ezekiel. I want you to tell me about my family. I want you to describe my father, uncles, and aunt as you remember them. As you know, I left when I was a small boy. I feel I have been cheated by not being able to be with my family, separated as it were by an ocean when my mother died in England." Sean did not see the terrible parallel in the life of the man with whom he was speaking.

Ezekiel was clearly uncomfortable with this request. He begged Sean to allow him to go back to the fields. Sean was rather sharp in his insistence, and reluctantly Ezekiel began to speak. At first his voice was soft and he spoke slowly. However, as he continued, the pace of his voice increased and Sean could tell that he was now remembering people who had not treated him unkindly, despite the fact that they held him in slavery.

For more than an hour Ezekiel told Sean of the O'Connell family. He answered questions as best he could understand them. As Ezekiel continued to speak, Sean was pleased to learn something more about his family, even though it was from the perspective of a slave. But, as Sean listened, he noticed the countenance on Ezekiel's face becoming sad.

Finally, there were no more questions to be answered.

"Thank you, Ezekiel. You must know that I hold you in high regard, even though you are my slave. I must ask you another question, though. Why did your face get so sad when you told me of my family?"

Ezekiel looked down at his hardened and callused bare feet. He said nothing.

"Answer me. Is it something I have said? Why have you become so sad?"

The silence continued.

"You black savage." Sean's voice rose, "Do not take my kindness as something with which you can trifle. My intent is to treat you properly, but you are a slave and you will answer me and answer me now, or I'll make you wish you had."

Ezekiel looked up at Sean. The look of sadness had been replaced with a different one. It was neither a look of anger nor defiance; it was something Sean could not define.

"Mas' Shawn, Zekiel face be sad . . . ." And Ezekiel then explained how, just as Sean knew little of his family, Ezekiel knew little of his people in what he called "the Land." He did reveal to Sean that his people were called "Proud Lions Walking" and that he was the son of a great chieftain. He told of being stolen by another clan and how many from his clan were beaten or killed when they tried to escape. Then they were sold to a white man and herded into what he called a "big canoe."

Ezekiel looked across the fields as though he were trying to see that place that lay across the ocean. After a few moments he continued, telling Sean how they were in the big canoe for a long time. Much of the time he couldn't understand what others were saying, because they were not his People.

Ezekiel was frightened, and they were packed so tightly that some nights people died on top of him, and he could hardly breathe. He related how they were made to jump from the big canoe. He was unable to swim, but a strong man had pulled him safely onto dry land.

He looked back at Sean as if he wanted to give him more answers, but all he could remember was that he had been brought to this place as a boy. And just like Sean, because it was so long ago, he had little recollection of his clan, the People.

That, he explained, was why he was sad—because his heart was crying out for someone to tell him about his People, the Proud Lions Walking. But no one could tell him and he had become sad.

Again, Ezekiel hung his head and continued to look down.

"I did not know, Ezekiel. I mean, I know you have no way of communicating with your family, but I never thought . . . that is . . . I did not know." Now Sean hung his head.

Several minutes passed and then Ezekiel said, "I tells mo', Mas' Shawn. "Zekiel don' lie. Zekiel knows 'bout clan."

"But, how could you possibly know about your people, Ezekiel? Who has told you of this?"

"Zekiel tells own self, Mas' Shawn. Zekiel knows Lion cub." As he said this his face seemed to glow. "Mas' Shawn, cub be Samson. Samson be Proud Lion Walking cub . . . an' Samson be havin' cub."

It took Sean a few seconds for the meaning to come to him. "Samson? Samson is a cub? You mean he is your cub? I mean . . . Samson is your son?"

Now Ezekiel was beaming, but then his countenance changed. Ezekiel said that, even though it was true that he was of the Lion clan, he didn't want Samson to know. He reasoned that it was better for a slave to think of himself as a slave and not one of the People.

"Why? How? I don't understand. Why would you not tell him you are his father?" Sean asked, his voice rising again.

Ezekiel explained his reasoning, and it struck the heart of Sean. He had never imagined that such profound thoughts could come from a black savage.

Ezekiel had said, "It is better for a bird not to know he is a bird if he must live with his wings cut off so he cannot fly. It is better for a man of the Proud Lion Walking clan to not know he is a lion if his teeth and claws have been taken from him. It is better that he thinks he is a slave and nothing more; then he can live as a slave must."

The things Ezekiel had shared puzzled Sean. They were a deep and strange mystery. Yet somehow, Sean seemed to identify with him even if he was unable to fully understand. The two men sat in silence for many minutes.

At last, Sean said, "He must know, Ezekiel. You must tell him. At least let Samson know you are his father. You'll not have to tell him about your savage family in Africa and about him being the grandson of a chieftain and those things . . . at least not now. But, he must know you are his father, Ezekiel."

Ezekiel looked incredulously at Sean. Never in all the years he had spent as a slave would he have dreamed of having this conversation. In fact, it was like a dream. First he was invited to sit on the porch with the master. Then, he was encouraged to tell him family details as if he were a close friend. Now he was talking to him as a real friend would—not demanding of him, simply encouraging him.

They sat silently again for some time. Then Ezekiel rose from the chair and stood silently for several minutes. When Sean said nothing more, he walked down the steps of the porch and back to the field.

As he walked, Ezekiel decided that it must, in fact, be a dream. *This white man was different,* Ezekiel thought, *but not so different—because I am still a slave.*

Chapter Fourteen

Ben's Endless Details

Even though he had no notion that Ezekiel thought him to be a very different sort of white man, Sean was determined that he would not allow himself to be seen as *too* different from the others who owned slaves.

Privately, Sean held Ezekiel and Samson with a sense of high regard, for which he thought he had no legitimate or plausible explanation. Of course, the private conversation he'd had with Ezekiel filled his mind with a heightened sense of appreciation for the men. However, whenever he found himself admiring the men, immediately he inwardly rebuked himself for such foolishness: *After all, these are slaves.*

He may not have been as knowledgeable as other slave owners, but Sean had been told by others one very important thing about slaves: they could easily become listless if they were not held to a stern working schedule. Sean smiled as thoughts about working schedules raced through his mind. *The phrase "easily become listless" sounds more like a good description of the years I have spent wasting my own life gambling and drinking than it does of Samson and Ezekiel.*

Although the fields were still muddy from the winter snow, the men continued to work in those areas that were dry enough. They were enjoying the early spring, even though it was still quite cold. Sean knew that he had to get tobacco seed soon; he planned to have the ground prepared for planting as soon as the plow could be used.

As Sean left the house, after his usual warm breakfast meal of corn mush and bark tea, he saw Dixon riding down the gated lane toward the house.

"Ben, my friend, where have you been this past week? I thought we'd have the seed by now. I've been looking every morning to see if the ground is right to plant. I have a field almost dry enough for the plow, and I've been expecting you before now."

"I know, I know, and it's what I've come for," Ben Dixon replied. "I've notices that are not the best sort. I observed that Edward Coale—you know the farm down along the Beacon Creek—was planting small tobacco plant seedlings instead of tobacco seeds. When I inquired of him as to this practice, he informed me of something very important that we had not learned earlier. I must take the blame for this."

"The blame for what?" Sean anxiously asked.

"Well, you see, Coale tells me that he plants seed-beds in protected boxes in a small shed that gets most of the day's sun beginning in January. Then he transplants the seedlings into the ground in early spring."

"What matter then? We will simply plant ours, using a different method," Sean replied.

"Not at all, Sean, because you see he told me that planting the seeds directly into the ground is too much a peril. Even if no frost were to strike, the seeds would be vulnerable to either too much moisture or too little. My friend, I fear that I've caused our ruin."

Shocked, Sean looked at Dixon and was speechless for a few seconds. Then he exclaimed, "But, you said you had *notices*. If there is more, you must tell me now."

"Well, aside from that, seems the man I bargained with last harvest for tobacco seed, Leg de Bouchelle, died with fever in early autumn and I had no announcement of any such a thing."

Sean seemed puzzled. "Well, of course I'm not pleased to learn of his dying, but what has that to do with our tobacco seed?"

"Well, it has much to do with our seed, and here's the hindrance. His young widow Anna remarried before winter passed."

"Aye, so did she? Then we can say that marriage for widows is common enough in the colonies. What of it?"

"Marriage is common enough and expected, but I think not in so rapid a fashion," Dixon answered. "It's not only an uncommonly early remarriage, but it's also somewhat scandalous. She married an odd man, named Peter Sluyter, the head of a group of religious zealots called Labadists. Now he's gained control not only of Leg de Bouchelle's young widow but of his land and tobacco seed as well. I should say that he controls *our* tobacco seed."

Dixon went on to explain the little he knew about how the Labidist movement had been founded by a French Jesuit priest and some mystic sort of fellow named Jean de Labadie. Labadie had claimed to be possessed of the spirit of John the Baptist and lived on herbs and wild plants until failing health forced him to leave the Jesuits and become some sort of secular priest.

"Come now, Ben, enough of this holy account of past events. I care nothing about Jesuits and Baptists and strange fellows. We have no seed, so be on with it man. What's the reason?"

"I'm trying to explain, but this is all a part of the collusion. Have a bit of patience, Sean. You see," Dixon continued, "Peter Sluyter was a follower of Labadie. When he came to the colonies, he traveled south along the Delaware River to the Chesapeake, where he met Augustine Herman.

"I've told you of Herman; he became one of the first landowners in Maryland. When he offered his mapmaking skills to Lord Baltimore, he was given a land grant for his efforts. The map of Maryland he created for Lord Baltimore was exchanged for a large tract of land that he received; it spread out from the Bohemia River."

"Am I to suppose that this has something to do with our tobacco seed?"

"Be a bit tolerant, Sean. You see, Augustine Herman and his son Ephraim signed a deed, giving Sluyter control of nearly 4,000 acres of quite excellent land in Bohemia Manor, and . . ."

"Enough of all that," Sean interrupted. "I have two questions: Why haven't we gotten tobacco seed? And where might we get it? A new winter will be upon us before you finish this unpleasant narrative."

"Here's the truth, Sean. Although it's against the beliefs of the Labadists to use tobacco, they've no qualms about growing and trading in tobacco and tobacco seed or in having and selling slaves. This Sluyter must have been a harsh disciplinarian. He'd allow no wood to be used for heat in the living quarters, except in the rooms he and his wife occupied."

"Yes, yes, interesting, and I'm sure that led to much discomfort, but what of the tobacco seed, Ben?"

"That's what I'm getting to. Meals were eaten in silence and any sort of affection between husband and wife or even the parents and children was frowned upon. Unquestioned obedience was required and rigidly exacted of every member of the community. This Sluyter held absolute authority in decision making."

Dixon went on to explain how he had become intrigued with growing tobacco several years earlier when a member of the Labadist community named Justine Dittleback told him about the profits to be made in tobacco. Justine assured Dixon that the Labadists had seed available; it was the very best of seed and it was for sale.

"So you see, Sean, when I discovered that our source of tobacco seed was lost with the death of de Bouchelle and the remarriage of his widow, I went looking for Justine Dittleback."

Not sure that he understood the meaning of what Dixon was telling him, Sean asked, "Well and good, well and good, but did you find him? Will we have seed, or will we not have seed? Will there be a crop for us?"

"Well," Dixon replied, "I made the trip to Bohemia Manor, but I was turned away and given no explanation as to why I couldn't speak with Dittleback."

"I see nothing here with all this chatter about these religious zealots to give me reason for hope of buying seed," said Sean with a disgusted air. He turned and began to walk back to the house, stopped, and turned again to face Dixon.

"There seems a simple solution here," Sean said. "Why don't we find another seller and get on with it? Even if we have to pay a higher price, at least we'll have seed."

"Be calm, my friend. I'm far ahead of you, so let me explain and you shall catch up."

"On with it then," said Sean. "I didn't know you enjoyed spinning such tales of trickery. On with it, man."

"All right, then. I soon discovered why Dittleback hadn't remained with the sect. He parted ways with them for several reasons. In particular, even though he was unmarried, he didn't appreciate the insistence on refraining from the expression of affection between husband and wife or even between himself and the maidens living there."

"Yes, yes . . . the tobacco seed, man, the tobacco seed."

"Well, he became particularly opposed to the severity of this rule concerning the expression of affection after he noticed the widow, Cynthia Wells. And he . . ."

The shock on Sean's face could not be hidden as he interrupted. "He noticed the widow Wells? What does this mean? Was she part of these religionists? Out with it!" He couldn't hide the irritation in his voice as he stepped closer to Ben.

"Am I trying to do anything less than that? Stop this interfering and allow me to speak and you'll soon enough know."

"Of course," Sean spoke in a softer tone, "Of course, the tale has become as clear as the babbling of a mad man. Oh yes, Ben. Yes, please 'mad Ben,' please do go on."

Ignoring the sarcasm, Dixon continued. "As I said, he noticed Cynthia Wells, the widowed sister of Reverend Topping. It all came about because it seems that very near the time that you arrived at Gunter's Harbour, Dittleback had gotten into an argument with Topping. Justine had gone to the port to pick up documents for Slyuter that had been sent from France. While passing the time, he fell into a discussion with Topping, who was awaiting the same sailing vessel."

"It couldn't have happened like that, because when Topping met me at . . ."

"Oh yes, then please go on and I'll wait as you finish my explanation," Dixon interrupted with mock anger. "I didn't say he was there the same day. I said that it was very near the time that you arrived."

"Yes, yes, I know. I said you should speak, so please do so."

"Well, the way Dittleback tells me, it started as little more than casual greetings, comments about produce, weather, how the crows and squirrels ravaged the crops before they could be laid up safely, and such. But very soon a derisive Topping turned the untroubled banter into a theological discussion. This led from a heated argument regarding the Calvinists and the Church of England and brought them to the papist beginnings of the Labidists. Then Topping challenged the manner in which the Labadists thought they could declare themselves independent of all human authority and be free to follow no other rule than the pure doctrines of the gospel. From that point on Topping, being a priest and all, took advantage over Justine and the casual tone of the conversation turned to argument, which came near to blows."

"I may miss my warm supper if you don't give me an end to this twisting tale," Sean urged.

"As best I understand, all of this humility, patience, and union of spirit that the Labadists supposedly preached was neither practiced by Sluyter nor understood by Dittleback. Though certainly not inevitable, it wasn't unusual that the casual conversation between Topping and Dittleback became a shouting match—one that attracted some attention."

"All this over religion? A shouting match in the name of God?" Sean asked. "Is it a wonder that people question God? I see it not so much as doubting God as being distrustful of those who claim to speak for Him."

"I must agree. Nevertheless, you can imagine that before long, Topping left Justine standing at the dock, proclaiming a chorus of rather unkind, disapproving comments as he drove off in his carriage toward his sister's house."

"Yes, but the seed, man; what of the tobacco seed? Will we have seed or not?"

"I surely hope to have seed, but I fear the time is too late for planting," was Dixon's singular reply.

Sean nodded his head in positive response, and they stood silently facing each other for what seemed a long time. Sean was trying to understand, and Dixon was wondering whether the plans he had devised were worthy.

Then Dixon continued. "Justine was frustrated by the anger that had welled up in him. So, he untied his horses and followed Topping's carriage in his cart. He wasn't sure what he would do when and if he caught up with Topping, but his irritation wasn't allowing him to think clearly. Dittleback told me that, although his team of cart horses was no equal for the speed of the Reverend's white geldings, he was determined to catch Topping."

"Ah, yes," Sean sighed with a hint of envy. "That matched pair of geldings. What an important part of obtaining tobacco seed that team of carriage horses is."

"So on he drove," Ben went on as if he hadn't heard Sean. "He splashed through a muddy creek that was still running swiftly with the last rain's runoff and came over the next rise in the road just in time to see Topping get down from his carriage to greet a beautiful woman. It was the home of Topping's widowed sister, Cynthia Wells."

"Are you saying that this Dittleback has something to do with the widow Wells?" Sean seemed shocked.

"This is part of the story, Sean; endure me awhile. Then, Justine pulled his horses to a halt. He was stricken by the woman's beauty and almost fell from his cart, and immediately the anger left him. He told me that in place of his annoyance with Topping there arose a sense of serenity he didn't comprehend. As he eased his cart alongside the carriage, Reverend Topping stepped behind the gated fence as if to distance himself as much as possible."

Sean saw the scene clearly in his mind, for he had experienced a similar response from the cowardly Topping. He was also reminded of the anger he'd had toward Topping just before the priest had been killed—anger that had almost caused him to make a tragic mistake.

Dixon went on with Dittleback's version of what had occurred.

"'And, can't you just see this happening?' Justine says to me, 'I pulled up there as meek as a rabbit and I says, Reverend . . . Reverend Topping, begging your pardon for interfering here, but Reverend Sir, I can't let this day pass without asking your pardon. I've no idea what got into my mind back at the landing, behaving as much as an insane person and . . .'

"'Well yes, I should think so,' Topping responds to me. 'You did behave like a demoniac and I wondered whether such carrying on was common with you. I can see now that it was common indeed, for it comes from a commoner. Being a gentleman, I'm unaccustomed to such crude behavior and I'm not only astonished at such mannerism but I am disgusted by it.' "

"So, Dittleback assures Topping that it won't occur again for any reason and gives Topping his pledge."

"'Yes, oh yes. I'm sure, I'm sure,' Topping replies. Then, under his breath he says to Dittleback, 'The pledge of a demoniac, a poor, deluded, common madman.' "

"'Well then, your lordship, I will excuse myself with your permission and that of the lady.' As Dittleback said that, he backed toward his cart and glanced to see if the woman would respond."

"Then, Topping replies curtly, 'Yes, yes, well enough then. Off with you and good riddance.' "

"Well, it was obvious that Justine hoped for some word from the beautiful woman," Ben explained. "He didn't know who she was, but he knew she couldn't be Topping's wife, for he was unmarried also. But, she had said nothing, so Justine Dittleback climbed on his cart and turned the horse back toward Gunter's Harbour. He told me that as he drove away he promised himself to make that trip again—very soon."

Sean stood there staring incredulously at his friend. "So then, this Dittleback is going to get our seed? I hope that's what all this nonsense means. I'll have to trust you Ben, for I see not any good judgment in it. No sense in it at all."

Ben just grinned at his friend and said, "Oh, it'll make sense Sean; it'll make sense. But first, we've a trip to make. It's best if your chores are done for today and tomorrow, for we'll leave before light in the morning."

Sean stood with a vacant expression on his face. He was thinking of the widow Wells and Julia, wondering if Dittleback had gone back to the Well's house and . . .. Then his thoughts returned to the tobacco situation. *Is this the way Ben plans to get us tobacco seed? I think he must have been drinking bog water.*

Chapter Fifteen

The Set of His Hat

The following day, Sean and Ben set off before
dawn to find Justine Dittleback. Dixon had
inquired and discovered that he had gone to Palmers
Island, once known as Kent Island, at the mouth of
the Susquehanna River. There he had joined with
a band of trappers who exchanged beaver pelts for
supplies at the trading post William Clayborne had
established.

It took the men most of a leisurely morning to
ride to the shore of the river. They had hoped to find
someone at the river with a boat or raft to ferry them
across, but they found no one. Having no means of
getting to the island, they built a lean-to, anticipating
having to spend some time there before someone
might come along who could get word to Justine on
the island.

Dixon snared a large rabbit, so they made a small
fire and roasted it. They were relaxed and spent the
afternoon talking of crops, seed prices, and slaves.

Although they had no experience growing tobacco, they tried desperately to persuade one another that their plan to grow tobacco was a good one. They agreed that they would find a way to salvage some of the growing season, but neither of them was convinced.

Then, just as dusk began to settle over the trees, they heard loud voices coming closer to their fire. Laughter and cursing led them to believe that the men they heard were drunk.

Someone called out, "Hello there, the fire! We're coming in and we ain't armed, so don't be harming none of us."

More laughter and cursing came after that announcement, followed by the sound of someone falling and even more commotion, curses, and louder laughter.

Ben and Sean were surprised to see that there were only three men responsible for making all the noise. As they came stumbling toward the fire, Dixon recognized one of the men.

"Justine," Dixon said loud enough to be heard over the laughter and cursing, "It's me, Ben Dixon, and this is young Sean O'Connell. Come to the fire; we've been looking for you."

"For you they've been looking, Justine," one of the men slurred. "Better run, Justine. Must be one of them husbands of one of them . . . hmmm, what was that last one's name?"

That question brought on more laughter and cursing, although this time they seemed less rowdy as they approached the fire.

"Dixon," said Dittleback. "It's you then. What is it? Do I owe you a farthing or two? Too bad, for I haven't a penny in my poke."

"Aye, that's no lie," another of the men shouted. "He's not a penny, nor have any of us. Rum and women — it's the only good for gold. Aye, men?" The man almost fell into the fire as he said it but caught his balance long enough to add, "Then we'll be off to the island as soon as we find us the boat."

With nothing more than that, the two men went crashing off toward the river. But Dittleback sat down cross-legged next to the fire.

"Just why would you be looking for me? What is it you could be wanting from me, Ben Dixon?"

He seemed almost sober, and both Sean and Ben were relieved that Dittleback's friends had gone on without him.

"I think you know exactly what I want. It's about tobacco seed, Justine. You know as well as I do that I can't get near the Labadists, but I know you're able to get seed."

"True enough, but I'd say that seed would be costly. It's not gone well with me and that Sluyter, you know. I can't just go walking up to him and say, 'Sell me some seed, Sluyter, and be quick about it.' No, I'll have to think this over and see who it is in the colony I can get to bring us the seed. But I can tell you that it'll cost dearly."

Sean sat there in the firelight, watching the man's eyes as he spoke with Ben Dixon. He didn't know the man but didn't much care for him, even if he was a source of tobacco seed. He couldn't help but wonder about the man's relationship with Mrs. Wells. He'd not liked what he heard the drunken men saying about their exploits.

However, the most troubling thing for Sean was not tobacco seed; it was that he was condemning himself for not following through with his promise to invite the Wells ladies to his home.

Ben was about to reply to Justine when Sean began, "Tell me Dittleback, what have you to do with the Wells family? Ben here tells me that you once ran aground with Mrs. Wells's brother, the deceased Reverend Topping. Is that true?"

"True enough it is. Yes indeed, true enough. I'd have none of that family, not even on a dead man's wager. Rather deal with the devil himself I would. I might say that maybe I did deal with the devil. That Topping thought he'd bested me with his protesting tripe."

Ben commented, "I'd say that's fairly accurate. Not many that trafficked with Topping ever felt good about the occurrence."

"Aye, but that's not all of it. I soon discovered that those Wells women were none better than he was. As much as called the Pope a devil himself; she as much as said it herself. I'll have nothing of that protesting, not I. I know devils when I see them, and the Pope it's not. I'll not pardon myself to you two either, although I know Ben here is one of them protesters. And you—an Irishman I hear—are you a protester, young sir?"

No one had ever asked Sean about his religious beliefs, at least as far as he could remember. He quickly responded, "I'd say that's a man's own affair and nothing to be trifled with by another. I'll thank you to watch what you ask me, and be cautious what you say about the Wells family and about my friend Ben here," he added, trying to conceal his interest in the Wells women.

Now where in the world did that come from? Sean thought, and he quickly followed with a question.

"So, you're saying that you had nothing to do with the Wells women then?"

"I didn't say that. I rather fancied the widow Wells at first, but . . . oh, . . . I seeeee." He threw his head back to laugh, but emitted a boisterous belch and almost choked himself. Recovering, he continued, "Then it's that you have your hat set for one of the Wells women."

"Don't be impertinent! I said no such thing!" Sean could feel the warmth of anger rising to his face.

"Here's the matter, Justine," Dixon interrupted, "We need tobacco seed and you can get it. Now, there's only one real question: What will it cost us?"

"Aye, that is the question, Ben. That is the question. But, I can't tell you this before I talk with those inside the colony. I'll tell you to be looking for no bargains. Sluyter's a clever one, and his is the upper hand as it comes with tobacco seed and everything else in the colony. The price will have to do with how easy we can get it out of the colony. Have your money pouches ready. Give me three days, and I'll have your answer."

"We haven't got time to delay things," Sean reminded Dittleback. "We have crops to plant. Can you get the seed in three days or not?"

Looking into the fire, Justine said, "If you're looking to plant seed now, I can see you're risking yourselves; even a fool knows it's too late for tobacco planting. But, I'll have your answer in three days is all I'll be saying."

He arose from his side of the fire and, without another word, he turned and disappeared into the darkness of the forest, heading toward the river.

The men looked at each other across the fire. Both men were thinking of seed. Ben was thinking of tobacco seed and Sean thought of the seed of invitation he had planted with the Wells ladies but had failed to cultivate.

He determined that he would begin to reclaim the opportunity he had planted. Tomorrow he'd make a trip to the Wells' home.

Just then they heard the raucous laughter of Dittleback and his companions, and it was clear from the way their voices carried that they were on a boat in the river. Ben said, "I think we'll be comfortable here for now. There's no need to head for home tonight. That can wait until morning."

The men made sure the horses were safely tethered near grass. Then they built the fire up a bit, covered themselves with their blankets beneath the lean-to and tried to sleep. The night was damp and cold, but Sean was having warming impressions of a young lady he was determined to meet again.

Before Sean fell asleep, his mind wandered as it reflected on the Wells women. *I don't like dealing with Justine Dittleback, but I think that I agree with what he said. I believe that perhaps I do have my hat set for those Wells women. Now, we'll just have to see what those Wells women think of my hat.*

Chapter Sixteen

The Invitation

Sean awoke to the smell of something cooking and the sound of muffled voices. Light was breaking in the east. Sitting up, he shivered with the cold of morning and hugged his arms to his chest. The fire had died down hours ago. The edge of his blanket was smoldering and he realized that he had rolled close to the fire during the night.

He stood and stepped on the smoking edge of his blanket. He determined that the sounds of the voices were coming from the riverbank. So, wrapping his blanket around him, he wandered toward the river, and before long he saw several men huddled around a fire; they were cooking something.

"Hello there at the river! Might I come to the fire?" The men looked toward the sound of Sean's voice. He heard them saying something to one another in low voices; then one of them stood and waved Sean toward the fire.

The standing man asked, "Are you hungry? We've enough for you and more. Would there be others with you, young sir?" The man was looking furtively behind Sean toward the trees.

Sean was almost to the fire now and about to proclaim his hunger when he saw what they were roasting. It was an opossum, tail and all, and two more lay to the side of the fire, waiting their turn on the spit. They looked like great rats, and Sean was about to lose more than his appetite.

"I'll be thanking you for your generosity, but my friends and I must be away. Business keeps us from enjoying a meal with you," he lied.

Just then he heard Ben's voice from the edge of the tree line, "Sean, we'll need to be off now, we've saddled the horses and the others are ready to ride."

Ben had heard Sean hail the men and he arose and went to find him, but as soon as he caught sight of the scene he didn't like the looks of the men. They were strangers to him, and as a precaution he was letting the men think that others were in the area—in the event that they might suggest some mischief.

Sean was very glad for the intervention that his friend wisely provided. He hadn't been thinking much of harm to himself, but he definitely was not prepared to eat a large rat.

"Perhaps next time we meet then. Thank you for the offer of your bounty," Sean said as he turned and walk hurriedly toward Ben. He could hear the muted sounds of the men's voices and their low laughter as he walked into the forest. "Aye," one of them shouted, "next time then."

"Good morning, Ben, and thank you for saving me from a meal with those rascals. They wanted me to eat 'possum."

"I'm thinking they had more than feeding you in mind, Sean. If we hadn't been together, a meal of 'possum would have been better than what those thieves had in mind." Then he quickly added with a smile, "Then you've never had 'possum?" Why, there's not a black savage I know of who'd turn away the opportunity for such delicate fare."

"Yes, of course, I'm sure. And may the black savages enjoy their repast of rat. Now let's make the conversation a bit more to my appetite, shall we? I've been thinking throughout the night, and I've decided to ride on to the Wells home before going back to Dawn Light. So, I'll ride to the ford with you, and then I'm off to fulfill my obligation to invite those ladies to my home. I should have made the trip long ago. Would that suit you?"

"Suit me? You ask as though it would make a difference whether it suited me or didn't suit me! Of course it does. Sounds like the only sane idea you've had in awhile. I'll tell you this: I have a wife who'll be glad to hear this news. But, there is something that troubles me, Sean."

"Yes, and what would that be?"

"What could possibly make you think that two genteel persons such as the Wells ladies would accept an invitation to the home of a man who doesn't shave and wraps himself in a castoff, smoke-smelling blanket?"

189

The expression on Sean's face revealed that he'd never thought of that. Then, realizing that Dixon was making sport of him, he burst into laughter and threw his "castoff blanket" at Ben.

They parted company at the ford of Little Beacon Creek. Even though neither man was aware of it, this was the very site where Topping had murdered the slave Mose—the man whose arm Sean had broken that fateful first night at Dawn Light.

Dixon rode on deliberately, anxious to see his wife and share the news of Sean's decision to visit the Wells ladies and, of course, also to tell her the good news that tobacco seed could be had, although he was not convinced that they could make a crop this year.

Sean rode with as much deliberation as, but with much more expectation than, Dixon. Tobacco was not on his mind. These were new feelings and thoughts he was exploring. Never had he spent so much of his time thinking of anyone but himself. Now, he was spending a good amount of his time thinking of Julia. He was determined to follow through with his plan to get to know these Wells ladies better—much better.

The sun was high as Sean came to the crest of the hill that overlooked the Wells' house. He could see someone seated on the porch enjoying the warmth of the sun. However, he was not close enough to tell who it was.

He remembered what Ben had said earlier about being unshaven and wrapped in a burnt blanket. Of course he wasn't wrapped in the blanket now, but he rubbed his unshaven chin and knew his unkempt condition would not work to his benefit.

He thought for a moment and then decided he had made a hasty choice when he had decided to make the trip to the Wells' home. He turned his horse about and headed back toward home. As his horse splashed through the shallow brook, a voice within said, *Sean, my boy, you've run too often. This time stay the course. The opportunity may never again arise.*

He reined his horse in, dismounted, went to the edge of the rivulet, and knelt down. He looked at his distorted reflection in the water and thought, *Surely I cannot look worse in person than I do in this watery likeness. I must do my best to present a good appearance.*

Sean removed his outer coat and the plain waistcoat he wore, and then he washed his face, hands, and arms as best he could in the cold, muddy water. Cupping his hands, he splashed water over his hair, combed it back with his fingers, and stood to dress himself.

I might not be well suited for royalty's court, he reasoned to himself, *but I'll have to do for a suitor.*

A *"suitor"?* He had no recollection of ever even thinking of that word and certainly had never seen himself as one. Now, here he was on his way to visit the Wells women. *Is this what I'm about? Am I preparing to court a young lady? And, this particular young lady—Julia? Because of the adverse involvement I've had with her uncle, the Reverend Topping, she has no reason to even hear an opening plea from me for her attention.*

But, Sean was determined to ride to the Wells' home and extend an invitation for the Wells ladies to join him for tea at Dawn Light. He remounted, nudged his horse's ribs with his heels, and reassured himself that he was committed to complete this mission as he rode down the hill. He ran his fingers once more through his wet hair and also tried to convince himself that this was not insanity.

Drawing nearer to the house, he could see it was the widow Wells seated on the porch. He called out, "Hello, and a good day to you, Mrs. Wells. This is Sean O'Connell, and I ask if I might have permission to come to speak with you?"

Shading her eyes, she looked toward Sean. She had seen him at the top of the hill earlier and saw him turn his horse about to leave. Then, she saw him coming over the hill again and knew at once, even from a distance, that the rider was Sean. Feigning surprise she responded, "My, but didn't you startle me!"

"Begging your pardon, Ma'am," he offered, "I meant not to frighten you."

"No, please think nothing of it. I must have been lost in thought and was not expecting you to come calling."

This was certainly true. She had not been expecting him, but she had been wishing—no, longing—that this handsome young man might come calling on her daughter once again.

It had been so long since anyone but a hired man had been part of their lives. Her brother, Jonathan Topping, had brought no peace to her life after the untimely death of her husband. There were no men near Julia's age that Mrs. Wells deemed worthy of her daughter and certainly none that she would allow to call upon them. That is, until now.

Sean dismounted, tethered his horse, and had his hand on the gate, waiting for permission to come to the porch.

"Come, come in then. Don't be so hesitant. There's no need to delay. Do come sit on the porch with me."

In a few strides he was on the porch, pausing before Mrs. Wells with a clumsy bow and taking the chair she offered. As he seated himself he looked about for a sign of Julia. He wanted to ask about her, but he didn't know how to go about it without being too obvious.

At last he said, "Well, I've finally come to invite you and your daughter to my home for afternoon tea, but I see she's not here today."

He looked about again as if to catch a glimpse of Julia. He hoped to hear Mrs. Wells say that, indeed, she was in the house.

"I do regret to say that I must greet you without the company of my daughter today," she said, hoping that he would not sense the deepest truth of her statement.

Sean's heart sank. After all this time and he could not see the woman that was filling his mind more and more. He knew enough to not ask her whereabouts, but his face must have revealed his disappointment.

"For you see," she continued, "she's gone to spend the day with our friends in Gunter's Harbour. Her friend Mary Davison came yesterday with her father to take Julia to their home. It's not a place I'd like to live, but there is always something going on in Gunter's Harbour. The ships are coming and going and there is the bustle of merchandising; it's quite an attractive pursuit to some, especially to those who are young. It was something my husband always enjoyed immensely."

Sean thought her eyes moistened as she mentioned her husband. Then, with a faraway look, she added, "I suppose indeed it must be rather enlivening for a younger person than I am. I do enjoy my solitude and private thoughts of my past with my dear husband. But enough of that."

Now what? he thought. *Should I say something kind about her husband? What can I say? Am I to ask if I can visit Julia there in Gunter's Harbour, or can I simply invite Mrs. Wells and her daughter to my home, even though I don't know if Julia would want to come?*

Knowing nothing of the intuitiveness of women, he was mildly surprised when she very matter-of-factly said, "I think it is most kind of you to invite us to tea. Even though Julia is not here, I am quite certain that she would consent that a visit to your home would be most agreeable. Why don't we decide what day you will be able to fetch us? As I recall, you offered to provide our transport from our home and back again, did you not?"

"I did? Oh, yes, I did. You will? How can I thank you? Oh, thank you, Mrs. Wells. You will come?" he repeated. "I mean, you *will* come! Oh, thank you. I'm very happy that you have accepted my invitation and that you will come. Thank you."

Mrs. Wells smiled gently at the clumsiness of this young man, desperately holding back a giggle. She could see that he was very pleased, and she was quite contented as well.

"Yes," she agreed, "Then, as you say, we will most certainly come."

Sean stared at her, wanting to hear her say it again.

She continued, "Then all we must do is to decide upon a day that will suit you. Our lives are not as busy as yours, I'm sure, and I believe we would be able to accommodate any day that you may choose."

They chatted together for several more minutes and then set a day for Sean to return for the Wells ladies.

"Oh, one thing more, Mrs. Wells. Might I be so forward as to ask permission to hitch the beautiful white geldings to your late brother's carriage and use it to transport you and your daughter to Dawn Light?"

"Why yes, of course. How silly of me, I never gave it a thought as to how we might get to your manor. Yes of course. Thank you for being so sensitive and asking. I never had seen you in a carriage, and I must confess that I wondered a bit about how we might travel. Although Julia is quite an able rider, I never ride horses, you see."

"Splendid. Thank you, Mrs. Wells. I'll arrive early enough then to harness the geldings. I assure you that I will care for them as if they were my own, and I'll put them to stable when we return as well."

She thought, *You don't know how pleased I would be if the horses and carriage were to become yours.*

As Sean arose to leave, she said, "I would never say something so bold if we were not alone here on the porch. However, I want you to know how pleased I am that you have called upon us. I know you've come to see Julia, but I am quite honored that you have been so kind as to stay to visit with me."

Then, smiling warmly, she added, "I do think that we need to say nothing further, Mr. O'Connell. But, as a mature woman, please allow this one last, bold proposal. Perhaps the next time you come calling, it would be good if you were to shave some of the beard from your face, dress your hair with fewer twigs, and wear clothing that is a bit more genteel."

Mortified, Sean looked down at his greasy breeches, stained hands, and muddy boots. "I don't know what . . ."

Then, with a gentle laugh she interrupted, "You must know that I am simply speaking in jest. I know you've been away from your home and you simply look the part of a well-traveled man."

Sean was glad to hear what she said, but he did take her comments quite seriously. He tried to respond but stumbled with his words, not because he was embarrassed for what she had said regarding his appearance but because he was thinking, *Even though I've not worn one, she likes the way I've "set my hat."*

He had no recollection either of leave-taking or of his journey homeward that day. Sean's mind was filled to the brim and somewhat overflowing with more pleasant, but considerably more unfamiliar thoughts, in regard to the person that had been absent during his visit.

What a fine day this has turned out to be, he thought, and he began to whistle, "Come all ye lads and lassies . . .." He couldn't remember the last time he had whistled.

Chapter Seventeen

Tea Time

The day had finally come. Sean had been having great difficulty trying to concentrate on the farming responsibilities since returning from his recent visit with Mrs. Wells. She had agreed to visit Dawn Light with her daughter, and this was the day.

The question of tobacco seed had yet to be resolved. Dittleback had not returned as promised on the third day, and they didn't know where to find him. However, even though the time was becoming very late for planting—perhaps past planting time—and he should have been concerned, Sean found that he could think of little more than the Julia's visit.

Samson and Ezekiel were quite aware of his distraction and reminded him daily that they needed to have seed to plant or it would be too late to make a crop. His irritation with their preoccupation with planting tobacco became something of a game with Samson and Ezekiel.

Fortunately for them, Sean was completely unaware that they were trifling with him, because he didn't suspect that they knew of his preoccupation with the ladies' impending visit.

"Get my horse ready. I can't be late," Sean advised Samson.

Being careful to stifle a smile, Samson responded, "Doesn't want me be in the fields this mornin'?"

"Would you listen? I said, get my horse and get it now. What on earth is wrong with you? Don't you understand anything? I've got to be on my way. Oh, and tell Kezie to come in from the field. I have to talk to her."

The last conversation he'd had with Mrs. Wells, regarding his unkempt appearance, had lodged itself in Sean's mind and he had carefully shaved, bathed his face and arms, dressed his hair as best he could, and made certain that he had presentable clothing to wear.

Only a few minutes had passed since he'd given instructions to Samson. But he wondered, *Now where is that lazy Kezie, and when will Samson bring my horse around?*

The door slammed, and Kezie's voice hushed Obadiah's chatter as they entered the house. As usual, Kezie was humming to herself as Sean came into the eating room. Kezie's humming was something he had first found annoying, but lately Sean discovered that he anticipated hearing her voice. The melodies she hummed were far different from any he'd ever heard.

"At last, you're here. Now, pay attention. Do you understand the instructions that Mrs. Dixon gave you?" He marveled at her ability to understand instructions, even though her speaking vocabulary seemed to consist of only a handful of English words.

She nodded affirmatively.

"I want to hear you say it. Can you make the tea as Mrs. Dixon instructed you?"

"Yas, Mas' Shawn, Kezie do."

What in the world have I done, he thought. *I've invited two enlightened English ladies to my home for tea, and what I have to offer them is who knows what, made by a girl who may know about making babies but not about preparing tea.*

He was so grateful that Mrs. Dixon had sent over a batch of her own tea biscuits for Kezie to warm at the proper time. He had talked the whole plan over with Samson and made sure that Kezie understood all the instructions. But, he thought he had been quite ignorant to think that Kezie would be able to serve tea the same way that Missy had done at the Wells' home.

"Kezie do?" I'm sure, but just what will she do? he wondered. *Ignorant, that's what I am. What an impossible thing to do: invite two genteel ladies to a house full of savages, and I'm not many steps higher. What have I done?*

Just then he heard Ezekiel's voice calling something to Samson. "Be doin' that," is all he could understand Samson to say in response.

Sean walked out to the porch and saw Samson holding the reins to his horse and grinning. "Wants I should goes with you to drive their team, Mas' Shawn?"

"No, I don't 'wants' you to drive the team. I'll drive the carriage myself." He was momentarily aggravated with Samson but then felt ashamed when he noticed how polished his saddle and harnesses were. "Thank you Samson, you've done a wonderful job for me."

Samson smiled and squatted in such a way that Sean could use his thigh as a step up to the saddle. Sean touched lightly on Samson's leg, then onto the saddle, took the reins, and said, "I should be back about an hour after high sun. Be sure everything is ready, because we'll take our tea early so I can return the ladies to their home shortly after dark."

"Be doin' it jes fine," but Sean didn't hear Samson's response as he snapped the head of the horse about and down the lane toward the road.

The trip seemed to take much too long. All of Sean' thoughts were centered on what might go wrong. *Perhaps they had changed their minds about coming. What if the tea Kezie makes tastes like bog water? Or, she might burn Mrs. Dixon's tea biscuits. Then of course, Topping's carriage might throw a wheel at some stage of the journey. Or, what if . . ..*

Finally, Sean found himself without more questions of things that might go wrong and began to think about how he might present himself to the Wells ladies. He hadn't noticed that he was ascending the low hill and was startled to find that he was looking down at the Wells home.

How must I greet them? Will they be in the house or on the porch? Do I ask if they'd like to leave now, or must I wait for them to say something before we depart? What in the world am I doing?

Just then he saw the two women step out to the porch. A few seconds later he saw Missy follow them. *Surely they're not bringing her along, he thought. Why would they do that?*

He pulled his horse in as close to the gate as he could, dismounted, and loosely tethered the reins to the fence.

"Good day to you, ladies. Isn't it a fine day? I'm glad to say it will be a very fine day, for which I am very happy. So, I'll say, good day. I'm sure you feel the same way on this fine day too, and I imagine that you'll enjoy the ride to Dawn Light as much as I have. Or I mean, as much as I will. So, good day to you and . . . ."

"Yes, and several good days to you," Mrs. Wells replied. She feared that if she did not respond he might go on with his nervous "good days" until dark.

"We've been expecting you and we are prepared to leave, if that seems suitable to you."

"Oh, of course, and it is a good day, ladies." As soon as he said it, he realized he had probably given enough greetings for this occasion.

Mrs. Wells said. "Julia and Missy took the liberty of hitching the horses to the carriage. You may want to examine the fittings to satisfy yourself."

"No. Oh, no. I'm sure they're fine, just fine."
Sean didn't add what he was thinking: *Julia probably
knows more about hitching carriage horses than I do
anyway.*

"We understand the difficulties of living without
the benefit of feminine influence in a home," Mrs.
Wells announced, "and we thought that perhaps
Missy might have suggestions for you. That is, she
might offer me some suggestions that I could then
pass along to you. So, we trust that it will be suitable
to you that Missy comes with us as well."

Sean didn't understand what she was getting at,
but he felt it best to simply agree with her. Trying to
show no opposition with the arrangement, he said,
"Well then, that's fine. It's a lovely, sunny day with
no appearance of rain clouds. So let me put my horse
up in your barn and then we'll be on our way."

He led the horse to the small barn, unsaddled him,
and left him tied near a small water trough with some
feed. Returning to the carriage, he seated the ladies,
carefully placing Julia so he could see her when he
turned his head. Of course he thought he had done
this very discreetly, but all three women smiled at
one another over his harmless impudence.

The trip back to his home was filled with pleasant
chatter. Mrs. Wells had a propensity to describe the
scenery as they drove along. It was very much like her
deceased brother, the Reverend Topping, had done
when Sean first arrived. She also was just as ready
to point out the close friendships they'd had with
residents of prominence. However, there was a great
difference in the manner with which she described

those friendships, and it seemed to Sean there was a difference in the purpose for which she said it.

Sean listened to Mrs. Wells, but he kept glancing at Julia. He breathed in the fresh air of spring. He had such an enlivening sense about this day. Everything looked so much brighter and greener than it had on his trip to the Wells' home.

"There it is," he said. "There's Dawn Light."

He expected to hear some favorable and flattering remark from Mrs. Wells. Instead she said, "How sad it is, Sean . . . excuse me, I mean Mr. O'Connell. Sad it is indeed, because I remember days when your parents, aunt, and uncles lived here in great happiness. What ever becomes of life? My dear husband and brother now dead and all of your family now gone—yes, what does become of our lives?"

Sean looked at Mrs. Wells but could think of nothing to say that would take the sorrow from her countenance and voice. "Yes. Sad, indeed," he replied.

He turned the team down the lane toward the house. As he expected, Samson, Ezekiel, and Kezie all stood in front of the house, waiting to see the guests. Obadiah was trying unsuccessfully to climb to the first branch of the smallest locust tree.

Wheeling the team to a stop at the steps of the porch, Sean said to no one in particular, "Let's get busy here and wipe these animals down and get them some feed."

Jumping down, he hurried around to help the ladies from the carriage. The men were holding the team steady. Kezie stared in wonder at the beautiful dresses the Wells women were wearing, and it was obvious that the attractive Missy intrigued her. But, no one knew that Kezie was thinking how outrageous it was that Missy traveled in the same carriage with the Wells women.

Sean took the women on a brief tour of the garden in front of the manor. Sean pointed out the buildings and sheds and the location of the spring, but he soon discovered there was no more to show them. Besides, he suddenly realized that the garden at Dawn Light looked more like briar brambles when compared to the well-tended garden surrounding the Wells' home.

Abruptly, Sean invited the women into the entry at the left of the porch. They entered a dark room. *Oh no, I failed to tell Kezie and Samson to light candle lamps. What will they think now? What an uncouth thing I've done. I must say something light.*

"I find it difficult to have anything done well here, what with the uncultured savages I have for help. I apologize for failing to have the rooms well lighted, ladies. Please wait a moment as I get candles."

Hurrying from the sitting room he called out, "Kezie, Samson . . . candles. Get them in here now!"

He had scarcely spoken when Kezie came into the hallway with candles but no spark to light them. "How often have I told you to keep the flints with the candles? Do you understand me?"

Kezie looked down at the floor and nodded.

"Speak to me. Look at me and tell me you understand," he shouted. Then, realizing what he was doing, he added in a gentler tone, "Here Kezie, give me the candles. I'll get the flint."

He returned to the sitting room with the candle lamps lit and invited the women to be seated. Julia and her mother sat close to each other. Missy stood until Mrs. Wells directed her to take a seat at the side of the room.

Sean moved a chair as close as he dared to Julia and tried to begin a clever conversation. He found himself talking in circles and the Wells ladies gave each other puzzled looks.

Mrs. Wells immediately sensed the need to salvage the situation and save this young man from his unrefined conversation.

"Well, Mr. O'Connell, I see that you have done quite well in your attempts to reinstate this manor to some of its glories from past days. I'm quite certain that you must be very pleased with the way things are developing."

She was very wise in encouraging him as she did, and Sean immediately took up the conversation from the place she initiated it. He was very comfortable sharing what he had done and explaining his plans for the future at Dawn Light.

The time seemed unimportant as the lively conversation moved smoothly from one subject to another. Missy helped Kezie with the tea, and Sean noticed how aptly she was able to mimic Missy's every movement.

"As you see, I've obtained some furnishings. However, I fear that I haven't the ability to add the genteel touches that a lady brings to a home. I would like to have that sort of feminine effect here one day."

When the words came from his mouth it was too late to retrieve them. Fortunately, his benefactor, Mrs. Wells, quickly rescued him.

"Well, Julia, are you going to read for us now? You brought the books, did you not?" Mrs. Wells asked.

"Oh, Mother, I don't think this would be a good time. The day is getting late and we must return home before the road becomes dangerous to travel."

"Nonsense, dear. I believe the gentleman would be delighted to hear you read, wouldn't you, Mr. O'Connell?"

Sean knew that question required an affirmative answer, but he was very willing to do anything to keep the ladies there a while longer—anything that did not require coercion.

"I've thought of little other than having the opportunity of hearing you read again, Miss Wells. Would you honor us with something?"

Julia also had been anticipating this opportunity, although her motives were different from those of either Sean or her mother's. She wanted to discover the spiritual condition of this young man. It was one thing to be kind and gentlemanly in the circumstances in which they had been placed, but he seemed to know very little about matters of a spiritual nature.

"Well, of course I will. Please excuse me for my hesitancy." She reached over to the nearby table for the books she had brought with her.

"On our first meeting, mother suggested Baxter or perhaps Donne, and I chose Anne Bradstreet. You'll recall, Mr. O'Connell, your surprise to discover that the poet was a woman. I've brought her small book today as well, and I've chosen one whose line begins, *By night when others soundly slept.*"

"Yes, of course. I do recall. And my recollection is that your mother asked you to read some of your own poetry. Will you do so today?"

"Perhaps another time. Today I think only to read that which I have already selected. Please listen not only to the melody of the sound but to the message the poet's words offer."

Turning slightly, so as to catch the light from the candle on the page, Julia began.

By night when others soundly slept
And hath at once both ease and Rest,
My waking eyes were open kept
And so to lie I found it best.

I sought him whom my Soul did Love,
With tears I sought him earnestly.
He bow'd his ear down from Above.
In vain I did not seek or cry.

My hungry Soul he fill'd with Good;
He in his Bottle put my tears,
My smarting wounds washt in his blood,
And banisht thence my Doubts and fears.

What to my Saviour shall I give
Who freely hath done this for me?
I'll serve him here whilst I shall live
And Love him to Eternity.

Julia carefully closed the pages of the book and turned to face Sean. "Do you understand the meaning of her words?"

Unwilling to admit he did not fully understand, he said, "Well, yes, of course. I think I understand quite well. I think perhaps she speaks of her husband and looks to him for protection and to spend eternity with him. Have I captured the sense of the poem?"

"I think you have listened very well, except that she is not speaking of her husband; she is speaking of Jesus the Christ."

"Of course," replied Sean, "That's why she called him 'My Saviour.' Very interesting thought, don't you think?" With that he turned toward Mrs. Wells, hoping for her usual intercession on his behalf. She simply looked at him with a pleasant expression.

Julia continued, "What do you think of our Savior? And, what of the line from Mrs. Bradstreet that promises, *'I'll serve him here whilst I shall live'*? This is how I look to my life, Mr. O'Connell. How do you understand your future?"

"Well, of course I'd say that none of us can really know about such things now, can we?" As soon as the words left Sean's mouth he knew that his response wasn't what Julia wanted to hear.

"I can speak for myself, but not for you," Julia replied. "I do know of such things now, else how could I possibly know of them later?"

Then looking at her mother she said, "I think we must be gone before it gets much later, do you not agree?"

"I fear she is correct, Mr. O'Connell. Where has the time flown?" Then rising, she said, "Come, Julia dear. Missy, the time has come when we must impose upon the young sir to transport us to our home once again."

Sean sprang to his feet as soon as Mrs. Wells stood. He searched for words that might correct his most recent response to Julia but could sense that he was too late. He walked to the door to call for Samson to bring the carriage about and saw Samson standing there, holding the bridle of one of the horses. Sean hadn't even heard the carriage being prepared.

Missy extended generous thanks to Kezie, and Kezie seemed to glow in the attention she received. The sun was getting low in the west and Sean's spirits were sinking low as well.

Sean was puzzled about what Julia meant when she had said, "I do know of such things now, else how could I possibly know of them later?"

The plans he had made to engage the women in clever conversation on the ride to their home did not materialize.

Julia thought much about how she had attempted to engage Sean in a conversation that she hoped would give her some indication that he was beginning to exhibit some spiritual insight. *Did I push too hard to gain a response from Sean?*

It seemed to Sean that the carriage ride to the Wells home and his solo return ride to Dawn Light both took much longer than they had earlier.

Chapter Eighteen

Brown Gold

Ben Dixon's voice called out, "Hello, the house! Gold for your majesty."

Sean hurried down the stairs, through the eating room, and onto the porch just as Dixon pulled his small cart to a halt. Jumping over the seat to the cart bed, he lifted two small bags for Sean to see. "Here it is, Your Majesty: your brown gold—at least, the beginning of gold."

"I knew it! Somehow I knew you'd be here today with the seed. Let me see it! Give me a sack."

Dixon slid from the bed of the cart, and as he handed a sack of the seed to Sean he said, "I've heard that a German doctor suggests tobacco to treat intestinal worries. And it's not just for horses and cows but for humans as well. In fact, he says inhaling tobacco smoke—he calls it 'drinking smoke'—serves better than messy oily enemas, and it's good for treating colic, hysteria, hernia, and dysentery, and who knows what else?"

Sean looked at Ben Dixon in disbelief. "Drinking smoke?"

"That's what two men from Virginia told me. Though they call it 'drinking smoke,' it's usually done through a pipe, or so they say. Can you imagine?"

"Oh, yes. I've seen that myself," Sean said. "Now that you say it, I understand. I'd thought that 'drinking smoke' meant simply that you'd drink a pint of ale and take a pipe with tobacco. What a marvelous thing this is. Why, I hadn't the slightest idea that this seed would be of such great use as a medicine."

Dixon continued, "Didn't I say I had seed for his majesty? Brown gold! We're going to become rich, Sean. I feel it will be so."

"I can't believe the seed is finally here." Sean turned to call out for Samson and Ezekiel, but they had heard the commotion and were already there.

"It's here," Sean repeated, holding the sack out to be sure they could see it. "It's here at last."

He untied the coarse string that sealed the sack, reached in, and took a fistful of seed. "It's gold, Samson! See Ezekiel? Gold! It's brown gold, isn't it, Ben?"

The two slaves stood smiling as they listened to Ben's and Sean's animated conversation.

"So it appears, my good man," Dixon continued, "You see now that it was worth the wait to get the very best of seed, wasn't it? And I call to your remembrance what I'd said last year. If we start out with harvesting adequate amounts of leaf, we can then go on to larger quantities the following years as our profits increase. We'll allow a short row of leaves to flower, collect the seeds, and never have to purchase more seed again. We'll be rich, friend. We'll be wealthy plantation owners."

"Yes, of course, I remember what you said. But, I must tell you that I thought little of it then. Hear me, Ben Dixon: I think a great deal of it now."

"Aye, and I tell you, Sean, I believe we'll have some pleasant new cures: cures for our empty purses for certain and cures for the maladies of man. I've heard from two men recently arrived from Virginia that, because of the clamor for tobacco in Europe for medicinal purposes, the Virginia planters are putting all their trust in the leaf."

Dittleback had problems getting the seed from the Labadie colony, and the prediction he had made that the price would be dear was accurate. Although Sean and Ben were aware that Dittleback would probably try to defraud them with an unjust price for the seed, they had no idea just how badly he had really cheated them.

But, to them it seemed to matter little. They were pleased just to have seed and get on with the planting. The two men that Ben had met were freed indentured servants from a large Virginia tobacco plantation. He had not only heard their stories of medicinal cures, but he had also discussed with them the art of planting tobacco seed.

Until recently, Ben had been unaware that planting tobacco was so dissimilar to planting corn or other crops. Nevertheless, he hadn't told Sean everything—either of his lack of knowledge that had started them down the path of this agricultural venture or of the planting discoveries he had recently made. He feared that Sean would become discouraged if he knew. His encounter with Edward Coale and the unfortunate information he learned about planting seedlings rather than seed had certainly dimmed Sean's farming instincts.

Ben had also learned that the seed they purchased probably was from tobacco grown by the Onondaga or Iroquois tribes.

Dittleback assured him that although different from Virginia tobacco, it was considered among the highest quality tobaccos, especially for medicinal use. Of course, Justine's comments regarding healing qualities were somewhat biased. They had been based upon the very information Ben had been sharing with everyone concerning the German doctor's opinions about the value of drinking tobacco smoke.

The men and their workers collaborated for more than a week in the fields, laboring each day from before dawn until the sun disappeared. Ben had two indentured servants, and they worked well alongside Samson and Ezekiel. The Virginia men that Dixon had met needed food, so they helped with the planting in exchange for meals and a place to sleep.

Each day when they went to the fields it seemed the land was ready for them. The weather could not have been better, providing occasional light evening showers and predictable sunny days.

By the time they finished planting the seed, some that they had planted the first few days had already begun to germinate. However, as the weeks progressed, the plants did not grow uniformly, and much of the seed failed to germinate at all.

Sean was very disappointed in this development and considered it an indication that their venture would fail. However, Dixon assured him that this was not an unusual occurrence when following agricultural pursuits, especially by planters like themselves who brought such a lack of experience to the land.

The Virginians assured Ben that the endeavor should not be considered a failed planting, especially for a first attempt. They also told him they'd be willing to stay on and help cultivate and harvest the tobacco crop.

The men from Virginia were cousins, Ethan and Edward Tubbs. They had been brought to Virginia together as boys to become indentured servants. During those days the English only enslaved non-Christians and at that time even a slave could become free by becoming a Christian.

Afterward, when the men had earned their freedom "dues," which included land, supplies, and a gun, they became free. However, because of the pressures that were being applied both to freed indentured servants and to slaves, Ethan and Edward did not want to remain in Virginia.

Once freed, many of the indentured servants had begun to pose a threat to the property-owning elite. As a result, many restrictions on available lands created unrest among newly freed indentured servants. In 1676, when working-class men burned down Jamestown, it made indentured servitude look even less attractive to the leaders of Virginia, especially the large plantation owners. Using slaves became a safer and certainly more profitable pursuit for the landowners.

The Virginia plantation owner had agreed to give the Tubbs cousins money as their freedom dues, and they decided to come to Maryland, looking to buy land. After Ben discussed with Sean the willingness of the cousins to stay on until the harvest, they agreed to hire the men from Virginia. However, this meant the Tubbs men would not be paid until the harvest was sold and Sean and Ben had their purses filled. The men consented to this and Sean provided living quarters for them in a shed at Dawn Light. What Sean could not foresee was that this decision was about to help him understand more of the providence of God.

Chapter Nineteen

The Set of His Heart

As far as Sean was concerned, things were not going well with the endeavor to become tobacco merchants.

Although the Tubbs cousins continually urged him to be optimistic about his agricultural future, Sean was not sure that he had been given the sort of character that would make a good plantation owner, even a rather small one.

Everything related to farming seemed based on the wiles of weather. If the sun decided to shine at the right time, if rains fell on appropriate occasions, if the air turned cold, if—if—if; there were so many "ifs" and Sean did not sense that this farming life, and especially the new tobacco endeavor, was dependable enough for him.

After all, his eyes were set on Julia Wells. However, he had no thought of asking Mrs. Wells for the hand of her daughter unless he could assure her that he had a certain way of providing a good liveli-hood for their future.

Ethan and Edward Tubbs had never married. Their hard lives on the Virginia tobacco plantation as indentured servants had precluded the opportunity of courting. Besides, there were no women to court.

However, as the Tubbs cousins worked the fields with Sean, Ben and his indentured servants, Samson, and Ezekiel, they could see that Sean was not cut out to be one to work with the soil. Of course, they never said anything in the company of the others, but they sometimes would talk late into the night about the farming situation at Dawn Light.

They had the practice of reading the Bible every night and often came upon scriptural passages that seemed to reflect the very things that had gone on that day in the fields at Dawn Light. Often, they would mention these Bible verses to Sean the next day.

At first, Sean resented the fact that the Tubbs cousins presumed to tell him things about the Bible. But, before too long he saw himself looking forward to what they might have to say as the day began. Sometimes, when they would offer no biblical passage, he would ask what they had read the previous night.

It wasn't long before Sean invited them to join him on the porch following their evening meal—for the purpose of reading the Bible. Before coming to Maryland, Sean had never seen a Bible or known anyone who owned a Bible. His earlier impressions of those who called themselves Christians were easily defined as mirrors of Reverend Topping. Of course, the situation with Topping had simply reinforced his many mistaken opinions concerning Christians.

But, those impressions were changing. It all began with Julia. *Imagine that,* he would think, *Julia, Topping's niece.* She had a special way of probing Sean's heart and mind with intrusive questions regarding his spiritual condition. He recalled how he had first tried to fence with her by using words that he hoped might show some understanding of things spiritual. She saw right through him.

Then later he would occasionally become somewhat belligerent, because he considered that Julia was prying too much into his personal life. Again, she saw right through his blustering.

But lately he looked forward to her questions and kind explanations. He seemed to be understanding more and more of what she meant when she talked of God and of Jesus Christ.

And now here were the Tubbs cousins, reading the Bible to him. He wasn't aware just why his interest in such things was increasing; however, Ethan and Edward Tubbs had a very good idea why this was so.

One evening Ethan was reading from the Bible in verse 6 of 2 Corinthians, chapter 9:

> *"But this I say, He which soweth sparingly shall reap also sparingly; and he which soweth bountifully shall reap also bountifully. Every man according as he purposeth in his heart, so let him give; not grudgingly, or of necessity: for God loveth a cheerful giver.*

"And God is able to make all grace abound toward you; that ye, always having all sufficiency in all things, may abound to every good work:

"(As it is written, He hath dispersed abroad; he hath given to the poor: his righteousness remaineth for ever. Now he that ministereth seed to the sower both minister bread for your food, and multiply your seed sown, and increase the fruits of your righteousness;)

"Being enriched in every thing to all bountifulness, which causeth through us thanksgiving to God. For the administration of this service not only supplieth the want of the saints, but is abundant also by many thanksgivings unto God; Whiles by the experiment of this ministration they glorify God for your professed subjection unto the gospel of Christ, and for your liberal distribution unto them, and unto all men; And by their prayer for you, which long after you for the exceeding grace of God in you. Thanks be unto God for his unspeakable gift. "

Ethan closed the Bible and looked at his cousin. Sean's eyes were closed and his chin rested on his chest. After a few seconds he opened his eyes and tears ran down his cheeks. He made no attempt to wipe them away.

He looked at Ethan, then Edward, and then back down at the floor. "Why haven't I seen this before?" he asked of no one in particular.

The Tubbs men simply looked at one another as he continued.

"I don't understand how, or why, God should have been so good to me when I've done so little for others. I want to purpose in my heart to give just like the Bible says these people did, because God has allowed me to reap so bountifully. Oh, I don't mean crops and such," he laughed softly. "I haven't done too well as a farmer. But, God has given me so much, including this very place of my birth, Dawn Light."

Edward said, "Well, that's a fine decision Sean O'Connell, a fine decision to purpose to give. Yes, a fine decision. Don't you agree cousin?"

"I do indeed," replied Ethan. "But, did you know that there's something that preceded the desire to give that these people had, Sean?"

"Well, yes, as I understand it was that they had sown bountifully so they reaped bountifully and had much to give."

"That much is true," replied Ethan, "but there's more. You see, these people we've read about in the Bible had accepted Jesus Christ as Lord of their lives. Did you notice the last words I read from that passage from the Holy Scriptures? He opened the Bible again and read aloud, beginning at verse 13:

"They glorify God for your professed subjec-
tion unto the gospel of Christ, and for your
liberal distribution unto them, and unto all

men; And by their prayer for you, which long after you for the exceeding grace of God in you. Thanks be unto God for his unspeakable gift."

When Ethan finished reading, he looked right into Sean's eyes and said, "You see Sean, these people had made themselves subject to God through Jesus Christ. They had received that *"unspeakable gift"* that God has provided through His only Son, Jesus. And Sean, it's my certainty that God has His hand upon you at this very time and wants you to receive His gift now, before it's eternally too late."

Sean stared at his hands, saying nothing. Then, he slowly raised his head and looked at Ethan as tears again began to flow down his cheeks.

"Yes. Yes, you're right, dear friends. I too want to receive His gift, and I want to delay no longer."

Then, as if commanded to do so, the three men bowed their heads in unison. Ethan prayed, asking God to hear Sean's confession and plea for life in Jesus Christ.

After several minutes of silence, Sean prayed and confessed his sin and his need for a Savior. From that moment, Sean's life was changed for the good and forever.

Chapter Twenty

Clearer Vision

Sean was showing less and less interest in making the tobacco production a success. He had taken to inviting the Tubbs cousins to discuss spiritual matters with him, because he had so many questions about his new life as a true believer in the Lord Jesus Christ.

Then, one day the Tubbs cousins suggested that he might be interested in selling his share of the tobacco endeavor. At first he was upset that they would think he was capable of giving over the enterprise. In fact, he suspected they may have preyed upon him and led him to believe things about the Bible in order to gain an advantage over him and work some scheme to get land.

However, his heart assured him that what he had done in accepting Jesus Christ as Lord of his life was authentic. These men were not working to bring about any disadvantage to him. They had been teachers and counselors to his soul.

He began to give their proposal consideration. Even though Ben Dixon was intensely opposed to Sean's idea of abandoning his share in the tobacco venture, there was little he could do about it.

In his mind, Sean proposed that if he could sell some of the acreage to a buyer he would then keep the house and some acreage. But, to whom could he make such a sale? The Tubbs cousins had an interest in the land, but he did not know if they had the kind of money required to make the purchase of a large tract.

Also, the problem was not really selling the land. That was one thing, but having a means of an ongoing income was quite another. He had no other skills except those he had learned at the gambling tables and, of course, his printer's apprenticeship in Dublin.

Even though his enthusiasm for the tobacco business had diminished, nevertheless, he never shirked in providing his share of the labor and time. When he made an agreement to do something, he would do it. Long ago he had sent money back to England to pay his distant cousin for having placed a headstone for his Aunt Elayne, just as he had agreed to do. And he would follow up with this commitment as well.

This warm July morning found Sean riding alongside Dixon; Sean was on his horse and Ben was on a sway-backed mount. They were accompanied by Samson and Ezekiel, who rode along in the freight cart. They were headed to Gunter's Harbour, where they would pick up supplies for the Dixon household, as well as for Dawn Light.

When they arrived at the Harbour, they pulled the cart as close to the docks as they could. There were two small sailing vessels at dockside, which had the small facility bustling with activity and loud voices, and laughter filled the air.

Ben and Sean dismounted and told the men to wait with the horses and cart until their turn came to pull in closer to the dock. Samson and Ezekiel gladly took advantage of this opportunity for some leisure.

Meanwhile, Sean and Ben thought to take in the local news and gossip with the possibility of coming up with something useful—perhaps a new style tool or goods to buy that might have been damaged in the sea journey and were not accepted by the merchant.

It seldom happened that they discovered such bounty, but one could never be sure. Besides, as Ben Dixon always said, "It's the chase that's important and not the catch."

The men walked slowly beside the dock and took in as much information as was available. They unhurriedly strolled along, enjoying light banter with the local men, as well as those who had come in on the ships.

Unexpectedly, a voice called out, "Ahoy there! Ahoy, young Mr. O'Connell! Ahoy, there!"

Sean looked around to see where the voice had come from, but no one seemed to be directing attention toward him. Then, again he heard, "Ahoy, young Mr. O'Connell. Up here, Sir! Up here!"

Sean looked up to the deck of one of the sailing vessels, and immediately he recognized the face of

Captain Laird Murphy who was aboard the *Southern Swallow*.

"Ahoy there yourself, Captain. What a grand surprise to see you!"

Then turning to Dixon he said, "This is the ship upon which I came over, Ben. Isn't this a surprise?"

The captain heard him and replied, "Aye, and an even more grand surprise for me it is, young sir. Come aboard will you, please?"

"I'd be contented and honored to do so, Captain; and with your permission I'll bring my friend Ben Dixon aboard too."

"Welcome he is, welcome he is. Come aboard men."

Ben waved his hand toward the gangplank and said, "No, Sean, you go ahead and visit. I just saw Justine Dittleback slinking around in the crowd. I'm sure he saw us and wants to avoid us, especially me. But, I'm going to find him and see about getting some of our money back on that seed that didn't come up. You go ahead, Sean. I'll catch up with you."

Sean boarded the *Southern Swallow* and was greeted with great gusto by Captain Laird Murphy.

"My goodness, young sir, but don't you look fine." He grasped Sean's hand and shook it mightily. "You'll excuse me for saying it, but you seem to have a good bit more color than you did when last I saw you."

Sean laughed, "Yes, Captain, I'll readily admit that on the last day of our voyage I had felt better at other times — much better. I was ready to set my feet on land again."

"I'm sure, I'm sure. My, but it's fine to see you again. What's it been now, two—no three years. Has it been three years?"

"I'm thinking it has been, Captain. It's good to see you again, and I trust you've been well."

"I have. Oh, I have indeed . . . well, except for some fine snags in the halyards. Let me tell you about it. And you, young sir, you'll tell me how your life's been caring for you."

The captain then called to his first mate, apparently a new man who hadn't been on the vessel when Sean had traveled, and told him to supervise the unloading. Then he and Sean went to his cabin where they visited and reminisced for a long time. Of course Sean told him of the terrible experience with the Reverend Topping, whom the captain had met on the first day, and of Topping's tragic death.

The captain said, "Sean, I've a bit of news as well, although mine's not as striking as yours. Having been successful in the printer's business yourself, I think you'll be interested to know that I have a printer's press aboard."

Sean felt his face flush, because he remembered the tall tale he had told the captain of his success as a Dublin printer. "You do? A printer's press? My now, but that's interesting. Why a press? We have no printers here."

"Yes, yes, I know. Unfortunate it is too. Sean, do you remember me telling you of how I brought the first printer's press over here to Jamestown? The printer first tried to operate his press in Virginia. But Governor William Buckley forbade the use of printing in a royal colony, because he reasoned that schools and printing brought nothing but heresy and religious sects into the world."

"I do indeed. I don't recall the printer's name, but I do remember that you brought the very first press here to the colony. Around 1680, wasn't it?"

"That's right, Sean. You've a good memory. It was 1682, and the printer's name was William Nuthead."

The captain leaned forward as if to speak in confidence. "I'm not one to make small of a person, Sean, but I must say this man's name fit him well." Then his face burst into a large grin and he sat back laughing.

The captain continued. "He had to abandon his printer's shop in Jamestown, for he caused a good deal of scandal with some of the things he printed. So then, I think it was about 1685 that he and his wife Dinah moved to St. Mary's, the capital of Maryland. He made a go of it there for awhile, but then they moved again when the capital went to Annapolis. But then, Sean, printer Nuthead . . . well, he up and died in 1695."

"Oh, I'm sorry to know of that," said Sean. He wasn't quite sure just what the point was and was about to ask what had become of the printer's press when the captain continued.

"Well, and it's sorry I am too, young sir. You see, Nuthead had ordered another printer's press from Germany. But, when he died his widow never gave no notice to the Germans what were building it. They moved that press from way over in Hamburg,

Germany to Southampton for me to bring over to the colony. I suppose you could say that I had something of a reputation for bringing printer's presses to the colonies."

The captain stopped to pour himself another cup of rum grog, but Sean waved off the captain's offer.

"Well then," the captain explained, "when I bring it here to Maryland, wouldn't you know, they tell me old Nuthead's dead. And the widow Dinah Nuthead, she says to me, she says she has one printer's press in Annapolis and that'll do her just fine."

"Well, what sort of business is that then?" asked Sean. "Wouldn't you think she'd have some responsibility in the matter to pay you?"

"Aye, Sean, it's what I say too. She has quite a head for commerce, I'm told, and I'm sure she takes great pride in being the only woman in the colonies who is a printer. I suppose that's a fine thing, but that doesn't help my purse one little bit. For now, do you see, I've got a printer's press and I know nothing to do with it that will be of any help to me."

"My, this must be turning out to be a very costly mistake," Sean offered.

The captain took a pull of his grog and said, "Aye, it is that. But I don't yet know what it will be before it's over. I don't suppose you've no need for a printer's press, have you, young sir?" The captain laughed nervously as he said it.

"Well, no I don't. But then . . . perhaps I do." Sean continued, "You know, Captain Murphy, I find it a strange thing to be happening today. The way I chanced into Gunter's Harbour on the very day that you're unloading your vessel, very strange indeed. Then you surprise me with a tale of what could be a great loss to you. I tell you Captain, there may be more providence in this conversation than what we know."

Sean really had no idea what he meant and he definitely shocked himself with the mention of providence in his life. Even though he had become a Christian, he didn't often dare think that way.

Captain Murphy was not aware of what was going on in Sean's life and of the decisions with which he struggled. So he asked, "Tell me, young sir, is there anywhere nearby where a man can get him a good meal and some clear rum?"

"I know of only one place that truly meets one of those requirements, Captain. You'll have to come to Dawn Light with me for some good food. How long will it be before you'll set sail for your return?"

"Well, that sounds like a very fine thing to do for me. We'll be the rest of the day and most of tomorrow and the next morning unloading and loading for the return. Then, with the tides we'll be another two or maybe three days before we set sail for Jamestown. Except for provisions and stores for the crossing we'll leave here empty, but we have to pick up cargo in Jamestown and Bermuda before heading east to England."

"All right then," Sean replied. "If your first mate can be placed in charge, I could send one of my men to collect you tomorrow afternoon. We'll have a good meal at Dawn Light and find you a bed tick to sleep on—one that won't rock quite as well as your ship.

Then, I can bring you back the following day so you'll be able to be here to assure that the *Southern Swallow* has been properly outfitted for your return."

"Aye, young Sean O'Connell. I can do that. Allow me to meet with my first mate and the crew and then you'll tell me when to be ready to leave. It can be whenever you plan to do so."

The men shook hands, and Sean told him that either he or one of his men would be back the next day, hopefully at mid afternoon.

As he walked down the gangplank onto the dock, his mind was spinning with rather strange thoughts—thoughts that he had never, ever, not in his entire young life, considered to be possible. He heard himself whistling and reflecting: *Sean my boy, this whole thing about providence may not be as strange as you once considered it to be.*

Sean found Ben Dixon lounging on a grassy knoll just above the docks. He sat up, rather startled as Sean called his name but swore he wasn't napping.

"Tell me, Ben, were you able to corner your friend Dittleback? What did he have to say?"

"Oh, my friend is he? Yes, I did corner the weasel, and I suppose what he said was true: said he had no way of telling whether the seed would grow any more than someone else might. Still, I pushed him for returning some of our money, because of the poor way the seed came up."

"So, then," Sean began eagerly, "how much did you get out of him?"

"There's the snag, Sean. If he can be believed— and I'm not saying I believe him—he's already spent the money. I see no reason to think he's lying. His income consists of making what he can, when he can, and from those he can—those just like us. I'd not be surprised if he and his companions didn't drink his profits before that week was out."

"About what I suspected," agreed Sean. "Even though he may have played us as fools as far as the price went, I suppose he had no way of knowing whether the seed would grow or not. But, friend, aren't we learning a lot about what *not* to do as tobacco growers?"

Both men laughed. After Sean told Dixon of plans he'd made for Captain Murphy to come to Dawn Light, Ben suggested they stop in at the Harbour House Ordinary for refreshment.

Sean agreed that it was a good idea, especially for such a warm day as this. He had many more good ideas to mull over as well. He was gaining a clearer vision of what his future might be and a better understanding of the meaning of providence, or so he thought.

Sean remembered how Captain Murphy had noted, "I've got a printer's press and I know nothing to do with it that will be of any help to me. I don't suppose you've no need for a printer's press, have you, young sir?"

And Sean recalled his own response, "But why a press? We have no printers here."

No printers. The thought took a few moments to soak in his mind. Then it came to him. *This sounds like the sort of opportunity I have been hoping for.* He also remembered thinking that there might have been the touch of providence in the conversation with the captain. He was beginning to like this new way of thinking about providence: divine intervention.

The captain came to Dawn Light as they had planned. It was a pleasant evening, because Sean had invited Ben and his wife. Preparation of the meal had been watched over by Mrs. Dixon, and Kezie had taken great delight in the attention this brought her.

After the meal, the Dixons returned to their home, but Sean and Captain Murphy talked into the night. They spent a great deal of time discussing the possibility of someone becoming a successful printer in the area. After all, aside from Philadelphia, the only other printer anywhere near was Mrs. Nuthead in Annapolis.

Sean told the captain about thoughts he'd been having. He mentioned that as he looked back to his days in Dublin as a young man he recalled being somewhat envious of the printer to whom he was apprenticed. Now, the thought of being a successful printer in a growing colony appealed to him.

At last, after a great deal of conversation concerning what Sean could afford, he decided to rescue Captain Murphy from his monetary loss by purchasing the printer's press that the Widow Nuthead had refused to receive.

Of course, the captain was pleased and so was Sean. Although Sean had no money he offered several hogsheads[6] of tobacco to the captain on his next voyage. They shook hands on the arrangement and went to bed. The captain slept peacefully, but

Sean's mind raced with thoughts of the possibilities that the future held.

After a hearty breakfast, Samson hitched the horses to the cart and they took the captain back to his ship. There were plenty of hands around to unload the printer's press and load it into Sean's cart. Everything was made of wood, including the huge screw that brought the press to bear upon the paper.

Sean was ecstatic, and he was certain that printing was going to be the way that he would expand his horizons: divine intervention.

But, he was wrong.

Chapter Twenty-One

To Print or Not to Print

It was several days after the *Southern Swallow* left Gunter's Harbour that Sean made the trip to Annapolis. He had decided to visit the Widow Nuthead and gain some impressions from her concerning the future of printing in Maryland.

At first, Sean thought of having Samson travel with him to Annapolis. It was a long trip and there were things he felt he should discuss with Samson—some very important issues that Ezekiel had shared with him. But he disliked having Samson away from his work for such a lengthy period of time.

So Sean made the trip alone. The day was clear, and Samson had fed and saddled the horse for the trip. Even though Sean was somewhat excited about going, he was hesitant about leaving. But, Ezekiel assured him that he would see to the work and care of Dawn Light.

"I'll expect nothing to go lacking while I'm away, Ezekiel. Ben Dixon will look in on you regularly and the Tubbs men will be working with you as well."

"Yes, Mas' Shawn. I do like you say."

"And you, Samson and Kezie, you listen to what Ezekiel says and . . ." Sean went on and on with instructions to Kezie. As usual, she stood there with a pleasant look on her face but always snatching glances at Samson, knowing she'd get his interpretation later.

This sort of thing no longer bothered Sean. He could always be sure that later on one of the men would talk to her in their dialect and explain what he had said. *Besides,* Sean reflected, *I think she understands more than what she lets on.*

Samson tied a large bag of food behind the saddle before Sean mounted and rode down the lane. Had he looked back he would have seen them watching him until he turned out of the lane and onto the trail that led toward the road south to Annapolis.

Sean was surprised that the journey to Annapolis went so easily. He rode at a steady pace and rehearsed some of the questions that had puzzled him about his anticipated new printing endeavor. He met other travelers in some areas, actually more than he had anticipated.

As he traveled, the days were clear and the nights moderate. He spent every night under the stars, although he had taken advantage of evening meals at two ordinaries along the way. In the morning he heated water and made tea from the bark that Kezie insisted he take with him, and he ate some dried breads she had sent along.

The only problem he had encountered was crossing the Susquehanna River. The boat that ferried his horse across tipped over, but fortunately the horse and waterman were close to shore and both arrived safely on land with no further mishaps.

But, the accident had infuriated Sean to the point that he made some angry suggestions to the watermen who ferried people and animals across.

"You don't have to be much of a waterman to know that a boat with such a shallow draft wouldn't be safe for a beast as large as a horse. Raise the gunwales on your boats and you'll make them much more stable."

The boat owners replied with curses for having to transport such an unruly animal that almost caused the ruin of their boat. Sean simply ignored their complaints, mounted his horse, and rode on.

Of course, he had been to Annapolis when he first arrived in the colonies. He had made that hurried trip to have his ownership of the land certified, but he had paid little attention to the town.

This time, as he arrived from the north, he was pleased to see how pleasantly the roads and streets had been laid out in the town. The people seemed to be reasonably helpful to him when he tried to locate Mrs. Nuthead. Most knew about her, but no one with whom he spoke had occasion to do business with a printer. Because of this, no one seemed able to direct him to her.

He was wondering if somehow he had been misinformed. Perhaps she had moved her print shop to another town. Finally, he stopped where several men were engaged in conversation outside a tinsmith's shop. When Sean inquired about Mrs. Nuthead, the tinsmith attested to knowledge of her location and proceeded to give Sean directions to a certain small building where Prince George and East Streets converged. He thanked them, thinking it sounded as though the tinker knew his way about.

He found the intersection of Prince George and East Streets and knocked on the door of a small building that looked as though it might be a printer's shop. But, no one answered. A woman sweeping the stoop of the next building asked Sean who he was looking for.

"I seek the house of the Widow Nuthead, the printer."

"Oh, 'at's the one yer after. Got business with 'er 'ave you?"

"I would appreciate your help," Sean responded, "but my dealings with her are personal. Do you know where she lives?"

"Aye, seems I do," she replied and returned to her sweeping.

"Well, then, would you be so kind as to give me her location?'

"S'pose I could be so kind. Or maybe a bit kinder if I 'ad me some brass," she replied without looking up from her broom.

"I think I'll find her then, without your help," Sean said as he turned his horse about.

"'Ere ye go now, don't be so 'asty. Ye're off in the wrong way. She's down yonder," the woman said pointing with her broom in the opposite direction, toward the Bay. "Just find ye Craig Street and ye'll come across the docks. Then ye'll be stumblin' over that Nuthead woman."

As Sean wheeled his horse about he said with a smile, "I knew you were a woman who would help a traveling stranger, and I thank you for your kind help and courtesy."

The woman stopped her sweeping, leaned her chin on the broom handle, and with a pleased look on her face she watched Sean ride away.

The woman's directions were accurate enough. He found the Widow Dinah Nuthead's small shop and, from the appearances of the building, she probably lived above the tiny workspace below. He dismounted and secured his horse to a ring driven into the stone steps leading to the entrance. An unobtrusive, barely readable wooden sign next to the door quietly announced the premises as "Printery Shoppe—William Nuthead."

Sean knocked on the door and he heard a woman's voice inside, but he could not understand what she was saying. He knocked again. The unseen woman repeated something this time a bit louder, but he still could not understand. So he knocked again.

A moment later the door flew open and a woman stood with her hands on her hips demanding, "I said, 'Who's there?' What do you want?"

The woman's head was covered with a dark cloth tied tightly at the back of her neck. She wore an apron that probably had once been used for cooking but now was covered with printer's ink. Her face was smudged with ink, her hands were black, and Sean recognized the smell of boiled linseed oil, used by printers to mix with carbon to make their ink.

"Please excuse me, Ma'am, but I'm trying to locate Mrs. Dinah Nuthead and wondered . . ."

"No need to locate me, young man. I know where I am. Now what do you want?"

"Please pardon this unannounced visit, but I've traveled almost four days to seek your advice in the matter of printing."

"Have you now? And to what end? If you have need of something being printed, I can tell you now that I'm much too busy doing printery for the government."

Then, holding up a sheet of rag paper she said, "And just look at this. It's that William Bladen, the clerk of the Lower House. He fancies himself an educated man. Now he wants me to print a book for him. I'd like to know how he expects me to find time to print a book. Can you tell me?"

"I would have no idea about such matters Mrs. Nuthead, but I would like to . . ."

"It's some sort of nonsense about 'merchantable leaf tobacco and casks' and such as that. Why, by the time I've done printing the book he'll need another, because the tobacco will have taken another price. I don't know why I ever decided to continue with this printery nonsense of my dear husband William!"

"I'm sure it must be somewhat overwhelming at times," Sean offered in an attempt to get on with his reason for coming to Annapolis. "But might I tell you about myself and ask you some questions?"

Mrs. Nuthead didn't exactly apologize for her outburst, but she did suddenly become more reasonable and somewhat cordial. When Sean explained his apprenticeship as a printer's devil in Dublin years ago and then his more recent decision to buy the press from Captain Murphy and begin his own printing business, she looked at him incredulously.

"Why in the name of any good sense would you purchase that press from Murphy? Didn't he tell you I didn't want it?"

"Well, yes he did. But, I thought that with my background in printing I might make a good living for myself and . . ."

"Young man, why do you think I didn't need another printer's press? What do you know about a good living from printing? Where will you get paper? I pay excessive prices for inferior paper from England—that is, when I can get it. They keep the best paper in London and then send us what no honest printer would use in England." After a brief pause, she continued, "And what would you propose to print?"

"I've thought a good deal of that and I've decided that there might be an opportunity for printing news and tobacco prices, and . . ."

"Well, there you are again. You've thought a good deal and you've decided have you? Who are these people who'll be able to read what you print? And, even if there might just be someone you find who *could* read, who *would* read your news broadsides?

And what tobacco grower doesn't already know the price of tobacco? Let me tell you something young man: Are you aware that my husband was the first printer in Virginia and Maryland?"

"Yes. Yes, indeed I am aware of that; and, if I may say, that is the one reason I wanted to meet with you and receive accounts of your vast experience."

"That's exactly what I am trying to tell you. The 'accounts of my vast experience,' as you say are none too pretty, despite the fact that my dear William has the very distinguished position of being the second printer to establish and sustain a printing press in the colonies. Of course, Massachusetts had the first. Early on we had thought to establish a good printing trade in Virginia. But, did you know that we had to bring our press from Jamestown to St. Mary's in 1685? And do you know why?"

"Well, I'm not altogether sure that I do."

"It was because the governor of Virginia thought our press was too dangerous. He thinks that when people learn to read they become rebellious. He assured us that our printing was going to cause all sorts of religious trouble—the rising up of cults and such nonsense. I have the very correspondence that Governor William Berkley gave to my husband." She began to look about and mumbled, "Now where is that letter."

She muttered to herself as she began leafing through stacks of paper. One stack fell off the table and she announced, "Here, here it is. Read it for yourself Mr. . . . uh, young man."

She handed the letter to Sean and he read:

*I think no printing should be done in any
royal colony. I thank God there are no free
school and no printing in Virginia and I hope
we shall not have these for a hundred years.
For learning has brought disobedience, and
heresy, and sects into the world, and printing
has divulged them, and produced libels
against the best government. 'The Honorable
Governor of Virginia, William Berkley August
3rd, 1683* [7]

"He may have been right," Mrs. Nuthead offered
when Sean had finished reading. "I don't know about
such as that. What I do know is that Mr. Nuthead
and I had to leave Virginia. As I said, we came to
St. Mary's in 1685 and produced our first imprint on
August 31 that year."

"Then, perhaps that was the hand of providence
that allowed this move, because then you and your
departed husband were able to practice the printing
craft here in Maryland."

"I know nothing of providence in matters such as
these. But, let me tell you: Maryland's not that much
the improvement. Here we're only allowed to print
government and legal documents. We can do that only
if the governor or a member of the Assembly sees the
document first. Such nonsense! And then there's the
matter of someone paying me for my trouble, and
trouble it is!"

Sean was somewhat surprised at this news and
could only say, "I had not any idea that there was this
sort of control over the craft."

"Well, I would say that there are many other things you know nothing of when it comes to the printer's trade. Are you truly familiar enough with printing to know that our imprint was produced before any of William Bradford's work was done up there in Philadelphia?"

"Well, no. Although I have heard of Bradford and his ..."

"Oh, have you now? As I was saying: then we had to leave St. Mary's when they moved the capital to Annapolis. Do you know what we print, Mr. uh, Mr. uh . . . .?"

"O'Connell, Sean O'Connell. No I don't, and that's what I wanted to learn."

"It's simple, young man. As I've already told you—you really need to listen more carefully—we print documents for the government and nothing more than that. Now, why would I need another printer's press when I have barely enough trade with one to keep myself alive? Can you explain how a printer in—wherever is it you say you come from—in any case there will never be the sort of commerce that would allow two printers in Maryland to make a living with their printing. How could it be young man, when my dear William and I have been unable to do so?"

"I had no idea that things were quite as grave as you've explained, Mrs. Nuthead. I can see that I have caused you some aggravation, and I certainly meant not to do so. Please forgive me."

"Nonsense, young man, my aggravation began long ago when my William died in 1695 and I became the first woman printer in the colonies. The way some speak and behave you'd think that was some sort of honor. I tell you that it's not. The government is slow to pay, paper is scarce to come by, and I assure you that this craft is not for the faint-hearted, unless your wish is to quickly become poor. I cannot say it any differently than to simply say: Do not become a printer. Now, I am very busy and you must leave. Please excuse me."

That was the end of Sean's long awaited interview with Mrs. Nuthead. She ushered Sean to the door and with a grimy hand on his arm, nudged him through the door and closed it behind him. Sean heard the door latch fall into place. The meeting definitely was over.

Sean stood at the side of his horse for a few moments, staring at the closed door, somewhat perplexed by the brief encounter with Mrs. Nuthead. He had traveled for more than four days and now had another four- or five-day ride back to Dawn Light.

He had learned very little, except what Mrs. Nuthead thought of his prospects as a printer, and he was beginning to believe she might be right. After all, if earning a livelihood by printing here in Maryland's capital was so difficult, what would make him think that North East would be any better?

The sun was low in the sky and Sean was hungry. What would he do now? He'd begin by finding the closest inn and finding some food.

Chapter Twenty-Two

Crossing the River

They made good ale in Annapolis, and Sean washed his food down with a pint. Innkeeper Jacob Smith at Smith's Ordinary was a genial fellow who knew a great deal about the history of Maryland and Virginia.

Sean was fascinated with his banter about topics that ranged from tobacco farming and local politics to oyster fishing in the Bay. The innkeeper even knew a fair amount about printing as well, because William Nuthead had been a frequent visitor at Smith's.

The hour was late and there were no other guests for the night, so when Sean asked if it would be possible for him to spend the night Jacob Smith was pleased to accommodate him.

Sean slept long after the sun arose the next day. He dreamed of little other than his lovely Julia. Sean had been quite amazed to discover that while his days might be occupied with matters of trade and farming, his nights were most often filled with dreams of her.

Not surprisingly, none of his dreams had anything to do with printing.

When Sean opened his eyes, the owner's wife was heating something in a small pot in the fireplace and it had an interesting and inviting aroma. Sean sat up. Innkeeper Smith had placed on the floor the scratchy, cornhusk-filled bed tick for him to sleep on.

"Good morning, Ma'am. I trust that by sleeping late I've not caused you any difficulty this morning."

"Not at all, and a very good and bright morning it is for you. I'm just now boiling some oyster stew and it may be that it would interest you. Are you hungry?"

"I am hungry, and the stew does smell tempting. But, I must tell you that I've never eaten oysters, not in a stew or any other way for that matter."

"Oh my, then this a day of good fortune for you, isn't it now? Just get yourself up and about. There's a washbasin behind the building and other necessaries. You care for yourself and I'll remove that bed tick; don't bother yourself about it. Then, when you come back in you'll have a special treat: your very first bowl of the most delicious oyster stew you may ever have." She smiled good-naturedly as she bragged about her cooking.

When Sean returned, he tasted her offering and thought that she was exactly right about her oyster stew. He inquired as to the ingredients and determined that he would see about having Samson do some oyster fishing and then have Kezie cook some of this new treat back at Dawn Light.

After eating, he saddled his horse and took leave of the Smiths, anxious to get back home. As Sean walked his horse along, the people of Annapolis were beginning to fill the streets. Most seemed single minded about where they were going, and Sean heard few personal greetings between the people.

He passed several brick structures, which Sean hadn't even noticed on his trip into Annapolis. *I haven't seen so many brick houses and buildings since leaving Ireland. In fact, I wonder if I shouldn't consider the possibility of making bricks for new structures in Gunter's Harbour.* But, of course, he knew nothing of making bricks.

At the edge of town he encouraged the horse to a gallop, thought better of it, and brought him to a slow trot. As his thoughts turned to Julia, he was somewhat surprised at how warm he felt, even though the sun was hidden by an increasingly overcast sky.

The trip back home was uneventful as he rode through the countryside and on to the Susquehanna River. Most days the sun was hidden by clouds, and on the third day a soaking rain fell. Thankfully, the nights were mild and without rain. Each night he fell asleep with a hodge-podge of thoughts racing through his mind—thoughts about his future.

Sean had determined that he would seek different watermen than those who had helped him make the crossing south. He didn't want to lose his horse when their boat capsized.

Unfortunately, when he came down the hill toward the river, there were no other watermen to be seen at the crossing—only the same men who had

251

been there a few days earlier. Sean spied them from a distance and recognized at once the man who seemed to be in charge.

He turned his horse and rode northward for several hundred yards along the river bank, looking for other possibilities before he realized that the men he had used earlier must have the only likely crossing for miles.

Wheeling his horse about, he rode toward the men. They had recognized Sean too, and, as he drew near, he heard their loud laughter and felt sure that their amusement was at his expense.

The man giving the orders said, "Well, well, lads, and what 'ave we here? Looks as if we 'ave some gentleman would like to cross our lovely river today. Would you look now lads, 'e 'as 'm a 'orse as well. What are ye thinkin' lads? Should the 'orse swim across? Or, may they both should swim. What say ye?"

The men began their loud hurrahing and laughing again and, as they did, Sean swung down from his saddle.

"A good day to you. You appear to be the same watermen that didn't know how to transport my horse a few days ago. And, even though both my horse and I can swim, I think you'll agree that we'd be better off if I cross with dry clothing and he crosses with dry hooves. That is, if there are any watermen here today capable of working their ferrying trade in a proper manner."

The man who had been doing all the talking stopped laughing. He hadn't expected this sort of response from Sean and said, "Aw now, 'ow's that a way to talk to honest ferrymen? Wasn't our fault that put yer 'orse in the water, what with 'm movin' about so."

"What I told you then I'll say again: any ferryman worth his trade would know that the gunwales on a ferryboat such as yours need to be higher. But, I'll risk you to ply your trade and your abilities once again today. Can you ferry my horse across?"

The men looked at one another and the thought of taking money from Sean was too tempting. "Well, we'll do it, we will. But I'll tell ye this time that if the 'orse takes a swim it's yer doin', not ours. An' we'll 'ave the brass on this side the river as well."

"How does this strike you then?" Sean offered. "If you get both my horse and me across safely and dry I'll pay you twice what you're asking on the other side."

"Now that's a grand idea, but I say we'll take the brass on this side."

"No, not this time you won't. You'll take me across as I said, and if my horse and I arrive dry and secure I'll pay you double for your hire, and that's an offer you must not lose. But I'll tell you this: unless we arrive on the other side safely I'll pay you nothing. How's that now? It's up to you—double or nothing?"

The waterman smiled an evil grin and said, "Well then, what's to keep us from taking our brass from ye no matter what 'appens to you or your 'orse?"

"Those in authority might not want to hear talk like that, and I believe you'll think twice of that idea. Now, shall we sail to the other side?"

"All right then, all right, but it's double you'll pay us or we'll double yer skull." The other men laughed at that observation.

As the men pulled the boats into the water, Sean insisted that the smallest man go in the boat with his horse. He watched somewhat anxiously as the horse began the crossing, but was pleased to see that the man in the boat with the horse seemed to be very careful as he pulled away on the ropes. However, he hadn't noticed the man in charge talking to the others.

Sean's horse was brought in unharmed to the other shore and he watched as the horse safely jumped from the boat onto dry land. With that, Sean and the other men pushed off and soon were on the eastern bank.

When he stepped onto the river bank Sean said, "Now, that's the sort of work I should expect from watermen who ply their trade ferrying people and animals. Well done, and to excellent craftsmen goes the promised portion."

With that, Sean reached inside his shirt and retrieved his money pouch, counted the coins, and handed them to the small man who brought the horse across.

The man seemed surprised at the approving remarks and was obviously quite pleased as well when he received double the price, just as Sean promised.

"Now, 'ere's the gentleman what we needs be makin' our business with, 'orses and all. Bring yourself around anytime for a ferry ride—a dry one."

With that, Sean mounted his horse and all of them began to laugh. But the man who had poled Sean's boat across reached out to grab him, pulled him to the ground and then struck him with something hard.

Sean rolled over and tried to get to his feet, but two of the other men fell on top of him. He remembered striking one of the men between the eyes and blood splattered on Sean's face. Then, another hard blow left him unconscious.

When Sean came to his senses it was almost dark. He was lying face down and, as he tried to roll over, a sharp pain on the side of his head let him know that something was terribly wrong. He tried to clear his eyes and thought he saw something moving not far from him. Managing to sit up, he saw that it was his horse, quietly nibbling grass.

Regaining his senses, he concluded that the ferryboat men had beaten him, knocked him unconscious, thrown him over his horse, and tied him loosely to the saddle. The rope they had used was still looped around his leg. It had come loose as the horse wandered about, and he had fallen to the ground.

With some difficulty he got to his feet to begin the last leg of his return home. Sean patted his side and noticed that the small money pouch was missing. Of course it could have fallen from his shirt as he was draped over the horse, but Sean guessed correctly that it had been taken by the men. For a moment he considered going back to the river, but better judgment called for him to return home.

His head throbbed as he rode along at a leisurely pace, and his thoughts kept going back to the conversations he had with the watermen. *"Now I've had no experience with such things as ferries and boats, but it seems to me that I may have some sort of intuitive sense about the gunwales of the boats those ferrymen used."* Even though his head was aching, for some reason this thought pleasantly surprised him.

He reflected on how he might use these recent experiences. *I'm not inclined to spend my life carrying people from one side of the Susquehanna River to the other, but there's a lesson here to learn. I've paid little attention to the watermen and their boats and it's not that I'd be interested in such a work. Yet, how might this business with the oyster stew enter in here? And besides, how would Samson fish us up any oysters if he had no boat. And, how would I go about getting a boat?*

These random thoughts came in and out, fully occupying his mind. As a soft rain began to fall he reflected on how good it felt on his face. His mind churned with the variety of possibilities to consider: potential schemes, brick making, oyster fishing, boat making, and ferrying—things to which he had never given a moment's notice or thought before.

Then, he looked up in surprise as he realized that he was approaching the lane to Dawn Light.

Chapter Twenty-Three

A Plan for the Printing Press

The night he arrived back home, Samson had called Kezie to dress Sean's head. The ferryboat men had struck him with something hard and sharp, probably a rock. Despite his injuries he slept well — better than he had in quite awhile.

Of course, as usual, he had dreamed of Julia Wells, but those dreams had been interrupted over and again with ideas that stirred up his mind in a troublesome way.

Ben Dixon had looked in on the manor while Sean was gone, but there was really no need to have done so. Samson and Ezekiel had busied themselves with their normal work, and Kezie had taken the opportunity during Sean's absence to do some things in their cabin that amounted to her version of interior decoration.

The sun was high before Sean awoke. The trip to Annapolis had taken a toll on his mind, and the beating had left its mark on his aching head and body.

Nevertheless, he had slept a deep recuperative sleep in his own home.

Kezie was the first to greet him the next morning. As he walked carefully down the stairs and into the small room that served as a cooking and eating room, he could hear Kezie humming one of her songs that had been hidden in her soul. There she stood in the doorway with a pleasant smile as bright as the day, and little Obadiah played busily at her feet. Obadiah chattered and banged on the floor with a wooden spoon.

"Good day, Kezie. Thank you for tending to me last night." She smiled, and he said, "I see that you've already eaten. Are the men in the fields?"

Before she could answer, Obadiah had heard Sean's voice and responded with louder chattering and a more determined beat of the wooden spoon upon the floor.

Kezie's smile broke into a hearty laugh. "Yes, Mas' Shawn, they be fields."

Obadiah took his mother's comment as an invitation to begin screaming and hitting everything within striking distance with the spoon. She picked him up, hugged him, and whispered in his ear. He began his chattering again, louder this time and all the while waving his spoon.

The now familiar aroma of her bark tea had a satisfying affect on Sean. He never even knew what kind of bark she used, but he had come to enjoy a hot cup of her tea in the morning.

"I'll have some of that smoked ham, if there's any left, and some water. Which field are they in today?"

"Don't be know. They be field."

"Yes, well, don't bother. I'll find them."

He picked up a large piece of the ham she had sliced, and with a cup of water he went out to the porch. He sat on the top step and took a bite of the tasty meat. Then he poured some water on a small rag that was lying on a bench and held the rag to the side of his head. It eased the pain.

Just as he was savoring the ham, Samson came around the corner of the house.

"Mas' Shawn. I hears you moanin' in the night. Sees now you up. Zekiel and me be in rock wall field and tend the ground."

"I asked Kezie about you. Is this the first day of work in that field?"

"No, Mas'. We be there not yes'day but nother day. We ready for seed. You'll see."

"That's just fine. But what of the Tubbs men? Are they helping too?"

Show us how to do. They be some fine field hands, Mas' Shawn. Knows how to do the work."

"Well, that is good. Why don't you take them some water now? I'm going to ride over to the Dixon's, because there are some things about which I'll need to talk to Ben."

As Samson went for water, Sean stepped into the barn shed for his horse. He decided to let the animal have a rest after his long journey and saddled one of the draft horses instead.

259

Riding down Dixon's lane, he wasn't sure just how he would approach Ben with the ideas he had been contemplating. After all, they had agreed to enter into this business of tobacco farming as a partnership, and now Sean was looking to other enterprises to make his wealth.

"Sean . . ., hello, Sean!"

He looked to his left and there was Ben riding toward him. He reined his horse in and turned to ride alongside Sean.

"How was your trip to Annapolis? Have you become a master printer after visiting with the printer's widow?" Then he added as he took a second look at Sean, "Did she beat you for asking too many questions? What's happened to your head?"

"Yesterday, I paid a dear price for a dry boat ride for myself and my horse. It seems that I may have taken my bargaining abilities too much for granted. The ruffians at the river took all of my money. Then they beat me for their trouble and sent me on my way like a sack of grain on my horse's back."

"I say we go back there now with some men, get your money, and have at those thieves."

"Not a good idea, Ben. They'd only deny it, and I doubt that we'd see them this day, anyway. Probably off somewhere spending the money they took. Perhaps one day we'll have the opportunity to meet them on our terms."

"I suppose you're right about that," Ben said.

"And I'm afraid it didn't go quite as I had thought it would in Annapolis either. When I . . ."

"Wait. Wait, Sean. Let me say something before you tell me about your new printing enterprise. Here, let's get down and sit awhile before we arrive back at the house."

They dismounted and allowed the horses to begin nibbling the grass. Ben flopped himself down against a pine tree and Sean carefully sat down and joined him.

"While you were gone, Sean, my wife and I talked about our tobacco partnership. She was never pleased with our decision. Then, with all of the trouble that Dittleback caused. . . ." After a brief pause he said, "I'll have to tell you that she gave me good advice, and I made the mistake of ignoring her."

"What's this all about, Ben?" Sean wasn't in a mood to hear one of Ben's long discourses. "I have some things I need to tell you."

"In a minute, Sean, in a minute. Here's the thing. I know that you've no real heart for farming the land and so I want you to know that I . . . well, let me say it this way: my wife believes that I should release you from the tobacco partnership we've set upon."

"What? Why is that?"

Ben thought that Sean's surprised outburst was based on anger, when quite the opposite was true.

"Well, you see," Ben began, "my wife and I believe that the printer's press you purchased from Captain Murphy was your way of letting us know of your disinterest in farming the land."

"No, Ben. No, no, you don't understand. Well, yes, I'll admit that farming has not turned out to be what I was hoping it to be. But, my trip to visit the

Widow Nuthead was nothing more than a confirmation that a printer's life was no more for me than that of a farmer."

"What? But how can that be? And now you've bought a printer's press, and I expect you've paid a dear price for it too."

"You're right about that. I felt that I was helping Captain Murphy by taking it off his hands, and at the same time I thought I'd found my life's work. How wrong I was."

Sean explained his visit with the printer's widow and how belligerently she had discouraged him.

"What I must do next is contact a printer in Philadelphia. Perhaps I can sell the press there. But, Ben, the trip may have been a real boon to my life. I know I'll never be a printer, but I have several other ideas. And, by the way, none have to do with farming."

They talked through the rest of the morning and into the early afternoon. Ben seemed to understand Sean's thinking and they discussed at length those ideas concerning oyster fishing and boat building—and even brick making.

Ben neither encouraged nor discouraged his friend in these matters, because he was wise enough to know that it was a decision Sean would have to make himself. Sean, on the other hand, believed that he needed advice and wanted to have the counsel of Ben and others before coming to his conclusion.

Sean laid out some of the things he had been thinking of. Ben was neither surprised nor disappointed over the report Sean gave about the outlook

of printing for his future. They discussed the possibilities of what to do with the press, which now they
both agreed had been a costly mistake, and they
talked about how Sean might recover some of his
investment.

They came up with a plan to contact some men
in the Philadelphia area. Ben was somewhat familiar
with a man named Rittenhouse who, along with the
printer William Bradford, had established a paper
mill—the first one in the colonies. It was above
Philadelphia near where the Wissahickon Creek
empties into the Schuylkill River.

Aside from Bradford, Ben knew of no other
printers in Philadelphia. He did know that Bradford
had been involved in a controversial tract he had
printed for some Quaker. The problem was that when
Bradford had printed the anti-slavery tract without
proper license he was imprisoned for a time and his
press was seized.

After his release in 1693, he moved to New York
and was named royal printer to that colony. Ben felt
that Bradford might have maintained contact with
those in the Philadelphia printing establishment.
His plan was to write to Bradford to see if he could
somehow help Sean in selling the press.

It certainly wasn't a perfect plan, but Sean was
grateful for Dixon's knowledge of the situation of
printing in the Philadelphia area and for his willingness to help in this way.

"Thank you, Ben. I had no idea where to begin
with all of this. How is it that you know so much
about these men?"

"Well, I'd not say I know so much about them. But, I do remember that my father had some business with them years before he died. It was even before I was married. I've no idea how the names remained with me, but there you have it. Why don't we get together and compose a letter and . . ."

"Yes, we will my friend. But, give me a day to think the whole plan through. Can we get together tomorrow—sometime past noon?"

"Past noon? I suppose we could do that, but why not right now?"

Sean grinned, "Because I have some personal business to attend to."

Ben laughed, "Ah, personal business is it? I'll say no more then except, of course, to ask that while about your personal business you give my greetings to the Wells ladies."

Sean had been trying to stay focused as he and Ben worked through their plan to deliver themselves of the printing press. However, his mind was on more important matters and it was racing almost as fast as his heart was beating, keeping cadence with his trotting horse.

He crested the hill leading down to the Wells home, and his eyes feasted on the scene that he had been dreaming of and hoping to see: Julia, on the porch with her mother. *Ah, the lovely Wells women.* . . .

Chapter Twenty-Four

Sean's Report of Good News

Sean's visit with Julia and her mother was more like a reunion. He had to spend an uncommon amount of time explaining his wounds and how he had been robbed and beaten, all to the shocked gasps and ongoing choruses of "Oh, no!" "How terrible!" and "Such evil men!" At last, they were able to talk of other things.

He had been away only a fortnight, but both ladies were eager to hear a report of the other events that had happened to Sean since they had last seen him. They were particularly interested in one certain item that he might have noticed as he traveled to Annapolis.

Mrs. Wells was first to ask. "Tell us, Sean, did you give occasion to notice if the ladies were outfitted in any new fashions?"

"New fashions? Well, I uh . . ."

"Mother, how would Sean notice such things? His was a trip related to commerce, and I should think he had other things on his mind besides ladies' fashions."

"Yes, of course. I was about to say that. After all, as I traveled, my mind was preoccupied with . . ."

"I know it must have been preoccupied, Sean. But, as mother asked, did you notice anything unusual about the garments of the ladies?"

"Unusual? I don't think so. Although I'd have to say that the Widow Nuthead was dressed in a rather uncharacteristic manner."

That seemed to get their attention, so Sean went on. "Perhaps her occupation had something to do with it. She wore a very dark cloth that covered her hair and it seemed to be tied in a rather tight knot at the back of her head."

"Oh, dear," Mrs. Wells interrupted, "that doesn't sound very attractive or comfortable, does it?"

Before Julia could reply, Sean continued. "She also wore a strange sort of apron over her dark blue dress. It looked a bit like an apron that, under other circumstances, might be used while cooking, but it seemed to be deliberately smudged with terrible black stains. And her perfume, well, it smelled somewhat familiar to me—a bit like boiled linseed oil and . . ."

"Sean O'Connell," Mrs. Wells scolded. "Do you see what he's doing to us, Julia? He has no pity for us, and he has no notion at all about telling us of ladies' fashions in the city." She smiled, and after a brief hesitation Julia smiled too.

"I'm afraid you're right, Mrs. Wells. The Widow Nuthead was the only lady that I paid any account.

That's not quite true, because a woman I met in the street spoke to me, giving directions, and the wife of an innkeeper also required some of my attention."

"Oh, did they now? Required your attention?" Julia asked, giving her mother a reserved look.

"Yes, they did. I believe that I can say with some confidence that the fashions I noted as I encountered these particular women would be nothing to recommend to either of you ladies."

"Then, tell us, Mr. O'Connell, sir, if not fashions, what *did* you discover?"

"Well, I can tell you this, Mrs. Wells: I learned that the business of a printery has nothing to offer me. Mrs. Nuthead made me understand, in no uncertain way, that I would be pursuing the wind if I were to follow the trade of printing here in Maryland."

"Then what of the device? What will you do with the device that you bought from the boat captain?" Julia asked. "Wasn't it your intention to use that contrivance to follow the print trade?"

"It was, and the contrivance is called a press. I must admit that it was an investment not well made. I have spoken with Ben Dixon about the matter. It seems—and somewhat providentially I might add—that Ben knows of families in the printing trade, possibly in Philadelphia. He believes that we may be able to sell the printer's press to a William Bradford, a man who has a paper mill, which of course is a necessity to the printing trade. Ben seems to think that this could be my best opportunity to sell the press."

"Then it appears that you have uncovered helpful information for your future," Mrs. Wells suggested.

"Yes, I agree. I might add also that many of the occurrences of the past several weeks have been somewhat providential."

"I notice that you have used that word more than once in the past few minutes, Mr. O'Connell. May I ask how you consider these occurrences to be *providential*?"

"Well, I, uh . . . perhaps I should begin again. I understand these recent events to be more than simply fortunate outcomes, although I certainly consider myself to be fortunate. I see these proceedings, with the printer's press and things I've discovered on my trip to Annapolis to have been directed by a higher authority than myself."

"I see," Mrs. Wells continued, "and to whom do you refer as this higher authority?"

"Mother, must we press Sean so? I believe he must be confused by our persistent questions."

"Oh, not at all, Julia. In fact, if I may ask for your time, I would like to tell you and your mother what has been happening to me in recent weeks. I find it quite extraordinary . . . and very satisfying."

Sean then recounted the details of the recent events that had led him to pray to receive Jesus Christ as the Savior and Lord of his life.

He spoke of his love and appreciation for the Tubbs brothers, because of the part they had in changing his life. As Julia heard these things, she captured the peaceful expressions of his voice, observed a new look in his eyes, and she felt a different peace too—and more.

Mrs. Wells was also pleased. She had liked Sean from the beginning. Even though her standard for this young man may have been lower than her daughter's criterion, her heart was pleased to hear the testimony of his conversion.

However, there was no doubt that it was Julia's heart that found the greatest pleasure. She had known from the beginning that Sean had been attracted to her. Yet, she also knew from experience that many potential suitors had shown that same attraction. But, with all budding pursuers, she always made it clear that she would accept no one wanting to woo her who did not share her love for God.

At last, Julia believed that God may have provided just the one for her. She felt that Sean not only knew and loved her Lord and Savior, but she believed that he loved her too. And Julia agreed with Sean's assessment. She would also call that providential: divine intervention.

Chapter Twenty-Five

Taking Care of Loose Ends

Sean had been rather excited to learn about the knowledge of printing in the Philadelphia and Boston areas that Ben had garnered from memories of his father. He certainly appreciated Ben's involvement in trying to sell the press.

However, when Ben wrote to Bradford asking for help in finding a printer who might be willing to buy the press, he found only a deaf ear. Thinking the first letter might have been lost or misdirected, he wrote again. However, Ben never received a response from the famous colonial printer from either letter.

As a result of their disappointing effort, Sean placed the printer's press in the back of a shed and covered it with a tarp, hoping that perhaps he would have another opportunity to sell the press later.

Despite long hours of backbreaking work, the tobacco crop had been a dismal failure. They had known early on that the planting had been done improperly, because Edward Coale had advised them of the proper way to plant and had warned them against applying any other method. Instead, they had planted their seed directly into the plowed fields.

Coale told them that he always planted tobacco plant seedlings in his field from seed he planted in January in protected boxes in a special shed.

They didn't know whether the failed endeavor was due to their improper planting, the result of poor quality seeds, bad soil, frost, or simply too little or too much rain that failed to produce a good crop. All they knew was that the plants that managed to mature consisted of poor leaf and very little of it.

Several other experienced tobacco farmers had assured Sean and Ben that they might as well plow this year's crop back into the soil. Nevertheless, more at Sean's insistence than Ben's, they harvested what they could of the leaf.

Sean also thought it would be good for them to learn something about the drying process and resolve any problems this year in anticipation of a good crop the next. So, they set up a makeshift drying area in the largest shed and the pitiful leaf shriveled.

Even so, Ben was not convinced that it was Sean's intention to be growing tobacco the following year, and he also knew that there was a problem at the Crown Ordinary that required resolution.

From time to time Sean recalled the emptiness and sorrow he had felt on that terrible day at the very door of the Crown Ordinary when the Reverend Topping died in that tragic accident. He also vividly remembered the warning he had given the innkeeper Hodge that he would return to examine the accounts that were to be kept while running the inn. He had threatened either to sack him or have him placed in stocks if the accounting papers were not accurate.

Nevertheless, Sean had been preoccupied with many other life choices that had kept him busy, although not flourishing. He had seemed unable or unwilling to bring himself to revisit the inn and confront the innkeeper. On several occasions he had ridden past the Crown Ordinary, but he never stopped.

Months passed, and he presumed that the man would have taken Sean's absence as some sort of weakness on his part. Then, undoubtedly Oswell Hodge would probably return to his old ways.

However, quite the contrary was true. The innkeeper, indeed, had taken Sean at his word. As the months passed, the man and his daughter had become more and more aware of the need to operate a proper inn, at least to the best of their rather limited abilities.

Hodge spent long hours poring over the accounts, making certain that proper amounts were set aside for taxes, and he kept back the owner's profits for Sean. Though not the cleverest of men, he remembered Sean's warning that if things were not in order he might be "looking for a new business—or the stocks."

His greatest fear was that Sean might somehow have discovered that, since the death of his uncle Edward, the innkeeper had not been properly paying Sean's Aunt Elayne. For this reason, he very generously set aside additional amounts for Sean as he calculated the income and expenditures of the inn.

So, after discovering that the printery business was not in his future and farming was certainly not in his blood, it was fortuitous for both Sean and Hodge that Sean should decide to pay a visit to the Crown Ordinary.

Sean had decided to arrive at the inn late in the afternoon, hoping to find that guests had stopped for a meal and perhaps a night's rest. He planned to observe how guests were treated at the inn.

He rode past a familiar spot in he road, the very place where he had burned the letter he had written to Ben.

"Thank you, God," Sean said aloud, "for keeping me from the evil I intended in that letter."

How grateful he was that, even though he had been a non-believer on that dreadful day when Topping had been killed, his conscience had kept him from following through with the wicked idea he had invented to humiliate Topping.

Sean's mount wandered to the side of the road, and as he brought the horse's head about he saw the inn ahead. He sat upright in the saddle, and as he did Oswell Hodge and his daughter Maudie came through the door. She had a broom in hand and her father was pointing to something that apparently needed attention. He looked up when he heard Sean's horse whinny.

"Oh my, oh my! Look smart now, Maudie girl. Do as how I've told you when the master comes. Get you inside and busy yourself."

"Busy with what, Father?"

"Don't be giving me none of that now. Do like I tells you, and do it now."

Looking confused, nevertheless Maudie obeyed her father and went indoors.

As Sean came within speaking distance, the innkeeper offered, "A good afternoon and Godspeed to you, fine sire, your honor."

"Yes, and good afternoon to you as well, Hodge. It is Mr. Hodge, isn't it?"

"It is, and a fine thing to call a man by his own name it is, Sir, your honor." The innkeeper struggled, trying to remember his master's name. "A fine thing, yes, indeed it is sir . . . uh . . . Mr. O'Connell." He smiled, relieved that he remembered Sean's name.

Sean dismounted and Hodge took the reins and secured the horse to a ring on the side of the building.

"I'd like him to have some water and oats. Could that be arranged?"

"Arranged? Oh my, yes indeed. I'll have that arranged. Maudie! Maudie girl! Where is she now? Never about when I'm needing her."

Maudie came rushing through the door, broom in hand. "Yes, Father, I'm coming. What is it?"

"'What is it? What is it?' It's about all she has to say these days, your honor, Sir." Then, looking sternly at his daughter, he said, "The man needs his horse tended. That's what. Now, take him out back for water and oats, and don't be mean with the measure."

"Yes, Father, I'll not be mean with the measure. Oats and water, Father."

Sean wondered if this sort of banter always went on, or if it was simply for his benefit that Hodge was being so insistent with his daughter.

"Are there guests this day?"

"Guests? Oh no, Sir. No guests . . . not today. I'm thinking it's a bit early and maybe some will come by later, but no guests today, Sir. No Sir."

"Well, perhaps that works to our advantage then. I've come to examine your accounts as I said I would. Can we do so now while your time is somewhat free?"

"Free? Oh yes, Sir. Free it is and always will be free for you, my good sir. I've been meaning to tell you how happy me and my Maudie are to be keeping this here inn, Sir. What a good man you are to let me do so, your honor."

Sean was sure that all of this overdone solicitous talk was to keep Sean from discovering what was really going on here at the inn. Nevertheless, he said nothing about such things.

"Yes, well I'm sure that's all well and good. Now let's get to the accounts."

With a flourish Hodge bowed, and with a sweep of his arm he offered Sean to enter the inn. He pulled the best chair to a table near the window and asked Sean to be seated. "Be right back I will, Sir, with the accounts as I have them."

Sean sat down and Maudie came running into the room. "Oh, I didn't know where you went to. Here you are though, aren't you? But, where's father?"

"He's gone to get the accounts."

"Gone to get the accounts? But he keeps them right here at the inn."

Hodge had overheard their conversation and reprimanded his daughter. "Maudie, haven't I told you not to talk to the guests unless I tell you to?"

"I'm sorry, Sir. It won't happen no more, your honor."

"It's not a problem. Let me see those accounts."

The innkeeper began to hand Sean a stack of papers, but then he said, "Wouldn't you want me to be explaining what these here accounts say, Sir? I'm the one what keeps the accounts, and I know more than anybody about them."

"I'm sure you do, but I intend to examine these documents myself. Then, if I have questions, you'd better be able to answer my questions—clearly and without any nonsense."

Suddenly, Sean realized what had probably kept him from returning to the inn to examine its finances: he knew nothing at all of keeping accounts for commerce of any kind, including his manor.

He took the documents and began to examine them. He knew that Hodge was watching, and occasionally he would shake his head as if to be in disagreement with some of the entries. In reality, he was quite amazed at how clearly the innkeeper had been keeping the accounts since Topping's death.

He called for light, and Maudie brought their finest reflector lamp to help him see in the growing dark.

"Hodge, come here and explain this to me," Sean said, and the innkeeper quickly responded to his request.

"Yes, Sir, your lordship, Sir. What needs be explained?"

"Well, you see, I notice that before Topping's death there were very few entries that showed 'owner's profit.' How is that explained?"

"Oh, I sees. Yes, sir, I sees. I says to meself on an early occasion, I did, that you'd be wondering about that, I did."

"Yes, then how is it explained?"

"Well, you see, Sir, it's like this it is. There ain't much to be said about it except that it was a great oversight. A great oversight, it was, Sir, and I had no way to correct it until recent, when I discovered me own self how to go about making them corrections, Sir, your honor."

"And . . . the corrections were made how?"

"Best way I sees how to do it, I says to meself is to just give the master, Mr. O'Connell, more than the required shares to him. That's what I says, so that's as how I made them corrections."

Without giving any indication that he was either pleased or unhappy, Sean simply said, "Then, Mr. Hodge, because of your past errors and your rather clumsy attempt to make restitution, I have determined to keep you on as innkeeper of the Crown Ordinary. Don't take this as weakness on my part. I'll expect that every guest who stops here will have nothing but good to say about the inn.

Another thing: I'll be paying visits from time to time—much like today—without so much as announcing myself. I'll always expect to find the inn clean, well provided, and the accounts kept up and accurate. Is this clear? Have I made myself clear?"

Somewhat shocked, but greatly relieved, Hodge replied, "Clear, oh clear it is, Sir. Thank you, kind sir. Many thanks to you it is from me and my Maudie. Your honor, I'll tell you this: that you can know that this here Crown Ordinary will be the finest kept inn what you'll find in Maryland. That's what it'll be, Sir. You'll see that them accounts they'll be just like you says, your honor—just like you says. 'Well kept up' is what they'll be."

Sean rode back toward Dawn Light with a deep sense of satisfaction. The visit that he had avoided for so long had actually been the very first opportunity he had recognized to provide forgiveness, grace, and mercy to someone who needed it. *Come to think of it,* he thought, *that's exactly what God has done for me in Jesus Christ. I think I'm learning.*

He smiled then, thinking, *So that's what "Do unto others" is all about!* He was enjoying it.

Chapter Twenty-Six

Important Decisions

S ean found himself becoming keenly aware of the watermen who plied the waters along the Chesapeake Bay and on the Elk and Susquehanna rivers. Even though his experience with the ferrymen had been somewhat dismal, nevertheless he had become very attentive to simple designs of the boats being used. As a result, he envisioned many improvements he felt certain he could implement. Nor did he simply imagine ways to perfect the type of boats being used, but he also had ideas of ways to improve the methods of those who made their living as watermen.

He had been fascinated when he learned that the boats being used were patterned after the canoes of the native Powhatan tribes. These canoes had been adopted by early English settlers, because they quickly discovered that, even while carrying heavy loads, the sturdy craft were capable of handling the rough waters of the Bay.

Constructing the canoes was uncomplicated and required nothing like the kind of productivity Sean had seen in Bermuda a few years earlier. Quite simply, the canoe was not much more than a loblolly pine or tulip popular tree log. Using the Indian's method, fires would be started on top of the log and allowed to burn slowly. As ashes formed they would be scraped away until the proper width and depth of the canoe had been achieved.

However, unlike the Indians, the settlers usually added a small sail to increase its speed. While offering the benefit of speed, the sails also provided opportunity for rolling over, if an inexperienced waterman was in control.

These boats could be as long as thirty feet and up to four feet wide. If a larger tree was available, an even larger boat was produced. There was an ample supply of logs in the area, so these canoes had become the standard workboat for the Bay. Most were built right at water's edge on the owner's or builder's property and construction required only simple tools. They were inexpensive to build and easily replaced.

Nevertheless, Sean had become something of a visionary. Unfortunately, since arriving in Maryland not many of his visions had been very practical and even fewer had seen fruition. Still, he was convinced that this vision—his ideas about boats, boat building, and the ways of watermen—was sound, feasible, and definitely had the potential to become profitable.

Now, he'd have to talk it over with Ben.

Sean thought that he had never slept on a more uncomfortable mattress tick, even though it was the same one upon which he spent most nights. His lack of sleep came from the fact that he had been mulling over his ideas for boats and the possibilities of a variety of water-related livelihoods all night long.

Each time he dropped off to sleep, another new idea would trouble him and he would awake to spend time pondering the notions.

However, that didn't keep him from getting up with the sun and drinking a mug of Kezie's bark tea and eating some ham. The men were already in the fields when he saddled his horse and left for the Dixon's.

As he rode, he concerned himself with presenting his ideas to Ben. He didn't want to prejudice his comments. He needn't have bothered himself with these thoughts, because Ben always gave him frank and well-thought responses, no matter how strongly Sean may have felt about something.

About midway down the Dixon's lane, he saw Elizabeth Dixon sweeping the porch. She looked up when she heard the horse, shielded her eyes from the rising sun, and then waved when she recognized Sean.

"Good morning to you, Mrs. Dixon," Sean called out.

She didn't like it when he addressed her as "Mrs." She guessed that she wasn't seven or eight years older than Sean, but his method of speaking to her made her feel much older.

"And a gracious good morning to you too, Sean. What brings you about at this early hour?"

"I'm hoping to find Ben at home. Have I good fortune today?"

"You have at that, my friend," Ben said as he strode through the doorway. "Get yourself down from that excuse for a horse and let's see what mischief we can do today."

He tethered his horse to a sapling and Ben came out to meet him. "Let's sit here, under this oak," Ben offered.

Sean had learned long ago that one of Ben's favorite locations for a good conversation was under a shade tree—at least if the weather was right. Today the weather was right.

His wife called to the men and said she'd bring them water and biscuits.

"Well, Sean, what have you on your mind this fine day? I can tell that something's troubling you."

"Not so much troubling me, Ben, as it is exciting me. And that's the good thing, as well as a caution. I need not tell you that I can get fairly carried away with some thought, plan my life around it—at least in my mind—and then suddenly I'm faced with the fact that I not only don't know what I'm doing but I have wasted my own time and the time and efforts of my friends."

Ben looked at Sean with a glare, as if to agree with his comment about wasting the time and efforts of friends, and then he burst out howling with laughter.

"No! Do you mean it? Is that what you do? Why, who would ever have guessed that you were that sort of man?"

"It's not as humorous as you think it to be, Ben Dixon. Since coming to Maryland, it seems I've had nothing but the best of fortune. I've inherited land, slaves, and holdings. I've gained the best of friends in you and met the kind of woman that I could spend my life with."

"Well then, that takes care of our discussion doesn't it? But wait, you're not talking about my wife, are you?" He smiled again.

Sean appeared to find no humor in that comment and went on. "Ben, I've had the worst of fortune as well. I cannot escape the notion that I had at least a part in Topping's death. It matters not that you and others tell me it isn't so. And this tobacco humiliation . . . you've been so kind to insist that we've all had a hand in it. I know you're right, but I was the one who was in such a hurry. I couldn't wait for seed. I couldn't wait to get it planted, and then I couldn't wait to run off and hide somewhere when I saw the result of our failed crop."

"Yes, I know. These are all sentiments you'll have to deal with yourself, Sean. I've told you my judgment about them all. Whether you were at fault with these things that trouble you or whether you weren't, you'll have to settle that. But here's my opinion: You've got to forge on ahead. Learn from your mistakes, and don't repeat them. My good friend, you do have to move ahead."

"I know. I know. Don't you think I want to do just that? That's why I'm here, Ben. I'm ready, as you say, to forge ahead. But, you must hear me and, as a trusted friend, please give me counsel."

"Of course, Sean. Out with it then, man. Let's hear your latest plan, and we'll hope I'll not have to save you from this one!" With that, he clapped Sean on the shoulder and accompanied it with one of his raucous laughs.

Even if Sean had tried to be annoyed with Ben's response, he couldn't do so. Since that first full day in Maryland when he met Ben, he had found him to be the kindest and most trustworthy man he had ever known.

Sean laid out the ideas he had been accumulating in his mind. As he spoke, he would jump to his feet, as though that helped him see his plan better. He went from talking about building boats similar to those he had observed in Bermuda to simply becoming an oysterman like many of the watermen on the eastern shore of Maryland and in Virginia.

The morning wore on. Mrs. Dixon finally called them to the house for a noon meal and they talked as they ate.

"I'm firm that the printer's press will remain under the tarp in the shed for now," Sean offered.

"I agree. And although we may not be convinced that a buyer will soon be found, somehow we'll see that you get your money back, Sean."

"I'll count on that, because I still owe Captain Murphy a few hogsheads of tobacco, which of course we won't seem to have any time soon."

"Next year, Sean. We may have a crop next year. In any case, I'm thinking you'll do well to try your hand at building one of these boats you've your mind on. But, I'll also remind you again that these men build their own boats. And I have to tell you, Sean, I can't imagine why anyone would have another man do something he can do himself."

"You may be right. Nevertheless, still I insist that even though they've been building their own crude boats, I'm convinced that my ideas to improve these small vessels will cause the watermen to seek after my boats."

"Oh yes, Sean. I've heard you be convinced about other ideas too, and one of them is in the shed under a tarp."

Just then Elizabeth spoke up. "All right now, Ben, we won't be bringing up any more things from the past, will we?" she asked. "For I have a few things to mention as well."

"I know, I know. We're just discussing things here, woman, and it's a man-to-man talk it is," Ben said playfully.

Elizabeth didn't respond. Instead, she bumped the back of his chair and hit him on the shoulder with a wooden spoon as she passed behind him.

"Here now, woman. I'll have none of that. Poor Sean here will see nothing but the gloomy side of marriage if you keep that up."

"Then stop I will," she replied. "After all, I'd say our Sean has some thoughts about such matters. Am I right, Sean?"

"We won't discuss that. Now, of what were we speaking? Oh yes, boats and such. Now that puts me in mind that I don't think becoming an oysterman is in your future."

"Well, that certainly gives me great relief to know that you have been able to see into my future," Sean said. "While you're there, would you be so kind as to tell me how I'll rid myself of the printer's press? Oh, and while you're about it . . ."

Ben interrupted Sean's sarcasm. "All right, I understand your meaning. However, I do see how you might be able to provide boats that would be of particular design for these watermen."

For a time they discussed the possibility of establishing Samson and Ezekiel as oystermen. However, both agreed that they would have to give that thought deeper consideration.

Ben questioned Sean quite thoroughly about every step of his plans and whether he had reflected on any of the possible harmful aspects of the future he had mapped out. By mid-afternoon they had come to some rather inconclusive decisions.

Still, there were two more decisions that required certain counsel. One had to do with the Tubbs cousins and their desire to farm their own land.

Sean explained, "This is how I've calculated the matter. I'm thinking that I could sell a portion of the land to the cousins and, with that money, have enough to purchase a small piece of land on the shore of the Bay."

"That would be a very good idea," Ben replied. "Because I had some thoughts about that matter—wondering how you'd move a large boat from the manor to the Bay. Good idea, Sean. And what parcel of land have you thought to sell them?"

"Actually, I've not given it enough thought to have settled on the land I might sell them. And, of course, involved with any decision regarding the land I would have to consider just what might be the fate of the future for Samson, Kezie, Obadiah, and Ezekiel. Besides, since Kezie lost the baby she has been rather unwell. I must consider them."

"Perhaps, but that seems to be the least of your worries, man. After all, even though you've treated them well, they're slaves."

"Yes, I know they are slaves, but they're slaves on my land, and I would make my plans based on what may benefit them as well. Right or wrong, Ben, I have that obligation, and I'll not overlook it."

At Ben's suggestion, the plan regarding the Tubbs cousins would be delayed. Once Sean and Ben were satisfied that Sean's plans were sound, had possibilities, and could be worked through, there was another matter.

In fact, this issue involved the most important decision of all, and Sean would require the advice and counsel of both Ben and his wife, because this was the one choice upon which all future decisions would be based.

It had to do with the life of a certain Miss Wells. It was the occasion that brought Elizabeth Dixon back to the table for this discussion and prompted her to decide that she would allow Sean the privilege of using her married title, "Mrs." because she had some very mature, wise, and important feminine counsel for this rather unaware young man.

Chapter Twenty-Seven

Sean Makes His Choice

Ben's wife Elizabeth had been delighted that Sean considered asking for their guidance in the matter. "My greatest concern for you, Sean, has been the length of time it has taken you to come to consider such a plan." She smiled as she said it, but Ben broke into laughter.

"I've wondered too, Sean. Because every time you spoke of her you had a strange habit of staring off into the sky. I agree with my Elizabeth. I'd say it's about time for you to make this sort of decision . . . if she'll have you." He tried to not laugh, but holding it back was too much for him.

Sean left the Dixon's with their best wishes for his success. As he rode along, he simply couldn't fathom why Ben would think this was such a light matter. He had been thinking about this very thing for a long time. *I'm not sure just when it all began, but I often thought that it might have been the very first day I met Julia and her mother—that day when*

I made such a fool of myself. I may not have recognized it with my mind, but I believe that my heart may have been miles ahead of me.

Now that he was firm in his decision, Sean decided that he would ride to the Wells house unannounced. He planned to arrive after their noon meal and ask for a private audience with Mrs. Wells. Sean O'Connell had matrimony on his mind.

He had rehearsed the impending discussion many times in his mind. From time to time he would revise his approach, for the purpose of making his bid for the hand of Julia more palatable to Mrs. Wells.

Suddenly he pulled his horse to a stop. "What a fool, I've been," he said aloud. "How do I know what she'll say?"

It had occurred to him for the very first time that every speech he had planned to make was based on Mrs. Wells responding to him with statements he had scripted himself. Suddenly, his brain filled with things that he might say that could offend Julia's mother.

This was no time to talk about such matters. His entire plan had been thought out without even considering what Mrs. Wells first response might be.

What if she would simply refuse to talk to me about the matter? How did I ever arrive at such a situation? There's no use in going on with this; she'll never accept me as a proper husband for her daughter. Sean was completely unaware that he had nothing to fear regarding this matter.

He was about to turn his horse about, when a cart came over the rise before him. Julia was riding with another young lady and an older man.

It was too late to turn around. The women were laughing as the cart pulled up before him, and Julia said something to the others that made her laugh even more.

"Why, hello, Sean. Were you on your way to visit me?"

Her friend smiled at Sean and said, "Well Julia, wouldn't you want to tell father and me who this stranger is with whom you're speaking?"

"Oh forgive me. Of course! Mr. Davison and Mary, this is a dear friend of mine—I mean, of ours—mother's and mine. Sean O'Connell, this is Mr. Davison and Mary Davison—also my good friends."

The newly introduced exchanged brief pleasantries, and then Sean said. "Well, I had best be on my way."

"And where shall your way lead, Sean? Were you coming to pay mother and me a visit?"

He wanted to deny it, but admitted, "Yes, I was. I know you weren't expecting me, but I thought to come unannounced to speak to you about a matter."

The women looked at each other knowingly. But, it was Mr. Davison who said, "Look here now, young ladies. It seems this good man has come to pay an important visit and I believe that you two can spend time together on another day. I'll just take you back home, Julia."

"Oh no, Sir," Sean almost shouted. "Not at all! I'll come another time."

"No, Sean, you must return to our home," Julia insisted. "As I began today's journey, I was feeling

293

somewhat unwell and thought that perhaps I'd best stay home this day."

"Oh yes, dear friend," agreed Mary. "Earlier I thought I saw a very unwell look about you, and I've no doubt you'd feel better at home—much, much better." She did her best to keep from laughing.

Mr. Davison turned the cart about and they headed back toward the Wells's home.

Mrs. Wells was seated in a rocking chair on the porch where Julia had left her a few minutes before. She had heard the voices just over the hill and wondered with whom Julia and the Davisons had been visiting.

Sean was quick to dismount and help Julia from the cart. They said farewells to the Davisons. Sean tethered his horse, and they walked up to the porch.

"What a fine surprise this is, Sean. I thought I'd be spending a lonely day, and now just look! My daughter is back and you are here."

"Yes, well I, uh . . . it's a fine surprise for me as well. Or, I should say that it's not so much a surprise, because I was on my way here—unannounced as you're aware, of course."

"That's nothing to bother yourself about, Sean, not on such a lovely day as this. Come, sit down both of you and let's talk."

"Yes let's talk, Mrs. Wells. That's the very reason I've come today: to talk to you, Mrs. Wells. Oh excuse me, Julia. I meant not to ignore you by what I've said. It's just that . . . I, uh. . . ."

"Let's simply place this rather difficult situation at some ease, shall we? Sean, I believe that I am very much aware of what brings you here today, as you say, 'to talk to Mrs. Wells.' If I am correct, and I believe I am, I can see no reason that Julia should not share in this very important conversation."

"Mother," Julia quickly interrupted, "Sean came to speak privately with you. Now. . . please!"

"Is this true, Sean? Must our conversation be so very private as to exclude Julia?"

"Well, of course I don't want to exclude Julia." He hesitated briefly. Then looking into Julia's eyes, he exclaimed, "I want to include Julia in every-thing—in every conversation I have and especially in my life."

The two women looked at each other in a way that Sean took to be utter shock. But then he knew he was wrong when Julia said, "Oh, Sean, mother knows what you've been wanting to say to her, and I'd dare say that she may be surprised that you've delayed so long. And I have as well."

Then Mrs. Wells added, "She's right you know, Sean. I saw the love in your eyes long ago, a love that you may not have been responsive to at the time but a love that promised something very special for my daughter."

Sean was incredulous. "How could you know such things? Oh, pardon me, I shouldn't question you so. You're right, of course, but how could you possibly know such things?"

"She knew, because I knew as well, Sean. From the first day we met, I knew you were a very special man. But, I confess that at the time I believed you could never be part of my life because you were not a Christian. And now, Sean, now . . . well, what did you want to say to my mother, and what is it that you will say to me?"

Sean's face was beaming. "Even if I could explain it, you would never be able to understand how I've struggled with this. I've practiced in my mind just how I would ask you, Mrs. Wells, for your permission to marry Julia. And then, this morning I lost my nerve and almost ran from doing so."

"You did?" Mrs. Wells asked in mild disbelief.

"Yes, I did. And then your daughter came over the hill and there was no place for me to retreat." He smiled as he looked at Julia and added, "Thank you. Oh, thank you for showing up when you did."

"Sean, will you please get on with this? What will you say to mother and me?"

"Mrs. Wells, I ask for your permission to ask your daughter to marry me, and . . ."

Abruptly, he stopped talking and dropped to his knee. "Julia, the first day I met you I stumbled over myself and landed at your feet, much like this. In that kneeling position I should have said then what I want to say now.'

"Then say it, Sean. Please say it."

Taking her hand he looked first at Mrs. Wells, as if for approval, and then back into Julia's waiting eyes.

"Julia Wells, I ask that you give this poor man your agreement to marry him. I would promise you and your mother that I will love and honor you always. I will provide for you to the best of my ability and defend you always in body and spirit. Julia Wells, dearest Julia, will you marry me?"

Chapter Twenty-Eight

Samson a Proud Lion Walking

Ever since God had freed Sean from the bondage of sin, he had an overwhelming urgency in his spirit to release Samson and Ezekiel from their bondage too.

He was well aware that in the 1660s several colonies, including Maryland, passed laws that mandated lifetime servitude for black slaves, even though previous English precedent had allowed freedom for those who converted to Christianity and then established legal residences there.

Sean knew what his heart required of him, but he struggled to find a way to free his slaves that would not result in their deaths—or his. He tried with as much discretion as possible to discover some way that he could accomplish this, but he found it difficult to ask questions or inquire of the status of laws without raising questions among those who insisted on keeping the status of slaves in bondage.

He had to be cautious not to raise questions that might give the impression that he was opposed to lifting any restrictions on slaves. On one occurrence he was at the docks at Gunter's Harbour, trying to determine his prospects of selling boats that he planned to build. He met Isaac Newby, a waterman with years of experience on the Bay.

"So, as I understand it, I suppose then, Mr. Newby, that you spend a good amount of time in the effort of making your boat. That must keep you from fishing and trading?"

"I suppose it could if I was alone. But, me son's son is given that task. He's good at it, that one, and I just keep on fishing—that's what I do."

"But, wouldn't it be helpful if you could both be about your fishing and not be bothered with the task of building a boat? It would seem to me that you'd fill your pockets more often than if just one of you fished."

"True enough, but who would build us a boat? Our neighbors are all watermen as well, about their oystering and fishing. I see you've never had a hand at such, have ye?"

Sean laughed. "You're right you are. You've a good eye. I've never been a fisherman, but I do like to eat fish—and oysters as well. But I'll tell you Mr. Newby, I could build you a boat that will make you a better fisherman than ever you've been."

They went on talking, and Sean thought he might have a future patron for his boat building.

Having established some rapport with the man, Sean said, "It's some fine laws they've made to protect us from the black savages too, isn't it? We don't need to see them about fishing with their own boats. Why, I've heard that some blacks in Delaware do fish for themselves. Have you heard as much?"

"I have," replied Newby, "and I'll tell you there'll be no such nonsense hereabouts. Why, did you ever hear that there are white women who have mixed-race children? We'll have none of that. Maryland's done it right, we have."

"Is that so? And what is it that you say we've done here in Maryland?"

"Why, we've laws to punish white women who have children by slaves and they'll have to sell them to be servants for seven years as they should. Their children are bound to serve until the age of twenty-one, if the mother were married to the slave, and till thirty-one if not married. Married! Have ever you thought you'd hear such? White women married to savages—black slaves? If it were my say, there'd be no seven years or twenty-one or whatever else they might say; they'd be slaves born and natural all their lives. That's how I'd be about doing it."

"I've never thought about it in such a way. And that sort of thing with whites marrying blacks is right here in Maryland, is it?"

Lowering his voice Newby confided, "I've told you, I'll not use the word 'marry' as they do. And, there's a Mary Davison married a slave and had two children. She's in another county now. Reason I'm knowing about this is she's the sister of widower

Thomas Davison, who has a young daughter, also named Mary — and them living right here under our noses."

Sean was careful to not reveal his knowledge of Thomas and Mary Davison, whom he had recently met while on the road to Julia's home.

Conversations such as this helped Sean determine how his chances as a boat builder might fare. And, as importantly, much of the information he obtained in a coincidental manner often provided him with a plan that he thought could accomplish his desires for Samson, Kezie, Obadiah, and Ezekiel.

It was this plan fomenting in Sean's mind that finally brought him to the place where he decided that he would tell Samson more about his own heritage.

Much as he had done that day when he asked Ezekiel to join him on the porch of the house, Sean chose a day when Ezekiel would be in the field helping Ben Dixon with the corn crop.

After his morning meal, Sean said, "Kezie, I want you to go to the barn and tell Samson to come to see me."

Kezie had recently lost her baby. No one could be sure what had brought it on, but she had experienced severe cramping for a few days and then began hemorrhaging. Because the slaves were accustomed to caring for themselves, Samson had not told Sean about her physical problems until the second day, and immediately Sean sent him to ask for Elizabeth Dixon's assistance.

Shortly after her arrival, Elizabeth helped Kezie as she birthed a stillborn boy. Although Sean knew they had to be grieving over the loss of their child, the slaves seemed to hide their pain and sadness, and he had no idea how to offer them comfort. And, even though Mrs. Dixon suggested that Kezie needed rest, when he told her to remain in bed a few days, she insisted on continuing her work.

The physical complications of the loss of her child had made Kezie somewhat awkward; nevertheless, she quickly reacted to Sean's request. She very proudly enjoyed responding to Sean when she could understand him, especially when no one was around who had to explain things to her. She rushed out the door but returned immediately to pick Obadiah off the floor. Then out she ran again—with her youngster on her hip.

Sean sauntered out to the porch and sat on the top step. Before long he saw Samson and Kezie running back toward the house. Kezie then slowed to a walk and Samson continued his steady trot.

"Needs sees me, Mas' Shawn?"

"Yes, Samson, come sit with me."

With a grin of enthusiasm, Samson took the porch chair that Sean offered, and Sean took another across from him.

Sean seemed sensitive to the fact that they were sitting in the same place where Ezekiel had revealed that Samson was his son. They had been seated quietly for several minutes when Sean began. "Samson," Then he fell silent.

"Yes, Mas' Shawn, I listens."

"Samson, there's some things I will tell you today that will change your life. But, Samson, I must also tell you that I don't know answers to many questions you may have, but I think that you'll … Samson, here's what I have to say," he blurted out, "Ezekiel is your father!"

"No, Mas' Shawn, Zekiel he don't be my father. He Zekiel."

"Yes, I understand. You must find it hard to believe, but Ezekiel *is* your father."

Samson looked at Sean in disbelief as tears began to fill his large brown eyes.

Without delay, Sean began to recount what Ezekiel had shared with him—about the way he had been taken prisoner as a slave and was sent in a slave ship from Africa to Maryland. As much as Sean could recall, he told Samson of how Ezekiel would have been a chieftain back in Africa, a chieftain of the clan called Proud Lion Walking.

Samson stood to his feet and looked about. Sean wasn't sure if Samson was about to bolt and run off or if he wanted to find Ezekiel and have him confirm what he had heard.

"Zekiel my father, Mas' Shawn? Zekiel he be my father?"

"Yes, it's true, Samson. And, I can tell you that when Ezekiel told me this he was very proud. Proud because he has a fine son such as you. And he is also proud of your son, Obadiah."

Then, with a puzzled look, Samson asked, "Why Zekiel don' tell me I be his son?"

"I'm sorry, Samson, but only Ezekiel can explain that to you."

Although Samson had good reason to be happy, yet he appeared distraught. He seemed unable to comprehend why Ezekiel had not told him these things.

However, Sean knew, because he remembered Ezekiel's words.

"He is my son," Ezekiel had said. "He is of the Lion clan. But, he cannot know. It is better that a slave thinks he is only a slave. It is not good to know that he is one of the People."

Sean had a better idea. He hoped that his plan would somehow allow these honorable men to live as free men instead of slaves and to both know that they were "of the people": of the Proud Lion Walking clan.

They heard the sound of a cart. It was Ezekiel returning from Ben Dixon's fields.

Chapter Twenty-Nine

Sworn to Secrecy

S amson had admired Ezekiel for as long as he could remember; in fact, for so long a time that he found it impossible to be angry with him for not having told him that he was his father.

The two men spent the rest of that day and far into the night with Ezekiel sharing his remembrances of days past and Samson asking more questions than he ever suspected were hidden in his heart.

It was a moving time as each man together confirmed the value of the other. Ezekiel soon found that Samson was made of the same strong personal fabric that he remembered of his own family in Africa. There was nothing they held back from one another as new and exciting information flew back and forth.

Samson had not awakened Kezie when he returned to their cabin, but he woke her as soon as he arose and told her much of what he had learned about Ezekiel—and from him.

Although the two men had talked long into the night, they met together before dawn the next day to continue enjoying Samson's new discovery and Ezekiel's fresh freedom. In fact, their excited chatter woke Sean from a pleasant dream.

He dressed and could hear Kezie in the room below happily humming her own song and Obadiah up to his usual noise making. He came down the stairs to the smell of bark tea and cornbread that she had baked earlier. The pleased smile with which she greeted Sean let him know that Kezie was aware that Samson had a father, she had a father-in-law, and Odadiah had a grandfather.

Samson poked his head through the doorway and asked, "Mas' Shawn, what field you wants us be in?"

"You wait there, Samson, and call Ezekiel in, because . . ."

Just then, Ezekiel looked into the eating room, "Yes, Mas' Shawn, I be here."

"Good! Then both of you just wait a moment while I get some ham and water for these cornbreads."

Kezie wrapped two pieces of cornbread in a napkin and carried a pint of water to the porch, placing it on the floor next to Sean's favorite chair.

Sean motioned for the two men to sit opposite him as he bit into the ham, stuffed cornbread in his mouth, chewed a bit, and then washed it down with water.

Looking first at Ezekiel and then at Samson, Sean began.

"I have something to say to you that you must never tell anyone else—no one! Do I make myself clear? Do you understand my meaning?"

Samson and Ezekiel glanced at one another. They were still somewhat numbed with shock over the mutual discovery of their father and son relationship. Without voicing it, each of them wondered, *Now what?* They sensed a hint of danger in what Sean was about to tell them, and they were not sure how they should properly respond.

"Yes, Mas' Shawn," Ezekiel began, "we don't be say nobody. What is we don't say?"

Samson looked at Sean and shook his head in agreement with Ezekiel's question.

"I must hear both of you say it. Will you swear that you will never tell anyone what I am about to tell you? That means you don't tell Kezie or Ben Dixon or anyone. No one must know what only the three of us will know. Do you swear?"

Then Ezekiel said to Samson in their African dialect, "This must be something very important—so important that even the Dixon man must not know. This is very unusual. But Samson, I also trust this man. We will agree to do as he asks."

Samson looked into his father's eyes with admiration and confidence and nodded in agreement.

"Yes, Mas' Shawn," Ezekiel offered. "We be saying we don't say to nobody. That's what Samson and Ezekiel says."

Samson looked at Sean, shook his head in agreement, and added, "Yes, Mas' Shawn."

"Very well, then, you have sworn yourselves to secrecy. This is a very solemn and important matter that I will hold you to; so here is what I propose. What I am saying to you and what I intend to do could cost me my land—and possibly my life. That is why I asked you to hold these things to yourselves and to no others."

He took a small bite of ham, finished the second piece of cornbread, looked at the men to be sure they understood, and then continued.

"The Tubbs men have a book called the Bible. We call this 'God's book,' and they read to me sometimes. The other night they told me some words from God's book that caused me to make a serious decision. A great king wrote the words in a part of the book called Second Samuel. In Chapter 23, from the third and fourth verses, the words written by King David are very important. I wrote them down so I would remember."

He wiped his hands on his breeches and reached into his shirt to retrieve a small piece of paper. "This is what it says:

'The God of Israel said, the Rock of Israel spake to me, He that ruleth over men must be just, ruling in the fear of God. And he shall be as the light of the morning, when the sun riseth, even a morning without clouds; as the tender grass springing out of the earth by clear shining after rain.'"

Sean paused for what seemed like a long time and then continued, "You see, it was as if God had been speaking to me, just as He did to that king. I am your master, and God says that I must be just when I rule over you; and I'm to do so in the fear of God."

Samson gave Ezekiel a puzzled glance. Sean saw it and tried to more clearly explain what he wanted them to know.

"I want to treat you with fairness as you serve me. You know that I have never beaten you. And, even if I have threatened it, I want you to understand that I could never do so."

The two men did comprehend this, and Ezekiel shook his head affirmatively.

"It is very important to me that you know that I am a man who will deal fairly and honestly with you. You see, I believe that the words from God's book speak of Dawn Light. When Ethan Tubbs read, *'As the light of the morning, when the sun riseth, even a morning without clouds,'* I understood that to be God speaking directly to me about the manor."

Without much conviction, Ezekiel said, "Yes, Mas' Shawn," as if he were expected to respond.

Sean wasn't sure if the men understood, and even though he wasn't certain about what else he wanted to say, he continued to explain.

"You see, if anyone knew what I was thinking and planning to do, I could lose much, and I have no idea what might become of you and Kezie and Obadiah. After my marriage to Miss Wells we will continue to live in the manor house just as if I was fully engaged in the farming of the land. However, such will not be true."

Sean told them of the stringent laws that governed the lives of slaves in Maryland. He also explained that even if there were no such laws preventing freedom for the slaves, the mood of the colonists was that slaves should remain in bondage.

"So you see, for the very sake of your lives, you must continue on as if you were slaves that belong to me. However, I want you to know that I intend to release you from bondage as slaves, and I will do this with a written document. Because this would be considered an illegal act, that is why it is so important that you not reveal this information to anyone. It could mean the difference between life and death.

"I will provide a way to keep this document safe and well hidden. My hope is that in the not-too-distant future my illegal act may be seen as just and legal by the officials."

Samson looked again at Ezekiel and it was apparent that the men did not fully understand the implications of what Sean wanted to do.

"As far as the community and the authorities will be concerned," Sean said, "you will continue to live on here as though you are still slaves. However, even though it may be difficult for you to understand, you must believe this: My desire and my pledge to you, insofar as it is humanly probable for me to do so, is that you will be granted complete freedom from slavery so you can live as free men, as much as might be possible under these present circumstances in

Maryland. I know that I've said very much, but do you understand?"

Ezekiel looked at Samson and said, "Mas' Shawn, I hear what you be say, but don't see how this be. If we be free men, why we must hide likes we don't be free?"

Sean was not sure that he understood all of the implications either. But he did know he could not continue holding these fine men in bondage, despite the fact that Ezekiel and Samson did not fully grasp the fact of what he planned or the desperate position in which this would put them all.

"We will speak of these things again, and very soon, but I remind you of our pledge to secrecy."

The men gave Sean their pledge of assurance and they left for the fields.

Sean knew that the Tubbs would have no reason to believe that Ezekiel and Samson were no longer slaves. *This could become a task that may come down hard upon me. I'll have to use the utmost care and can only hope that the Tubbs will continue to see Samson and Ezekiel live and work with much the same sort of free lifestyle they had seen before at Dawn Light.*

This plan would undoubtedly provide many dangers of which Sean was presently not aware. And he was uncomfortable with the fact that Julia would not know of his plan. *Perhaps after we've been married a while,* he thought, *I can tell Julia, but I dare not reveal this to Samson, because I would not want him to believe that he could do the same with Kezie.*

Samson and Ezekiel had no experience in commerce. For the present, Sean would have to provide needed counsel to them, but he would have to do this in a way that would call minimum attention to their trading.

The more I think of this the more it seems my plan could become a noose around my neck, as well as the necks of those whom I wish to free. Nevertheless, the risks are well worth the anticipated results.

Sean did not tell Ezekiel and Samson of other plans he had concerning them. If his boatbuilding business were to become successful, he imagined them participating in the craft as well; and, who knows, perhaps later on they might become oystermen.

Ezekiel and Samson stepped from the porch. As they walked away, they spoke in their dialect with subdued voices.

As Sean watched them, a smile of satisfaction came to his face. Suddenly, as if it were a cloud bursting with a downpour of rain, God filled his heart with the recollection of a Bible passage that Ethan had read just the night before from Proverbs 2:6-9.

"The LORD giveth wisdom: out of his mouth cometh knowledge and understanding. He layeth up sound wisdom for the righteous: he is a buckler to them that walk uprightly. He keepeth the paths of judgment, and preserveth the way of his saints. Then shalt thou understand righteousness, and judgment, and equity; yea, every good path."

Sean thought, *I must spend more serious time praying about these things—about righteousness, judgment, equity, and the path God has chosen for me.*

Chapter Thirty

A Good and Godly Heritage

The day was soft and warm, and scattered clouds flew swiftly northward on the cooling breeze coming off Chesapeake Bay.

As Sean and Julia entered the cemetery, the sun that dappled through the trees caused them to shade their eyes. Sean took the occasion to wipe a tear that had formed in his.

For some reason he had never been prompted to visit the grave of his father. He had ridden past the small cemetery quite often, but he had never considered going to the gravesites.

When Julia questioned him about his neglect in visiting the gravesites, he simply declared that he had never felt a need to do so.

Mildly surprised, Julia said, "Oh, I've wondered why you never mentioned the gravesites of your family. And why is it, Sean, that you have never felt the need?"

Sean looked at her, and his face reflected the answer he had already given. "Well, I, uh . . . it simply has never occurred to me that I had a need or that I should have a need to do so. Was that wrong?"

Julia knew that she should say no more, and at that moment she saw two mourning doves sunning themselves on the ground nearby. She placed her hand on Sean's arm to keep him still, and they watched as the doves picked up bits of small stone and then groomed each other. Then, startled by some movement, the birds flew off in a flurry.

"Aren't they such lovely and peaceful creatures?" Julia said, "The very sort you'd expect to find in the quiet of this place of rest."

"Yes, I suppose they do make fitting visitors to this place."

"Sean, did you know that in the Bible book of Genesis, at the end of the great flood, Noah released a dove to see if it was safe outside the ark?"

"I have never heard that. How could a dove determine if it was safe? After all, they're such timid creatures."

"Yes, they are. However, Noah sent a dove to see if the waters had gone down, but the dove returned. So he waited for seven days before he once again sent the dove forth. This time the dove returned with an olive leaf in its beak, so Noah knew that the waters must have subsided. He waited another seven days and sent the dove out again. But that time, Sean, the dove did not return. Then Noah knew that God had prepared the future for Noah and his family."

"Imagine that," Sean responded. "A dove provided such important information. Noah must have been very wise to have thought of such a way to assess the conditions about him. I wish God would provide such simple ways for me to make my decisions."

They continued among the graves, which seemed to have been placed randomly. As they slowly strolled about, examining the names on the markers, Julia led Sean to the grave of her father. There they stood silently for several minutes. Then Julia sighed and led him away. She discovered the markers of Sean's family before he did.

"Here they are, Sean! Look at these—and all in a row. . . *Alan O'Connell* and *Sarah O'Connell, our daughter.* Who was Sarah, Sean?"

"I don't know. I remember that I was the only child at Dawn Light. No, of course, she must have been my cousin, Uncle Alan's daughter. But I don't remember her or his wife, my aunt. I've no idea at all what became of her."

"Perhaps Sarah died at birth and you were simply too young to understand. Oh look, Sean: *Nathan O'Connell.* Wouldn't this be your father?"

Sean looked away as if avoiding the sight of his father's name on the stone might somehow indicate that he was still alive somewhere.

"Oh, I'm sorry, dear Sean. I thought you'd be pleased to see his marker."

"Pleased?" His voice was gruff. "No, I'm not pleased."

At first Julia thought she must have offended him.

He continued in a softer tone, "I cannot say that I am pleased, but I am very grateful because of your insistence that I come to the cemetery. Julia, I'm grateful that you're here with me as well." As he said this, his eyes moistened and he slipped his arm about her waist and gently kissed her on the cheek.

Ignoring his tenderness, Julia exclaimed, "Oh, look, Sean! There's *Thomas O'Connell* and *Edward O'Connell*. Edward was your last uncle to have died wasn't he?"

"Yes, of course. That much I know," Sean tried to respond in annoyance, but he was much too pleased that Julia had persisted in getting him to visit the cemetery.

"What is that Scripture you told me about, Julia? You know, the verse about having a good heritage or some such thing?"

"I'm delighted that you remember, Sean. My, I must say that you're becoming quite a student of the Word of God."

"I think that you might be saying more than what I really am. I know this: I'm certainly not a student of much of anything."

"You mustn't speak so, Sean. You certainly have learned a great deal about the Word that God gave us in the Bible. You've learned so much about so many things since I first met you. Yes, you're right about a '*goodly heritage*', and it was King David who wrote of it in verse 6 of Psalm 16. Despite those things that King David had done in his past, he knew that he could run to God for mercy and salvation, and he said, *"The lines are fallen unto me in pleasant places; yea, I have a goodly heritage."*

"That's it! *A goodly heritage!* Julia, coming here today makes me aware—perhaps more aware than I've wanted to be—of my own life. Now, dear Julia, I'm becoming more sensitive than ever, not only of my past without Jesus Christ and without you but of our future together.

"Julia, are you as excited as I am about the possibilities of the heritage that we can leave as we live our lives in honorable and lasting love together?"

"Oh, I am. I think of little else, Sean, and I can scarcely wait for our wedding day."

"And I am the same. With the wedding but a few brief weeks off, I think about this often. Decades from now, perhaps the children of our children's children will read our names on stones such as these and be honored that they are our descendants."

"Yes, Sean, I consider such thoughts often." Smiling, she added, "But perhaps without as much glee as you express about these gravestones."

He laughed at how his demeanor must have seemed to her.

"I reflect often on what the Bible says too, dear Sean. We do want to have a 'goodly heritage' and we will. But, more important is the fact that now, because of Jesus Christ, we'll leave those who follow us with a *godly* heritage."

They stood together quietly looking out upon the Chesapeake Bay. The soft breeze was bringing images to her heart that were unseen by Sean.

Still looking toward the bay she said, "Whether Dawn Light remains with us or not, the day is bright, so very bright, because we will be together. And Sean, do you recall the line from Anne Bradstreet's poem that I once read to you? *'What to my Savior shall I give, who freely hath done this for me? I'll serve him here whilst I shall live, and Love him to Eternity.'* "

Julia paused, then looked up at him. "Most importantly Sean, our future is eternally bright with God."

With an assuring smile he lovingly gazed into her striking green eyes. "I agree, my dearest Julia. With you and the Lord God, the days ahead promise to be so very exciting and brighter still—brighter and better than ever I've dared imagine."

They turned as they heard the drumming of wings taking to the air and looked up to see the doves circle over their heads then fly off toward the Bay.

"Julia, just as with Noah, let's take this as a sign that the future is safe for you and me and our family. We are in God's hands."

ENDNOTES

[1] Quay (pronounced *key* or *kay*) — A wharf constructed parallel to the bank of a waterway where ships and other vessels are loaded.

[2] Whipstaff — Ships of the 1600s had no wheel for the helm. They were steered by a vertical shaft called a whipstaff, usually found aft, on the starboard side of the ship. The whipstaff was attached to the rudder bar and, when pivoted, it moved the rudder to turn the ship. The ship's wheel did not appear until the mid-to-late 1700s.

[3] Perch — A variable measure used for stonework. One perch is approximately two rods. A rod equals 16.5 feet, making a perch equal to 33 feet. These 4,000 acres would be approximately 6.25 square miles.

[4] Socage — Middle English word meaning: "A tenure of land by agricultural service fixed in amount and kind or by payment of money rent only and

not burdened with any military service." *Webster's Ninth New Collegiate Dictionary.*

[5] Fealty—Middle English word meaning: "The fidelity of a vassal or feudal tenant to his lord." *Webster's Ninth New Collegiate Dictionary.*

[6] Hogshead—Large casks used for liquid, food, or other commodities. Specifically, "hogshead" refers to volume measurement that, in the 1600s, could vary greatly from 45 to 100 gallons or more.

[7] Quoted in *A History of Printing in Colonial Maryland*, 1686-1776 by Lawrence C. Wroth, (Baltimore, 1922), p. 1.

Printed in the United States
91317LV00001B/1-30/A

9 781604 770957